"Are you well, M___ ___"

Her lack of contro___
Anna found herself ___
where he stood. He l___
for a moment she tho___ ___ might try to kiss
her.

She hoped.

She prayed.

She tried to clear her mind of whatever bewitching spell he was placing on her.

"If you are to swoon, Miss Fairchild, let it be over something pleasant, like this, and not over that boring old Lord Treybourne."

She began to laugh, but his kiss covered the sound of it. He touched his lips to hers, softly at first, and then with a bit more persistence. He tasted of something mint. Then, as quickly as he had begun, Mr David Archer stepped away.

Anna could form no words to speak after that experience. She was fully aware that his behaviour had been too forward, and that she should reprimand him. The problem was that in her heart of hearts she would welcome his mouth on hers again.

And again.

THE EARL'S SECRET

Terri Brisbin

™MILLS & BOON®
Pure reading pleasure

First published in Great Britain 2007
Harlequin Mills & Boon Limited,
Eton House, 18-24 Paradise Road, Richmond, Surrey TW9 1SR

© Theresa S. Brisbin 2007

ISBN: 978 0 263 85199 1

Set in Times Roman 10½ on 13½ pt.
04-1007-78657

Printed and bound in Spain
by Litografia Rosés S.A., Barcelona

Terri Brisbin is wife to one, mother of three, and dental hygienist to hundreds when not living the life of a glamorous romance author. She was born, raised and is still living in the southern New Jersey suburbs. Terri's love of history led her to write time-travel romances and historicals set in Scotland and England. Readers are invited to visit her website for more information at www.terribrisbin.com, or contact her at PO Box 41, Berlin, NJ 08009-0041, USA.

Recent novels by the same author:

LOVE AT FIRST STEP
  (short story in *The Christmas Visit*)
THE DUMONT BRIDE
THE NORMAN'S BRIDE
THE COUNTESS BRIDE

Acknowledgements

The idea for this story came about while listening to a panel of librarians at a Romance Writers of America® Conference in Denver a few years ago. They painted such a vivid depiction of the early history of book reviews that I thought—Hmmm, there's a story here. Not long after that, while watching some old romantic comedies that involved secret identities, hidden agendas and love, I began to plan out that story.

My thanks to John Charles, Shelley Mosely and Kristin Ramsdell for their inspiration for this story and for their ongoing support of the romance genre and its authors.

Chapter One

London, England

"**B**loody hell!"

The piles of papers from his various business interests that lay on his mahogany desk scattered across the surface and onto the floor as he tossed down the latest copy of the *Scottish Monthly Gazette.* An uncommon anger built within him and he could not resist picking the rag back up for just one more glance. Surely, he had misread the editorial. Surely, the writer had not used his name. Surely not.

Yet, upon examination, David Lansdale saw that his ire was in part well-deserved, for there on the second page, as part of the *Gazette*'s editorial essay, was not only his title, Earl of Treybourne, but also spurious remarks against the arguments made in his own essay the month before in the respectable *Whiteleaf's Review.*

"My lord?"

David looked up to see his butler at the door of his study.

"I did not want to be disturbed, Berkley."

"I understand, my lord," Berkley replied with a deferential bow, "but Lord Ellerton has come calling and shows no signs of being deterred in speaking to you."

He has most likely seen this, he said under his breath as he glanced at the newest issue of the *Gazette*. And, no matter how much his friend tried to offer commiseration, it always sounded like gloating.

"Then you must be a stronger deterrent, Berkley. I do not wish visitors at this time." Allowing his displeasure to show, he reiterated, "No visitors."

Berkley, the consummate butler, approached the mess of papers David had made of his desk and the surrounding area of floor, and bent to pick them up.

"Leave them, Berkley. It is more important that you keep everyone out...."

With a nod, Berkley left and quiet descended for a few moments as David gathered the strewn papers and put them on the desk. David turned his attention to the confusion of paperwork and began sorting it back into the neat piles it'd been in just moments ago. Lord Anthony Ellerton would be more pest than pestilence, but his company was simply not welcome at this moment. David would apologize later for the brush-off, later when he had handled this mess.

And after he prepared to face his father's wrath over this attack.

His stomach gripped as he thought about his father's reaction. The Marquess of Dursby was a dour, humorless man at best. He could only hope the marquess was in better spirits when he opened the copy. Or that he avoided reading the Whig-supporting publication completely. Now that was a thought. If his father kept to his regular Thursday schedule, he would most likely skip dinner at his club for a quiet night at home.

David sat down at his desk and placed the object of his displeasure in the drawer so he did not have to face it straight on. At least not until he had a plan to answer the questions and comments in A. J. Goodfellow's newest essay. He leaned over and held his head in his hands, knowing it was much too early in the morning for such a disastrous feeling.

The sounds of another arrival stopped him before he could wallow much longer. Heels clicking across the wood of the entryway coming closer to his study's door grabbed his attention. That kind of fuss, the kind of attention his staff was giving to whomever approached his door, could mean only one thing and it was not that Ellerton had successfully pressed his case for admission. David prayed in the moment before the door opened.

His prayer was not answered.

"The Marquess of Dursby," Berkley called out as he stepped aside and allowed David's father to enter. With a bow, he pulled the door closed and a sense of impending doom spread through the room.

"Father," he said, standing at once and bowing. "I am surprised to see you this early in the day."

His father simply nodded, not deigning to answer the question implicit in his greeting. The door closed quietly; Berkley at his post.

"Would you care for something to eat or drink, sir?"

"I do not waste my time on such things when the fate of the nation is on the line."

"I would not say it is as grim as that, sir."

"And that, Treybourne, is most of your problem. The responsibility granted to you—"

"Forced on me, rather," David interrupted. In private he could admit that being the spokesman for the Tory party's position in this war of words had not been his choice.

He looked at the man who fathered him and marveled that in spite of their close resemblance in appearance—same brown hair cut shorter than current style would dictate, same chiseled angles in their faces, same pale blue eyes ringed in midnight blue—their personalities and approach to honor and family were completely different. And when serving as the target of his father's attempts to intimidate, he thanked the heavens above for the differences.

"A nobleman honors his word." The words were more demand than statement, more insult than declaration. The Marquess of Dursby did not look lightly on shirking one's duties, especially when the family honor was involved.

"And I will carry out what I have agreed to do, sir."

David clenched his jaw and waited for his father's displeasure to be demonstrated. Never a man to waste time, the marquess seized the topic.

"You should have seen this rebuttal coming, Treybourne. Anyone with a modicum of education or experience in the oratory and debating arts would have known."

Crossing his arms, David stared off into the corner of his study while his father continued in his well-controlled diatribe over the latest Whigs' arguments and the insults leveled at the Tories through him.

"You are not paying attention, Treybourne, another of your weaknesses. How do you expect to quash this opponent and make it clear that his party is seeking that which will undermine the good of the nation?"

David did not answer immediately, for he was cognizant that his father would point out another fault of his—that of taking action without adequate thought and planning. Since no amount of arguments or evidence could sway the marquess once he adopted an opinion or position, David saved his efforts for when it would matter.

"What answer would you like from me, sir? If you do not feel that I can accomplish your aims, then give this honor to someone else in whom you have confidence."

This was not new ground for them. Every time his father berated him over this role as party spokesman, he asked to be relieved of it.

In truth, he only did it for the money it brought to him. And for what he could do with those funds. Activities that would have his father in palpitations if he knew the extent of them. Projects which were too important to let this animosity between father and son interfere.

"I will continue to honor our arrangement as long as you do—ten thousand pounds per annum for your own use, unquestioned, though I do wonder over what sordid uses they may be, in return for you using your persuasive abilities to convince those in Commons and in Lords who are in thrall to the Whigs of the error of their ways."

David swallowed deeply when he thought of losing the funds. He would not control the family's strong and still growing fortunes until he ascended to the marquessate, at his father's death, so he was still beholden to his father's whims and wishes and demands.

If there were some other way, he would have gone it long ago, but writing various essays and giving speeches as an MP from one of the Dursby pocket boroughs was the easiest legal way to get the blunt he needed.

"I usually take a day or two to mull over the newest article before writing my own, sir," he offered as he turned back and met his father's steely gaze.

"Excellent," Dursby said. "Remember you can always call on my man Garwood if you need assistance."

He would never use Garwood for anything. "My thanks, sir."

Then, with but a curt nod to warn that his visit was at an end, the marquess turned and walked to the door. He cleared his throat and waited for Berkley to open it for him, and then the sound of his heels on the floor of the entryway told David of his hasty departure.

The entire encounter took less than ten minutes of his time, but he felt as though countless years had passed since his father's arrival. David relented on his own practice of avoiding spirits before midday and sought the decanter of brandy in the cabinet. Another regrettable lapse in control, but for now, David decided to fortify himself before his next battle...with the Scottish essayist known as A. J. Goodfellow.

A few hours later, when Berkley dared to encroach into the study to remind him of his dinner and evening engagements, David felt no closer to a suitable retort to the written assault contained in the magazine. Leaning back in his leather chair and rubbing his eyes with the heels of his hands, he considered sending his regrets to Lord and Lady Appleton even at this late hour.

No, the ball this evening would be attended by those who would know not to mention the essay in polite company. Conversation would be filled with talk of horses, soirees and the latest on-dits of acceptable gossip and not the weightier topics of politics and economics. Though he knew he was the subject of much discussion among the best of English society, David also realized it was more about his income per annum and the titles he would assume at his father's death than the arguments in his essays.

Women controlled the ballrooms and gatherings of society and their interest was nothing so complicated as the latest bill in the Commons or Lords. Titles, wealth and lands were the yardstick of judgment and, with enough of those, most or all of a man's foibles could be overlooked. And he had enough of all of those.

So, as Earl of Treybourne, he would take refuge there for the night. Indeed, for once, he preferred the questionable and possibly foolhardy adventures in the ton's social schedule to facing an adversary more dangerous than any he'd faced before. That self-knowledge worried him more than his father's appearance here before eleven in the morning.

Chapter Two

Edinburgh, Scotland

Anna Fairchild walked briskly over the Water of Leith from Stockbridge toward the New Town. Anxious to get to the offices of the *Scottish Monthly Gazette,* she barely spent a moment returning the greetings of those familiar faces she passed as she made her way through the fashionable area toward Frederick Street. There would be time to stop and chat on another day, but this one was special. This one could determine her success or failure in her endeavors.

This was the morning after the latest issue had been delivered to households and news sellers all over Edinburgh and London. By now, A. J. Goodfellow's nemesis, Lord Treybourne, had read the answers to his essay and was probably still reeling over it. This was the first time that Goodfellow took the earl on directly and Anna could not wait to see the results. It was Nathaniel's reactions that she was not so certain about.

Her usual journey of about thirty minutes from the home

she shared with her sister and her aunt near the newly built Ann Street houses to the offices on the corner of George and Frederick Streets seemed to rush by, much evidenced by her out-of-breath condition upon arrival at the door. Anna looked around the office and found Nathaniel speaking to his secretary. Taking a moment to remove her pelisse and bonnet and to put her appearance back to rights, she smoothed several strands of hair loosened by her brisk pace and the city winds back into place in the rather severe bun at the nape of her neck.

Anna nodded to the two clerks working busily at their desk, opening and sorting the piles of letters already arriving at the office. She presumptuously blamed part of the amount of letters on the contents of yesterday's issue and her decision to publish it, Nathaniel's objections notwithstanding.

"I can see the pride in your gaze, Anna." Nathaniel stood by her side near the doorway.

"Is it unseemly then?" she asked, trying to resist the urge to gloat a bit over the success of their gamble.

"A near thing."

"We wanted to gain more attention for the magazine and, by the looks of that—" she pointed to Messrs. Lesher and Wagner at their work "—it's been successful."

"But at what cost?" He let out a sigh. "I have just this morning received an 'invitation' to speak to several of the Whig leaders about the latest essay."

"I would think that you would be pleased by that, Nathaniel. Part of this plan was for you to gain some notice and begin to move toward election to Commons. Surely, this will build your reputation and possibly even gain you a patron toward that end."

"Perhaps."

"Perhaps? More likely you will find yourself engaged in a debate on the floor of the Commons with the target of that essay."

"Trey?" he asked.

"Trey?" she echoed now recognizing the familiarity that he'd never exposed to her before.

"We attended Eton and Oxford together. I thought I had mentioned it to you when we started this endeavor."

Anna forced the first three thoughts, ones not appropriate for mixed company and certainly not from a woman of gentle birth, back into her mind and spoke her fourth one. "Perchance you should have made your prior acquaintance clearer to me a bit earlier than this moment?"

Her tone drew the attention of the clerks, Nathaniel's secretary and several delivery men and visitors to the office. Anna closed her mouth and lowered her eyes modestly. Now was not the time to jeopardize all that they worked so hard to accomplish. Nathaniel nodded toward his office. She walked inside, and waited for him to follow her in and close the door behind them.

"Anna, I am certain I mentioned it to you when we planned these essays." He stepped behind his desk and waited for her to be seated across from him. "And I repeated my concern over mentioning him by name this early in our campaign."

It had been Nathaniel who had first named it "their campaign" and it had appealed to her sense of organization and judgment. Theirs was a campaign. Not a military battle certainly, but a moral and economic one.

She thought on his words and those expressed when they reviewed the essay. "Will Lord Treybourne retaliate?"

Anna smoothed the wrinkles of her forest-green gown over her lap and tugged off her gloves. Tucking them inside her reticule, she laid it on his desk, on top of one of the numerous piles of magazines, newspapers, leaflets and other printed matter. When he did not answer, she looked up and met his gaze.

His worried gaze.

"Financially?" she asked.

"I think not," Nathaniel said. "The Lansdale family seat is in Dursby in western England. They own properties all over England, even a few here in Scotland. We have nothing financially appealing to tempt them to attack. But…"

"But?" Nathaniel was not usually an alarmist in matters of business, one of the very reasons she valued his input.

"I do not remember Lord Treybourne as such a stickler for propriety when we were at the university. His position surprised me and still does. This makes him unpredictable to me now."

"Ah, life at the university! I have read that even divinity students succumb to the temptations of that life and all it offers. And young men are susceptible to many pressures," she said, allowing a slight smile to curve her lips. "The Marquess of Dursby has long supported Tory positions. It is natural, I think, for his son to do so as well."

"The Prince Regent did not always agree with his father," Nathaniel countered. "Anna, I think you must be reading all manner of improper material if the subject is such an inflammatory one as the occupations of young men at university."

"But when forced to it by the economics of his lifestyle, he certainly discarded his long-held beliefs and conformed," she replied. "And my reading material, other than the *Gazette,* is none of your concern."

Although, at first, a frown dug deep angles in his forehead and drew his eyebrows together and his eyes turned a darker shade of green, Nathaniel smiled at her. "If you would accept my offer of marriage, it would be."

He had pulled their two separate topics of conversation into one and brought it to an abrupt halt. But, it was the true affection in his eyes that caused her stomach do a flip and her heart to beat a bit faster. Anna looked away to try to calm her rapidly beating heart, after hearing such a declaration.

"There is no new ground to turn on that matter, Nathaniel. You know that you and Clarinda are my dearest friends and held in the highest regard. Marriage, although desirable and necessary for most women my age, is something I simply am not seeking."

She thought him long ago disabused of the idea of marriage between them, so this new request surprised her. Was he truly worried that Lord Treybourne or his father, the marquess, would seek to destroy their fledging publication over this disagreement of position and politics? Nathaniel's expression gave her a moment of tension before he nodded his head and smiled.

"I think you simply avoid the controls that would be in place if you marry—your husband would certainly curtail your work here and at the school. And control your money," he added. "That is what I think you fear the most."

He most likely had no idea of how close to the truth his words were.

Anna had struggled for years to keep her family together after her father's death and during her mother's illness. Her own education at the fashionable Dorchester School for Girls outside Edinburgh made it possible for her to support them through those difficult years. Then, with her mother's death and an unexpected, though modest, inheritance, she was able to invest a portion of it in Nathaniel's dream—a monthly magazine. Now, the funds from their increasingly successful endeavor supported both of them, as well as several charities for the poor.

"Shall we return to the topic that brought us here this morning, Nathaniel?" He seemed to have lost the trail of the conversation so she refreshed his memory. "Lord Treybourne," she repeated the name of A. J. Goodfellow's adversary. "Are you overly concerned about his reaction to the essay? Or just worrying, as is your custom when each new issue is published?"

"I fear something of both, Anna. The Trey I knew at school was always direct about his displeasure. If he believes I—we, that is—have crossed a line with this, I think he will contact me directly about it. As to the new issue, I am pleased to tell you that our subscription demand has risen more than ten percent over the last month."

She quickly calculated how much that would be, after the additional expenses, and smiled. "That is excellent news!"

"I have the figures here for you to review at your convenience," he offered.

"With your assurances, there is no need for me to do that." She did not doubt his honesty, just his willingness to see their plan, their campaign, through. Anna understood that their motivations for investing in the publication were completely different, but she also realized early on that they could both accomplish their own aims together.

"Nathaniel, I do think you should go to London."

He seemed startled by her change in topic again and the frown said so. "You do? But Clarinda is coming to visit next week. And Robert."

Anna stood and walked to the window, peering through it to observe the activity on the very busy corner outside the offices. Nathaniel politely rose as well. She waved him back to his seat and stared out as she organized her thoughts.

"I do not think you must accomplish this trip in haste. Truly I think that waiting until after Clarinda returns home is the best timing. Lord Treybourne will be busy this next week trying to frame his response to Mr. Goodfellow's address. You should not appear too overly concerned with his reaction, but I suspect it would be best to meet him at a time advantageous to you. One when you can speak of gentlemanly subjects and leave when you have made your point."

Nathaniel laughed at her words. "Gentlemanly subjects, eh? Will you give me a list and the point I must make as well?"

"You tease me now, Nathaniel. I trust you to handle Lord Treybourne and his inflated ego and opinion of himself."

To her consternation, he laughed harder and louder, crossing his arms over his waist, until tears flowed down his cheeks.

"Oh, Anna," he said, wiping his eyes. "You are so comfortable with your ways and your attitudes that you have no idea of what faces you if the Earl of Treybourne takes the bait. When you teach, your students listen because of your experience and expertise. When you advise me on publishing matters, I heed your words because I know you and trust you. But, Lord Treybourne, especially if his father the marquess is involved, will be the most formidable adversary you have faced."

Anna felt her spine stiffen at his words. Not specifically an insult, they bordered closely upon an affront to her. Being called a bluestocking was no new matter to her. Indeed, it kept many undesirable acquaintances at bay and many unwanted inquiries unasked and unanswered, so she relished the label for the freedom it granted her. And, she was not embarrassed by her abilities or education. They had served her well and saved her family, as well as countless others, from a life of dismal and unrelenting poverty and its dangers.

Nathaniel rose now and approached where she stood, taking her hand in his. "I suspect that if you ever face Lord Treybourne in the flesh, you might begin to believe that marriage to me is the lesser of two evils."

"Since, dear Nathaniel, you will take care of facing down the devil, I mean the earl, *in London,* I will worry not over the possibility of it." Anna slid her hand from his and patted his. "It is part of the appeal, of course, of our unorthodox arrangement."

He looked as though he would argue or add to his warning, but he stepped back to allow her to pass. Dawdling here without purpose when others waited on her arrival was rude and not to be excused without good reason, so Anna reached for her reticule and walked past him.

"And A. J. Goodfellow?"

"A. J. Goodfellow will continue to chip away at the hardness of society regarding the poor and unfortunate."

"So, the arrangements remain the same?" Nathaniel asked, as though there were some measure of doubt in the situation.

"I do not think there should be any changes at this point. We should stay the course," Anna offered, waiting to hear his decision. They faced this each month since A. J. Goodfellow had delivered the first essay to the magazine. And each time, she held her breath, hoping that Nathaniel would not lose heart or courage in their work. Anna distracted herself while waiting for his answer by putting on her bonnet and gloves.

"Stay the course," he repeated, with a nod.

She let out her breath and turned the door's knob to open it. "Well then, I bid you a good day, Mr. Hobbs-Smith."

"And good day to you, Miss Fairchild."

Their feigned formality was for the benefit of any strangers or visitors in the outer office, for both clerks and Nathaniel's secretary knew that they were well-acquainted. They might not know the nature or extent of that acquaintance, and most likely were under the misapprehension of some romantic involvement, but she and Nathaniel did not hide their friendship nor most of their working relationship while in the office.

The men employed there did not, however, know that the woman now being assisted into her pelisse and being escorted out of the offices by Mr. Hobbs-Smith was none other than the political essayist A. J. Goodfellow.

Chapter Three

"Lady Simon is thrilled by her success this evening."

"If you mean the excessive heat, too many people and late hour, I would have to agree with you, Ellerton."

David tried to make his way to the edge of the ballroom where there appeared to be more room to move…and to escape this crush. His third ball this week, this one was no less crowded, heated or unpleasant. But it was a somewhat safe escape from the topic of his predicament.

"You are too modest, Trey. You are the jewel in her crown."

Coming from anyone else in the ton, the words would have been mindless simpering. From Ellerton, however, they were more of a warning. And it was a warning too late in coming, for their hostess was in pursuit and caught them just as he reached the outskirts of the crowd.

"Lord Treybourne! Surely you are not departing so early?"

Lady Simon wore a dress clearly meant for a younger, more lithesome figure of womanhood, one that did not compliment her voluptuous curves. Instead it pointed out the glaring changes that older women sometimes experienced. She leaned forward, displaying what she must have assumed was a pleasant view of her décolletage. "My niece, Catherine, had hoped for a dance."

She nodded in the direction of the dancing couples, and those not dancing. A young woman whom he'd not met stood, glanced his way and fluttered her eyelashes at an alarming rate.

"I fear I must, Lady Simon," he said, taking her hand to keep her back at a decent distance. "Please introduce me to your niece at our next encounter. I have other commitments I must keep now," he whispered in a conspiratorial tone as he threw a glance at Ellerton.

"Oh!" she murmured in a disappointed tone. "Oh!" she uttered in a now more excited one. Tapping on his arm with her closed fan, she nodded. "Masculine pursuits, sir? Ones best not spoken of in mixed company, I suspect?" In spite of her words, her heaving bosom spoke of her desire for him to elaborate on just what their plans were. Her niece was now forgotten in her efforts to discover his plans.

"I thank you for your kind invitation to this evening's fete, madam. Now, I will bid you a good evening."

He peeled his fingers from hers and backed far enough away to bow politely. Luckily for him, Anthony was familiar with the situation and was already heading in the direction of the door. David followed quickly, nodding at several people as he passed briskly through the crowd and toward freedom.

The hair on the back of his neck was rising when he stopped momentarily to take his cloak from a footman and he looked around the entryway to see if he were being watched. Not wanting to take the chance of being stopped again, David tossed the cloak over his arm and strode through the door and down the steps to where Ellerton waited on the sidewalk.

He reached in his pocket and drew out several coins. Handing them to the nearest footman, he instructed, "Find my coachman and tell him to catch up with us. We will be walking in that direction."

It was the only practical thing to do since the line of coaches stretched several blocks away from the Simon mansion. His club was too far to walk to from this neighborhood on the edges of the more fashionable ones, but they could wait for an hour or more for his coach to approach in the lines. Once away from the crowd and the possibility of being overheard, he broached the subject with Ellerton.

"I am thinking of a short trip to our hunting box in the Cairngorms, Anthony. Would you care to join me?"

"Is Commons done its sessions?"

"I have been told we will not be called back until the first or second of October. Surely enough time to enjoy the pleasures of shooting and hunting."

Ellerton did not respond immediately and, indeed, said nothing, even as the Dursby coach approached in the street. David gave instructions to the coachman as they climbed in and sat on opposite sides. The coach rolled down the street for a few minutes before David decided to pursue an answer.

"My father will not be there, if that's what you're waiting to hear. He is escorting my mother to the estate in Nottinghamshire."

"That was a concern, Trey. The marquess does not care for my company."

"He cares even less for mine, so we are safe for the moment."

"Ah, not carrying the party standard high enough?"

"Why is it that you do not take this seriously?" Their families were both Tory supporters, yet Ellerton's father did not involve himself in the power maneuvers.

"My father has long been more interested in his lands than speeches. Overseeing the latest innovations in his crops gives him great joy and fulfillment."

David could understand the draw of other facets of life away from the morass of backroom meetings and grabbing for power of politics. Perchance Ellerton's father had the right of it? Realizing he'd still not received an answer about the trip, he pressed again.

"I plan on leaving on Thursday morning. You can send word if you will join me."

Anthony stared out the coach window at the passing houses and city blocks for a few moments before answering. "I have never seen you run from something before, Trey."

He chose to deliberately misunderstand. "The season is over and only those few who have not snagged a husband are still being shown around town. After five balls, four salons and six dinners in this last fortnight, I have certainly fulfilled any possible obligations as a bachelor and target of marriage-minded mothers of the ton."

"So this is about taking a respite from the rigors of society and not about avoiding the unpleasant topic of a certain publication?"

He could continue to dissemble to avoid the admission of his weakness, but Anthony was one of few people in the world whom he could trust.

"Actually, instead of running away, I am running *to* the problem."

"At your hunting lodge?" Anthony eyed him suspiciously. Shifting on his bench, he frowned and then shook his head. "Of course, it is no coincidence that our path to your property in the mountains goes right through Edinburgh."

"Unless the roads have changed and I have not been advised of such an occurrence."

Anthony was not addle-pated and he immediately understood...and laughed out loud as he did.

"Keep your friends close and your enemies closer, eh?"

"Although I battle in the light of day, my opponent chooses to hide in anonymity. A situation I thought to change."

"Now that's the Trey I remember! Never one to avoid a good fight." Anthony reached over and smacked him on the shoulder. "And I am honored that you asked me to accompany you, as your 'second,' so to speak."

David smiled at him, but his words made him cringe. He had hoped to keep this a discreet visit to Edinburgh to discover more about the elusive Mr. A. J. Goodfellow. His man-of-business had been unsuccessful in his efforts to find out the man's background or family or even his whereabouts.

Now, David would use his own connections—his school friend owned and published the *Scottish Monthly Gazette* and would surely be able to help him uncover this writer. Well, Nathaniel might be able, but David was certain that it would take more convincing on his part for his friend to reveal the information.

"I would consider this a quiet reconnaissance mission of sorts, if you please. My man has already made most of the inquiries, I thought only to follow up on several more promising leads."

Anthony sat up straight and put a finger over his lips. "I can be as quiet as the grave, Trey. You can count on my discretion in this matter."

Deciding not to discuss the arrangements or his plans further now, he nodded his acceptance and turned his face toward the windows. He had much to do in the two days before he left town.

He'd written his response to the inflammatory article and it would be delivered to the publisher on Thursday. With the publishing schedule as it was, his essay would arrive to readers while he was in Edinburgh. The best time to observe Nathaniel and his allies and their reaction to it. The best time to flush out the elusive Mr. Goodfellow.

The coach arrived at his club on St. James, and as they climbed out, David was making lists of tasks to be completed before he could leave London.

Engrossed in her review of the newest textbook she'd chosen to use to teach reading at the school, the knock surprised her. Before Anna could call out, the door of Nathaniel's office opened and a stranger entered. She did not see his face as he turned momentarily to close the door, but his fine clothing spoke of money and his bearing of power. He was as surprised as she must have been at finding an unexpected person in place of the one they sought. She pulled some papers over the book and then rose and walked around Nathaniel's desk to meet him.

"Good morning, sir," she said, holding out her hand to him. "May I help you with something?" He eyed her extended hand and frowned. Ah, a high-stickler. Most likely from London.

"Good morning. I am seeking Mr. Hobbs-Smith," he said with a cursory bow, but without taking her hand. His accent confirmed his origins.

"Mr. Hobbs-Smith has not arrived yet. I am Miss Fairchild. Can I be of service?"

Anna observed him as he thought on her words. Tall, taller even than Nathaniel, this stranger carried an air of anger and danger as he shook his head. When his gaze met hers, the piercing blue stare rendered her breathless. She'd never felt such a concentration of attention before and her words jumbled in her mouth, unable to right themselves. Finally, Lesher opened the door and whispered of Nathaniel's impending arrival, breaking the spell being woven that robbed her of her wits.

"Can I offer you some refreshments? Mr…?" Anna waited for some name to attach to this man. She needed to know his identity.

"This is a business matter, Miss Fairchild. No refreshments are needed." He tugged off his gloves, crushed them impatiently in his grasp and examined every inch of the office. Lifting the hat from his head, he tossed the gloves inside it and laid it on the desk.

Did he think her an imbecile to not know the expectations at a business discussion? She was simply trying to be polite and he was treating her as though she were a…woman.

Anna detested the imperious attitude of those of his class, which she supposed must be noble. The only working women he encountered were most likely his servants or store clerks or those who earned their money on their backs.

She gasped as her thoughts went in an inappropriate and unexpected direction. What had ever conjured up such things?

"Are you in distress, Miss Fairchild?" he asked. His gaze did not soften, but there was something resembling concern in it now.

"I am well, sir. I only just remembered a previous commitment." She hoped the blush was not so apparent to him as she went back to the desk, rearranged some of the papers there and picked up her book. "Mr. Hobbs-Smith is soon to arrive. If you will excuse me…"

Anna's escape was in sight, her hand on the knob of the door, when it opened and revealed Nathaniel standing there. She pulled it back and allowed Nathaniel to enter.

"Nathan…Mr. Hobbs-Smith, you have a visitor," she announced to warn him of the presence behind her.

"So I was told," he replied, tilting his head toward those in the outer office who stared and waited, not even bothering to hide their curiosity.

Nathaniel walked past her and she shut the door. Now her own interest forced her to stay and discover the intent of the mysterious stranger. When she turned back, she found Nathaniel, with his mouth hanging open and his eyes wide, simply staring at the man as though he'd seen the very specter of death.

"Mr. Hobbs-Smith," the visitor exclaimed as he reached for Nathaniel's hand. "And I was not certain you would remember me from our previous acquaintance."

Nathaniel did not refuse, exactly, but offered no enthusiasm or resistance to his greeting. Watching the man closely now, Anna was certain she glimpsed some devilish enjoyment in his gaze at Nathaniel's obvious discomfort.

"Ah," Nathaniel finally mumbled as he shook the man's hand and then tried to release it. "My…my…" he stuttered.

"Mr. David Archer, at your service," the man replied, still grasping Nathaniel's hand.

A gentleman only? Not a nobleman? Glancing at him, she noticed the expensive material and fine cut of his coat and boots, the well-groomed appearance and haughty bearing. Surprised at her misjudgment, Anna waited to learn more.

"My memory failed me, sir. Forgive me," Nathaniel said. Realizing that she was still in the room, he turned and began to introduce her. "And this is…"

"Miss Anna Fairchild," Mr. Archer said. "We have met already. Since Miss Fairchild has another commitment, I would suggest we allow her to leave."

The dismissal, bordering on curt, was however accomplished very smoothly. Now that her escape was assured, Anna realized she did not wish to leave. Something was amiss here, for there was a strong and palpable ambient between this man and Nathaniel, and she wanted to know the truth of it. When Nathaniel did not voice an objection to her departure, she knew she would not be able to stay.

She would simply need to discover more about this man and this business he pursued when she dined with Nathaniel and Clarinda this evening. With his sister as her ally, Nathaniel would stand no chance of keeping secrets.

Mr. Archer's disconcerting way of gazing at her, as though he could see and hear all her thoughts, convinced her of the wisdom in a strategic retreat. Glancing from one to the other, she noticed for the first time that they were opposites in many ways in appearance.

Nathaniel was tall and thin, with sea-green eyes and blond curls that made many a woman swoon. She knew because she had witnessed it many times—his angelic good looks and pleasing manners nearly defeated her own efforts to stay out of the bonds of marriage.

Mr. Archer would make women swoon, but she suspected that it would be in fear or from intimidation, for Anna could feel the effects of his intense blue gaze and muscular build on her own calm senses. Although his clothing was the height of fashion and design, he wore his light brown hair cut shorter than was the current rage. Somehow, though, it fit him, for attempts to soften his appearance with longer hair or the curling style that Nathaniel sported would have met with failure.

Lightness and darkness.

Angel and devil.

Nathaniel and Mr. David Archer.

Intrigued more than she would like to admit, Anna knew she must depart. "I will return at one, Mr. Hobbs-Smith."

"Very good, Miss Fairchild."

Anna closed the door and stood there waiting, impolite as such behavior was, to hear anything spoken between the two men. She wanted some clue as to their past acquaintance, as Mr. Archer referred to it, or to their business. When silence was the only answer, she glanced at the textbook in her hands and knew she would have to wait.

As she made her way to the school, she hoped and prayed that Nathaniel was not so jostled by this man's arrival that he revealed too much to him. Nathaniel tended to become unnerved under too much pressure. They must stick to the story they'd concocted to cover the truth.

Too much and too many depended on it.

Chapter Four

~~~~~~~~~~⌘~~~~~~~~~~

David did not immediately meet Nathaniel's gaze, his very stunned gaze, preferring to allow his old friend to stew in his own juices for a bit. Instead, he turned from watching the lovely young woman leave and walked over to the nearest set of bookshelves, pretending to examine several of the volumes stacked there. He fought the smile that threatened as the sound of Nathaniel's shallow, nervous breathing became louder and unmistakable. When he deemed that enough time had passed and that Nathaniel was suitably ill at ease, David pivoted and faced him.

"Your venture seems to be quite profitable for you, Nathaniel." He nodded at the impressive collection on the bookshelves that lined three walls of the office.

"Trey...I can explain—" he stuttered out.

"I would not have expected your father to support you in this endeavor," David said, interrupting Nathaniel. "My father speaks highly of the baron's Tory attitudes."

"My father is extremely Tory in his attitudes until money

is involved. Then he has little problem with his son being involved in industry."

A certain bitterness filled Nathaniel's voice as he answered, and David wondered at it. The Hobbs-Smiths would certainly not be the first family of noble origins to be punting in the River Tick. And that situation undoubtedly caused the baron to allow, or at least overlook, this endeavor of his son's if it brought in funds or did not drain those already burdened. A sore subject for any man, so David changed it to one of a lighter nature.

"Who was that woman? Miss Fairchild?"

"Anna?"

Nathaniel's cheeks colored as he spoke the woman's name. Her first name. And spoke it as someone very familiar would say it. David observed his old friend as he appeared to search for an acceptable explanation.

"She—Miss Fairchild, rather—is an old schoolroom friend of my sister."

Ah, completely acceptable but devoid of any reasons for the woman's presence here and her sense of familiarity, even *control,* over this office.

"She, Miss Fairchild, seemed more a fixture than a visitor here. Does she hold a position with you?" David asked, allowing all the nuances of his words to strike Nathaniel. Although why he thought she might be someone in a more personal relationship with Nathaniel, he did not know. Something in the way she was uneasy with his presence. Something in the way she pursued her line of questioning as to his visit. Something in the way she moved about the room.

"Although it is not widely known, Trey, Miss Fairchild

helps me with some of the articles in the *Gazette*. She is a teacher and has great skills in writing and editing."

"So, she is your secretary then?"

While he waited on a reply, David walked over and sat down in the chair facing Nathaniel, who was now standing behind the desk. Then, he leaned back and crossed one leg over the other.

"I am not certain what you are trying to insinuate about Miss Fairchild, but I do not appreciate your efforts to somehow besmirch her reputation because of her presence here."

This was not the Nathaniel he remembered. This one was boldly standing up for a woman's honor. Interesting.

"Consider your remonstration a success, Nate," he said, nodding. "I am simply trying to ascertain who does what in your business so I know where to address my own complaints about a besmirched reputation."

David was gifted with a rapid change in Nate's appearance and behavior. He'd not seen a man faint in a very long time, but Nate appeared ready to do so. Then, in an instant, the man gathered himself together, stood and cleared his throat.

"I am in charge here and any compliments or complaints should come to me."

Although the distance between them was only a yard or two, David felt as though he were facing Boney across the battlefield on the Continent. A definite chill fell between them and David wondered if he had misjudged his friend. Better to step back from the breach and approach it differently than to lose a battle so early in this engagement.

"Then I will address them to you if need be." He stood,

reached over to his hat for his gloves and pulled them on. Placing his hat under his arm, he casually said, "While I frame those possible complaints, you could give me Mr. Goodfellow's directions if you would be so kind."

"Mr. Goodfellow?"

"As his publisher, you must know where I can find the man."

Nathaniel stuttered through several possible replies as David watched and then settled on one. "As I said, if you have a complaint, you may give it to me and I will see that it is handled."

Collecting information was his first priority and David sensed that his attempts would now be unsuccessful. He nodded and strode to the door. "I will most certainly do that," he began, pulling open the door. "I will call on you in a day or two to discuss our business."

A few days and Nathaniel would be ready to babble. In their schooldays, he never performed well under pressure and so David did not doubt that he would be rattled enough from this encounter to allow some items about the elusive Mr. Goodfellow to escape. A few days and David would have a better idea of his opponent and how to undermine the fellow's efforts in the press.

Lifting his hat and placing it low on his forehead, David turned away without another word and left the office without closing the door.

A few days and the information he sought would be his.

The Earl of Treybourne!

Nathaniel waited for Collins to pull the door closed and

then collapsed into his chair. Meeting the earl in London at a time and place of his choosing was one thing. Having him walk into the office in Edinburgh with no warning, and while Anna was present, was quite another. So much was at stake. Nathaniel clasped his hands together to control the shaking.

With a glance at the clock, he ignored the hour and decided that a wee dram would help immensely. Reaching for the bottom drawer of his desk, he took out the bottle kept there for those necessary moments such as this one. He poured a small measure into a glass, also kept for emergencies, and swallowed it down quickly. The strong, burning liquid slid down his throat and into his stomach and he waited for it to settle his nerves. Another mouthful and he decided that two were enough…for now. As he calmed, his jumbled thoughts also began to clear and he saw what had escaped him before.

David Lansdale, the Earl of Treybourne, was here in Edinburgh and using another name.

Could he not wish his identity known?

Nathaniel's spirits rose a bit at this insight. Trey had something to hide and a reason to hide it. Could it be? A weakness in the formerly impenetrable armor of the Lansdale family?

Of course, if he were playing least in sight, it would be extremely difficult to locate Trey. As he realized this, Nathaniel jumped to his feet and ran to the window, hoping to catch sight of Trey's coach or even horse. Throwing open the window, he searched the streets below.

The crowds and busyness of the thoroughfare made it impossible to see him, if he were still close by that is. Sinking back into his chair, he knew that he would wait on Trey to make his next appearance. Running his fingers through his hair, Nathaniel closed his eyes and leaned his head back. A dull painful tension made his forehead begin to throb with the promise of headache.

Why was Trey here *incognito?* Why not come and threaten him and his fledgling publication with all the influence and power of the Earl of Treybourne and his father, the Marquess of Dursby? Surely, he was not afraid of the essays he—the *Gazette*—published about him? Certain that the earl would not stoop to underhanded tactics or any dishonorable actions, Nathaniel shook his head. This surprise appearance made no sense unless…unless…

The earl was worried!

Nathaniel could not keep his mirth contained now and he laughed out loud at all the possibilities in this situation. From their time together at the university, he would never have expected Trey to act in this manner.

Knowing that Trey had a weakness and was worried enough to avoid being recognized in his perceived enemy's territory lightened his mood. He would go about business in his usual habits and be better prepared for the earl's next approach. Nathaniel reached over and tightened the cap on the whisky bottle before replacing it in the lowest drawer. But the earl's subterfuge caused him another problem—Anna.

Did he share this knowledge with her or wait to discover Trey's intentions? If Trey simply wanted to pace and growl over Nathaniel's publication of essays that were, at the least, uncomplimentary, so be it. Nathaniel could handle that on his own and Anna need not know that her—their—nemesis in print had stood before them. If Trey wanted something more, some capitulation on his part as publisher or some revelation that might expose Anna and put her person or her reputation in danger, then Nathaniel knew he could rise to the challenge and protect the woman he hoped to marry.

For no matter how much she protested to the opposite, Anna would come to a point in her life when she needed more than causes to offer her the sense of fulfillment she pursued with relentless intent. She would, at some time, come to realize and understand that a woman's happiness and sense of purpose in life came from her husband and family. And Nathaniel knew that his offer of marriage would be accepted.

He could afford to wait. The magazine was growing in popularity and Anna was beginning to be weighed down by her commitments to those less fortunate served by her school and the demands of formulating and writing the articles to further her causes. It was only a matter of time before she realized the value of marriage and husband and, perchance, the earl's appearance would hasten that epiphany. He could only hope for such a thing.

David entered his rented lodgings south of the Old Town and handed his hat and gloves to Harley. His valet, the only one of his personal servants to accompany him here to Edinburgh, appeared quite put-upon as he now was forced into service as doorman and footman and butler. Unwilling to expose his presence, the Earl of Treybourne's presence, here in Scotland, he'd decided against hiring on too many servants to staff the house. Servants talked and word would soon spread if he were not careful. He hoped to gather the needed information and be at his hunting box before anyone other than Nathaniel and Ellerton knew he was spending any time at all in Edinburgh.

This house was not as spacious or well-appointed as the one he maintained in London, but it would do. In spite of the grumblings of one servant, it would actually do quite nicely. Located a short distance from both the Old Town and New Town, these premises would allow him access and, alternatively, privacy, as needed.

"Harley, did you send word to the man I requested?" David strode into the study and tugged at his cravat. He stood by the desk and searched through some papers, looking for the name his man-of-business had suggested to him as someone who could conduct discreet investigations.

"I did, my lord. He should arrive at half past one." Harley looked him over and wrinkled his face in disdain. "I shall lay out some hot water and fresh linen."

Rather than argue the point about his appearance, David nodded and sat down, examining the papers he'd brought. Discretion would indeed be necessary and he was glad that he'd sent Ellerton on to the hunting box to await his arrival. Since their mutual friend Jonathan Drake, the Earl of Hillgrove, would join him in the Cairngorms, Ellerton would remain occupied and entertained by the diversions offered there while David had the freedom from surveillance to pursue his other interests, namely one Mr. A. J. Goodfellow.

And while he learned more of the lovely Miss Fairchild.

Uncertain of where that thought had originated, David shook his head. The woman Nathaniel chose to pursue as his wife was of no concern to him.

The image of her sable-brown eyes flashing indignantly at his manners, which had been curt and just short of rude, filled his thoughts. He'd been too focused on his business and his study of Nathaniel to truly take notice of the woman who had occupied Nate's office as though it were her own. He remembered the way her full lips pursed and thinned and how her eyebrows narrowed as he refused to disclose his reasons for the visit.

Miss Fairchild was no wilting flower. And, although he could not afford to be distracted from his purpose, David knew that he would enjoy this excursion to Edinburgh a bit more for her presence there.

Chapter Five

Anna should not have been surprised by the change in weather. The winds blew in from the north and rattled through the streets, making her hope that her bonnet's ribbons would hold tight. Although August usually meant warmer temperatures, each day could bring a variety of conditions. Today, thick clouds rolled over the city, promising showers that would make her travel both more difficult and longer than she wished.

It was as she turned the corner and headed for the office that she spied Mr. Archer standing across the street, on the corner of the North Bridge. Meticulously groomed in spite of the wind, he almost seemed to be waiting for her as she made her way from the Old Town. Why would he be waiting for her? More importantly, should she pass him by or acknowledge him?

Anna stopped for a moment and adjusted her bonnet, thinking over how best to handle this. For the last two days ___ ___ deflected any questions about Mr. Archer in an ___ ___ ___ would have demonstrated his disinter- ___ ___ Anna knew him better and realized at once that he was trying to minimize her curiosity about this Englishman and his business at the *Gazette*. Any question of ignoring the man under consideration ended when he appeared directly before her.

"Miss Fairchild," he said. His deep voice held no hint of the near-unpleasantness of their first meeting.

"Mr. Archer."

"I had no idea that the winds could be so strong here." He tugged his top hat down and tilted his head as he smiled. That smile created the most attractive dimple in his chin. And it lightened the serious expression in his eyes.

"Is this your first trip to Edinburgh then?" She watched as his eyes narrowed and then he shook his head.

"No, not my first. But my first in a very long time." He turned then and looked down Princes Street in the very same direction in which she needed to go. "Are you going to the *Gazette*'s office?"

It was foolish to feel as though she need conceal her movements from him. Anna nodded, "I am. And you?"

"The very same place. May I offer you my escort there? From the strength of these gales, you may need some assistance in staying out of the street itself."

The buffeting winds were something unexpected by the city's planners when they designed the layout of the streets between the old 'Nor' loch' and the Firth of Forth. Anna was about to deny any need for escort or assistance when a rather strong gust whipped by her and wrenched her bonnet from her head. Saved at the last moment by Mr. Archer's quick action, she accepted her hat from him and then she placed her arm on his when he offered, without argument.

"Perhaps you could familiarize me with the New Town as we walk?" he asked as they began to walk south on Princes Street. "So much of it is changed since I last visited."

Anna pointed out shops she frequented as they ambled along, as well as the houses belonging to several well-known peers, scholars and writers. From what she'd heard and read, Edinburgh's Old Town was completely different from London. Instead of separate areas for the various classes of society, *Auld Reekie* tended to have them in layers in the same buildings and blocks—the richer and more prestigious one was, the closer to street level and the more spacious one's accommodations were. New Town was more similar to London, with the rich in specific squares and streets and those who served or did business with them in others.

Mr. Archer listened attentively and asked questions as they covered the distance from the bridge to the office. Surprised by his polite demeanor, she found herself deeply engrossed in their conversation as the blocks raced by and even the nasty weather faded away. When they would cross a street, he would block the worst of the wind by placing himself in the way of it.

Although she was certain that only moments had passed, Anna drew to a halt in front of the door of the *Gazette*'s office. Startled by their arrival in so short a time, she searched for the words to end their excursion. Before she could, the door opened from inside and Nathaniel stood glaring at both of them.

Glaring in a most possessive fashion.

Her cheeks grew warm at such a gaze and she blinked a few times trying to regain her composure. Nathaniel was a different man in these last few days, in both his manner and his attention to her. Why, last night at dinner with Clarinda and her husband on their first night in Edinburgh, he had complimented her appearance and invited her to the theater! Behavior like this reminded her of how a gentleman courted a lady.

Lud! What had rekindled Nathaniel's interest in such a hopeless thing? Before she could speak, Mr. Archer spoke up.

"Good afternoon, Mr. Hobbs-Smith. I found Miss Fairchild being pushed about by the winds on the North Bridge and have delivered her safely to your door." Holding out her hand to Nathaniel, Mr. Archer bowed and stepped back.

"Anna…Miss Fairchild, come in," Nathaniel said, backing up a pace from the door so that she could enter. That measure of welcome disappeared as soon as she was behind him, for he stepped forward, quite clearly blocking Mr. Archer's entrance. "If that is all, Mr. Archer?"

"Actually, I have a request of you." Mr. Archer moved forward, forcing Nathaniel to back up a bit from his stance. "The rooms I have let are much too small in which to entertain, but I would very much like to continue our discussion from a few days ago."

Nathaniel appeared to wilt at the words, but then he rallied and stood straighter. Although none of the words were directed at her, she nonetheless felt the scrutiny of both men as they lobbed comments back and forth like a battledore and shuttlecock match.

"Might you suggest a dining establishment or perhaps a club where we can have supper?"

A simple request, really, but apparently it raised Nathaniel's hackles. Out of the corner of her eye, she could see his hands fisting and relaxing, fisting and relaxing. She fought the urge to slide hers into his in front of Mr. Archer. Before Nathaniel could answer, he added, "Not to be rude, of course, Miss Fairchild, but this is about business matters between Mr. Hobbs-Smith and myself."

Not to be rude? He was insufferable and rude and he knew it. In what she would consider a challenge, he made certain she knew she was excluded from the proffered invitation. How had his manners changed so in just those moments? He'd been attentive and polite during their walk. What was between him and Nathaniel that brought on this behavior? Maybe Clarinda would know?

"I would never presume to interfere in your business, sir," she answered, not unhappy that a sharp tone entered her voice then. "If you would excuse me?"

Anna turned then and walked away from them. She held herself to a certain standard of behavior since her carefree, even hoydenish days before her father's death, and at this moment she felt the very unladylike urge to stamp her feet and screech. Better to retreat and not embarrass herself and Nathaniel. She would discover the truth of the matter from Nathaniel and, if he prevaricated, from Clarinda.

Only a few minutes passed before Nathaniel joined her in his office and Anna attempted to ignore both him and the question burning within her. As though he could sense her disquiet, Nathaniel followed her lead and they were able to clear up a number of outstanding matters related to the improving status of their publication. Finally, her curiosity overtook her control and she blurted out the words she'd fought to keep in.

"Who is Mr. Archer?"

Nathaniel frowned at first and then leaned back in his chair with a resigned air. She watched as his gaze moved to the bottom drawer of his desk and wondered what was contained there and why it drew his attention.

"Mr. Archer is a past acquaintance of mine from my time in London. His appearance here unannounced simply startled me."

"Startled you? I would describe your reaction to the sight of him in much stronger terms than that." Anna drummed her fingers on the smooth surface of the desk and met his gaze. "And his business here in Edinburgh?"

Nathaniel ran his fingers through his hair and frowned. "Did he not speak of it during your walk here?"

Evasion.

Nervousness.

Guilt.

She could read all three of those in his gaze and wondered over it. In their years of acquaintance and friendship and in their working relationship, she'd never felt as though he'd been less than honest. Until now.

"We spoke only of the city."

Nathaniel paused now before answering. She watched as he took in a deep breath, as though trying to calm himself, and then he smiled at her. "Mr. Archer seeks to buy some property here and wants my assistance in the matter."

"Ah, property here in Edinburgh," Anna replied. "And will you aid him in his search?"

"I told him that I know more about the countryside between the city and our estates than I do of the city proper, but it did not seem to dissuade him."

Now this was interesting. From the expression on his face, Nathaniel was not pleased. Had his previous dealings with Mr. Archer been such a negative experience for Nathaniel that he would exaggerate his true knowledge to avoid any future involvements? Apparently he would.

"Then why not simply acquiesce and help him? Surely, you know enough or can direct him through your man-of-business to someone who could assist him? Perhaps protesting too much will draw more of his attention and interest than you seem to want to bear?"

Nathaniel thought on her words and nodded. "Once again, Anna, you display a sense of common wisdom that aids me. It is a splendid idea that could shorten his visit here as well."

So, Nathaniel wanted Mr. Archer gone? Anna had never seen Nathaniel react so strongly to a situation. Always the one with an innate calmness in the most trying of matters, she puzzled over it. And, although he directed the conversation to other matters, Anna would have to discover more about the mysterious Mr. Archer in her own manner.

"Did you see him?" David asked as he climbed into the hackney.

"I did, my lord."

David shook his head. "While in Edinburgh, Mr. Archer will do." He did not want word to spread of his identity and presence here. Nathaniel was the only one who knew at this point and David would keep it that way in order to effectively seek out the man who was presently making his life miserable. At the man's nod of agreement, he continued. "I am interested in his daily business regimen only. Details of a personal sort are not necessary."

David did not wish to gather invasive information about Nathan's life unless it was related to the business he carried on as owner of the *Gazette*. No need to know if he kept a ladybird or his private activities.

"I understand, sir," Keys replied. "And the woman?" he asked, nodding in the direction of the *Gazette*'s office across the street from where they sat. "Should I have someone follow her?"

David glanced over at the door to the office where he'd last seen her, Nate's form standing between them in a clearly defensive position. With her cheeks aglow from their brisk walk and her dark brown eyes flashing, Miss Fairchild presented a pleasing appearance. He watched as she tried to glance around Nate's tall form. His cutting tone had quashed her further interest, but he did not doubt for a moment that the intelligence and curiosity he glimpsed in her would not be stopped for long. Smiling, he wondered if Miss Fairchild were even now pestering Nathaniel for information about him, and the thought of it gave him pause.

"Miss Fairchild?" David shook his head. "You need not assign anyone to that task, Keys. Narrow your efforts to Mr. Hobbs-Smith and his secretary."

Keys looked as though he would ask another question, but the man thought on it and then reached for the carriage's door. "As you say, sir."

"Two days, Keys, three at most and then report back to me."

"It should be a simple thing, sir."

Keys closed the door and David leaned back against the

seat. He was not comforted by the investigator's confidence. If it had been a simple task, it would have been accomplished by now.

David watched as Keys blended in with those moving along Princes Street and saw him approach a man standing near the storefront of a mercer. After a few whispered words, they both disappeared into the crowds.

Turning back, he stared at the *Gazette*'s office window, seeing nothing but vague images moving inside. Watching on for another few moments, he reprimanded himself when he realized what he was doing.

He was hoping to see Miss Fairchild there in the window.

Shaking from the distracting thoughts, he was even more dismayed to realize the reason he stopped Keys from considering Miss Fairchild as a subject of the investigation. David reached up and tapped on the roof of the carriage. As the hackney rolled forward and joined the rows of horses, carriages and pedestrians, David shook his head. He knew to a certainty that if she needed to be observed, he had to be the one to follow her.

Bloody hell! This could make a mess of things.

Chapter Six

"No, Becky. Try it like this," Anna said, demonstrating to one of her students the new letter of the alphabet on a slate with chalk. "Glide your hand up and curve down to the right." As Becky tried valiantly to imitate the motion, Anna completed the letter for the rest of the class. "*Q* is always seen with the letter *U*, so move quickly into it—" she glanced at the group to see which ones picked up on her pun and smiled "—up, down, up and down."

The ten women in the room gave their full attention to the task she assigned and Anna circled the room, stopping to help and to guide those having difficulty with the formation of the letters. After a few minutes of practice, she smiled. If effort were the only method to judge, each of these women would be a success.

"I don't think I like this letter, miss," the youngest one, Mary, called out. "It's too swirly-like."

Others joined her in her complaints, but Anna laughed. "Practice this one, girls, for the others to follow promise even more swirls and curls. Do not let frustration over the dif-

ficult overwhelm you—we are nearly to the end of the
alphabet and your writing improves with each letter."

Although some agreed, others did not look as certain.
Anna looked over the group and wondered which of them
would truly find a way out of their current straits. In spite of
the intelligence that hid behind many of these pretty faces and
the commitment that brought them here, some would not
attain the position of lady's maid or companion that they
sought. There were simply too many poor and not enough positions in which they could find employment.

Her eyes burned with unexpected tears and she blinked
against them. Surprised by the strength of her reaction to the
plain realization of her charges' plight in life, she cleared her
throat and nodded to Mrs. Dobbins, the housekeeper who
stood waiting in the back of the room.

"It is time for luncheon, girls. You should be proud of your
work this morning."

"Thank you, Miss Fairchild."

Their voices rang out in a well-practiced, exquisitely timed
chorus that still brought a blush to her cheeks. From Mary,
the youngest at fifteen, to Becky, the oldest at twenty, the
young women gathered up their books and slates and waddled
out of the room, following Mrs. Dobbins to the meal that
awaited them. Each woman was at a different stage of her
pregnancy, making their progress out of the room resemble
a procession of chubby geese.

Just before leaving, Becky stepped away from the others
and approached her. Leaning in, she whispered, "It weren't
your fault, Miss Fairchild. She made her mind up to leave and
there weren't nothing you could do to stop her."

Anna's first reaction was to correct Becky's grammar, but it was the small pat on her hand that made it impossible to speak. She simply nodded and accepted the girl's comment for the attempt at sympathy it was. Becky rejoined the others on their way to their meal and Anna was left alone.

Gladys had a wild streak in her and came by her unfortunate situation from not so much attempts to defile her virtue as from her attempts to give it away...over and over...to several men willing to partake of her favors. From her arrival here, Gladys had fought the strictures and schedule and never settled in as the other girls did. And, Anna suspected from overheard whisperings among the others, she continued to seek out the companionship of men.

Many men.

Any man who smiled at her or offered her a kind word.

Most especially any man who offered her some bauble or a few shillings for her time and attention.

In essence, Anna's first and only attempt to rehabilitate a...a... Anna had difficulty thinking of her as a prostitute for it seemed such a harsh word, but Gladys was a light skirt and her presence here had been an unmitigated failure. Gladys slipped away only two nights before, giving only a quiet farewell nod to Becky, who'd befriended her during her short stay.

A growing maudlin feeling grew within her and Anna wiped at the gathering tears. In the last three years since opening this home and school, she'd watched dozens come and go. At first, she'd lost herself in each one—learning about their lives, the details, even their hopes and dreams. But as she found her heart broken for each one, Anna learned to hold back and keep a distance between herself and the young women. Doing that hurt her in some ways, for it seemed to be her nature to open herself to these unfortunates. She knew what they faced, for her own experiences demonstrated all too clearly how much they were at the mercy of those who had no mercy to give. In order to be effective in her work, Anna needed to separate herself a bit.

Anna walked to the desk near the door and organized her papers and books. Not truly a schoolroom like the one in which she'd been educated, this large chamber had served as a drawing room in the better days of the house. Usually, poor-houses and those for unfortunate women like the ones she sponsored here were large, uncomfortable and more than un-pleasant places. But then, most did not agree with her notions and methods of helping the poor, choosing instead to throw them together in filthy places no better than warehouses with no attention to anything except the meanest level of survival.

With the backing of several extremely wealthy patrons who asked little and preferred to be known for their charity rather than to be involved with it, Anna had been able to buy this house, furnish it, staff it and provide a modest living to the women who called it home for those few months before their bairns were born. That time was a time away from the harsh life they'd lived and a time to learn new skills that would, hopefully, give them a better opportunity for employment. Confirmed bluestocking that she was, Anna knew that education was the way out of poverty.

Sitting in the high-back chair at the desk, she reviewed her schedule of the next few days. Alternating mornings and after-noons here and at the *Gazette,* and overseeing her aunt's household and her sister's education and upbringing left her little time for anything else. With the promising returns on her investment in the publication, she hoped to buy a second house and to expand her work. But that would take more money than she had. And more time than she could spare right now.

If only His Majesty's government in England and here in Edinburgh would do more. If only more of those who benefited from wealth would contribute to those less fortunate. If only…

Anna shook herself from such a path of hopeless consideration. Between her work here and her efforts through the *Gazette,* she was doing as much as was humanly possible. Certainly more than many, including the arrogant Lord Treybourne, who not only held to his lofty opinions but also preached them to others and undermined her work as surely as a crack in a building's foundation would.

Piling the books one on top of the other before her, she felt a shiver of anticipation as she realized that his response to the last Goodfellow essay would be published in just a few days. All of Edinburgh, indeed all of England and Scotland, would be aflutter with discussions of it. Last month, a brawl had broken out at a pub frequented by the literati of Edinburgh over the opinions stated in Lord Treybourne's essay. Goodfellow had defenders of his own who stood up with their voices and their fists and more than one ended up in the arms of the law due to the violence.

Anna had hoped for educated discourse, not crude brutality, but if it brought more attention to the plight of those she tried to help, it served a purpose. Hopefully, this month's exchanges would raise the level from coarse to thought-provoking once more.

She placed her bonnet on her head and tied the ribbons. Gathering her books and reticule into the basket she used for such things, she carried her well-worn spencer over her arm, not knowing yet if the temperature would necessitate its wearing. The sun's rays that invaded the room through the front windows and threw dappled shadows on the floor promised not, but Anna knew better. Pulling open the door, she was greeted by a rush of fresh, warm air. Tugging it closed behind her, Anna stepped down onto the walk and glanced up the street.

There, not fifty yards away, stood Mr. Archer! This was the third time this week that she'd found him along the path to the *Gazette*'s office, but this was the first time he was so obvious in his intent to intercept her on her way there. Impeccably dressed, looking quite dashing for midday, he spoke with the coachman who held his horse's reins in the street. He noticed her almost as soon as she saw him.

"Miss Fairchild! Good day," he said as he walked toward her. "If you are going to New Town, may I offer you a ride?" He tipped his hat and waited on her response.

"Have you been waiting for me, Mr. Archer? This is the third day in a row that our paths have crossed."

Riding with a gentleman of short acquaintance was most likely on the edge of prudent behavior, but the carriage was open and would discourage any untoward behavior. Not that she thought him planning such things, but, as her aunt had warned her countless times, a lady must be cognizant of such possibilities at all times.

He glanced over her head, seeming to take note of exactly which building she'd exited from. Ah, so he'd positioned himself close to where he thought she was and then waited on her appearance from one of the houses. Now she knew without a doubt that he was following her, but for what reason? Before she could ask, he lifted the basket from her arm and held out his arm to her.

"Although the rooms that I am renting during my stay necessitate this route to get to the New Town, I do confess to a nefarious purpose, Miss Fairchild," he said, his arm steady beneath hers in spite of such an admission. Only the wicked glimmer in his eyes predicted a less-than-serious matter. "I have noted that you keep yourself to a very busy schedule, but I had hoped to entice you into a bit of leisure."

"Leisure? I am afraid that I have commitments to honor, sir." She stopped and lifted her hand from his. "I am expected at the…"

He raised his hand, with one finger pointed in front of her face, and for a moment she thought he was going to touch her mouth. Anna stopped, shocked by the thought that he would do such a thing and by the sudden craving within her for him to do it. Mr. Archer seemed surprised by the pause and stood frozen for just a moment. Then he smiled, the wicked one that curved his lips into something forbidden, the smile filled with all sorts of meaning. The one that made her stomach quiver and her cheeks flush.

The dangerous one.

"I would never presume to interrupt your day or your plans without some notice. That would be unforgivably impolite." He walked once more toward the carriage and nodded to the driver, who opened the door. "I have procured an open carriage, Miss Fairchild, so that you would have no fear of allowing this familiarity in public."

"Familiarity, sir?" She found it difficult to take a breath at the thought of any such a breach of behavior with this man. For a brief moment, she admitted to herself that this man could tempt Gladys to share her favors without payment. He could not mean such a thing?

"Riding alone with a man who is neither family nor friend, Miss Fairchild. I have come to realize in my short time here that, although some rules of polite behavior seem to be more relaxed here than in London, some conventions must be observed."

"Just so, sir." His consideration was startling. And well-planned. What were his motives? "I would certainly be less than polite to refuse then."

He stepped up into the carriage and helped her in. Once she was seated, he placed her basket securely between them on the seat and told the driver they were ready. Anna sat back and enjoyed the luxury she did not partake of very often. Hiring a hackney or sedan chair for traveling about town was too costly when every pence and shilling needed to be watched. Instead Anna chose to invest in some sturdy walking shoes and the largest umbrella she could manage by herself for those days when the weather was, well, typical Edinburgh weather.

"Do you have students there?" he asked as they pulled away from the curb and into the moving lines of carriages and horses.

"Pardon?"

"I know that, in addition to assisting Nathaniel at the *Gazette* office, you are a teacher. I simply wondered if that is where some of your students live?"

Anna knew that there was nothing on the building to identify as something other than a private home. She did not want to discuss the girls and their situations with Mr. Archer.

"Yes, Mr. Archer, some of my students do live there. How did you know I taught?"

He glanced down then and ran his fingers over the books in her basket. She watched as they glided over the surface of the one on top and wondered how it would feel to have those long fingers and tanned, strong hands glide over her...! She coughed, trying to regain her composure.

Aunt Euphemia must be correct in her criticism that spending too much time with those in the lower class and those women of certain reputations was spilling into her own sensibilities! She'd warned Anna that exposure to those who lived a different life with different standards of conduct would impair her own moral judgment. Now, from the strange inklings she had any time she saw this man, Anna was beginning to think Aunt Euphemia was accurate in her assessment of such dangers to a young woman of good upbringing.

"Firstly, I noticed your selection of textbooks and your attention to them when we met at the office. Then I asked Nate."

"Nate? I've not heard him called that in some years. Have you known him a long time then?" It was time to get answers to her questions if he were seeking answers to his.

"Yes, our paths first crossed when we were only boys."

"I had no idea, Mr. Archer. Nathaniel has said very little about you."

His laughter rang out at her words and she watched his face become even more attractive than when it was stern. The carriage rolled along and he quickly regained control of his levity. "I would imagine you have not made that easy for him, Miss Fairchild. Your curiosity fairly leaps from you and I am certain Nate has been doing his utmost to keep quiet around you."

He had not meant his words as an insult, but from the frown that now marred her forehead and the question in her deep brown gaze, she'd taken them as such.

"I meant no insult, Miss Fairchild. Your dissatisfaction with my introduction at our first meeting was apparent even to me. You wanted to know more and neither I nor Nate have provided you with substantive answers."

"My aunt would warn me that such curiosity is unseemly. I hope you will forgive such a gauche display."

"If I was being honest, I would tell you that I find such candid curiosity a refreshing change."

His stomach tightened at the expression on her face now— her eyes alight and a smile that made her full lips curve delightfully. Dimples, unseen when she was not smiling, appeared and tempted him even more. The urge to lean over and taste those lips nearly overwhelmed him and his body tightened in other places.

"Nathaniel has obviously not had time to warn you about how relentless I can be when pursuing matters of interest, sir. Refreshing is not a word he would associate with such pursuit."

The carriage clattered over the cobblestoned street and came to a stop before the office on the corner. Disappointed that they had not had time for more conversation and realizing that he had not yet extended his invitation, he waved the driver aside with a the tilt of his head.

"Miss Fairchild, would you be able to spare a small amount of time tomorrow morning to accompany me to see the Honours of Scotland?"

"Tomorrow morning?" He could see her candid interest in

such an outing. They need, it seemed to him, only work out the details.

"All of London knows the story of their recent discovery and I have been told that they are most impressive. I thought to see them while here, but I understand, of course, if you would find such a visit boring since you have seen them already?"

He could see her considering the invitation and wondered what held her back from accepting it. Ah, the conventions of polite behavior once more? He did not want her to decline and he found that he was willing to make whatever concessions were necessary to gain her company.

Bloody hell! What was happening to him?

"I could ask Nathaniel to accompany us if it would put you at ease. Or perhaps your aunt could be convinced to act as chaperone?"

"I fear that Aunt Euphemia would never be able to endure the strenuous walk up to the Castle's treasure room." She paused for a moment, drawing her lower lip between her teeth, worrying it, and he lost the ability to think as he watched her mouth. "I know just the right person to join us."

"Very well, shall I pick you up then at your home? If you would give me your directions, I will bring a carriage at ten in the morning. If that is not too early or too late?"

Miss Fairchild shook her head, sending a few loosened tendrils bouncing on her shoulder. The urge to wrap the hair around his finger and test its softness surged through him. "The time would be perfect, but would you mind meeting me here instead? I have some errands to finish before that time."

David stepped around her and out onto the sidewalk, reaching back in for her basket and then her hand. Once she was standing next to him, he told the driver to wait and escorted her to the door. "I look forward to the morning then, Miss Fairchild."

She opened the door and turned back to him, expecting, he was certain, him to leave. He did not. "Good day, Mr. Archer," she replied.

Miss Fairchild startled when Nathaniel appeared in the doorway. She looked from one to the other and then in a surprising move, she took a position between them as though expecting some sort of altercation to erupt between them.

David wanted to laugh, for if he decided there was cause for it and it was time to do bodily injury to Nate, her slight form, lovely as it may be, would never stop him. Instead, he took note of the sincerity on her face, the slight frown of concern in her forehead, and stepped back.

"Nathaniel," he said, nodding his head. "I have a carriage at the ready."

Miss Fairchild glanced at Nate, the question clear in her expression. Again, her deep brown eyes narrowed and David could almost read her list of questions there. The air around them fairly crackled as she exerted a steely control over her urge to ask them. Nate waited for her to pass and then walked outside.

"Until tomorrow, Miss Fairchild."

David tipped his hat and then followed Nate back to the carriage. He'd already instructed the driver, so, without delay, they were on their way into the gnarled lanes of traffic that continuously filled the thoroughfares of the growing city.

"Trey…"

David interrupted him with a glance before he could say

any more. "Mr. Archer, there really is nothing to discuss," Nate argued.

He shook his head. "Two acquaintances surely have many things to catch up on after such an absence." David did not wish to conduct his true business in a hackney in the middle of the thoroughfare. Keeping his identity a secret was difficult enough without jeopardizing any gained success in that regard. "Tell me of Clarinda."

Although Nate had spoken frequently of his sister, David had never met her. From their exploits as children, he wondered over how she had managed to overcome her rough edges and catch a... "Whom did she marry?"

"Lord MacLerie."

"His father is the Marquess of—"

"Duran. Just so." From his curt answers, David knew that he was going to have to pull every bit of information from his friend piece by infinitesimal piece. He let out a frustrated breath. Nate's glare grew stronger.

"I thought this was to be about our issue of mutual concern, not a time to catch up on family ties."

"I have not seen you in what... seven years? I simply wish to be polite and set the standard for our behavior in this exchange."

Nate did not answer then, instead he turned his head and watched as they passed by a number of new buildings under construction along George Street. According to all reports, the New Town would continue to grow for at least several years to come. Nate had been quite canny in his choice of location for his enterprise. The carriage rambled on back over the North and South Bridges and away from both parts of Edinburgh toward Nicolson Road.

"Is your father still in the country?" David paused and waited for a reply. "If I might ask?"

Nate gave up his resistance to talk of such matters and nodded. "Yes. He prefers it during August when the city seems to wilt under the heat or be battered by storms." David looked over when Nate finished and met the glaring gaze in his old friend's eyes. "You already know this. Why play this game of cat and mouse with me when we both know that you, or perhaps your father, have had someone looking into my affairs for the last month? Give over and do not pretend that this is of no importance to you?"

They reached their destination—the house he was renting—and he led the way out of the carriage and to the door. Aggrieved but efficient Harley opened it as they approached.

"Good day, my lord. Mr. Hobbs-Smith, it is a pleasure to see you, sir." Harley took their hats and gloves and led them to the small study. "Would you care for tea or some other stronger refreshments, my lord?"

David smiled as they entered the chamber and Harley simply retrieved glasses and a decanter from the cabinet and filled them with a strong local whisky. Three fingers deep in each glass told him that his valet knew the subject was serious. A moment later, they were alone. He watched as Nate took one mouthful of the liquor and swallowed deeply. His first foray was not long in coming.

"So, why is the Earl of Treybourne hiding his identity and staying in a shabbier part of town instead of the duke's new acquisition on Charlotte Square?"

"Cutting right to the heart of it, then?" David drank a

healthy portion from his glass and set it down before him on the desk. "I am not accustomed to fighting unknown enemies. When my man of business—" he paused and nodded an acknowledgment of Nate's correct assessment of his attempts to uncover Mr. Goodfellow from afar "—could not discover anything about the interesting Mr. Goodfellow from London, I decided it was time to investigate myself."

"Trey, Goodfellow sends in the essays each month, timed so that they arrive within the week after yours is published in London."

"You do not know his whereabouts?" he asked, watching for signs of subterfuge in the response.

"I do not know where he is." Nate stood now and dragged his hand through his hair. Then, after a moment, he seemed much more confident. "You should know that I support the position behind the essays."

"I am not completely surprised by that. You always did have a leaning to the liberal side of the aisle."

Nate stared at him. "As did you, if I remember correctly. When did you accept your father's politics?"

About the time I began accepting his money, David was ready to admit, but he held the words inside. No need to give the man who was placing his own strategies in danger too much ammunition for the battles to come. David just lifted his head and met Nate's gaze, conveying the message nonetheless.

"Politics aside, it is the manner in which you've pursued your aims that most alarms me. After all, I identified myself from the first word to the latest. Remember also, your Mr. Goodfellow attacked first."

David watched as Nate drank the rest of his whisky in one

gulp. Was he hiding something or simply uncomfortable with his part in embarrassing an old friend?

"Goodfellow fights for a good and worthwhile cause, Trey. I will not force his efforts from the forefront of discussion."

David stood and walked to the window, peering along the drive leading to the house. Being on the outskirts of Edinburgh, the separate house afforded him a measure of privacy that staying closer would not. Finishing his own whisky, he shook his head. "I am not asking for that, Nate. I do not mind a fight." He smiled. "As a matter of fact, I relish the challenge of pitting oneself against a worthy adversary. But the methods of this Mr. Goodfellow are what have me riled."

Since he privately supported the same causes that his opponent advocated, David hoped the discussion could continue. But the tone of the latest had brought out the worst in his father's circle and that would mean trouble—for him if he did not win the argument and for the ones behind the attacks. The Marquess of Dursby would not endure having his heir's reputation and his family's name embarrassed on an ongoing basis. Hell, his father did not allow it for a single incidence, hence the secrecy of his own actions and causes.

"I can no more stop Mr. Goodfellow than I could stop the tides, Trey." Nate stood as well and shrugged. "I will attempt to argue for a lessening of hostilities, if that will suffice?"

David thought to argue, but hesitated. Staring out the window, he considered the offer, for it sounded sincere and well-meaning. Crossing his arms over his chest, he let the draperies drop back into place and turned to face Nathaniel.

David certainly understood the business situation at work here—the *Gazette* was more popular now that the feud had begun than before. As its publisher, Nate would face financial difficulties, if not ruin, if he pulled the essays. A more civil battle would be a step. He had no doubt that he could prevail as long as a certain level of decorum was maintained. If the strength of his arguments did not sway many, the weight of his position in society and the wealth behind it would. Knowing the realities of the world, he did not doubt it for a moment.

There was only one thing that stopped his immediate agreement with the terms offered. His essay would most likely arrive in Edinburgh by the day after tomorrow and he suspected that it would not calm the rough waters. Indeed, now that he thought on the tone and wording of his piece, he knew it would stir up more of a response. He'd risen to the insults and issued his own.

"Communicate with Mr. Goodfellow through whatever means you employ to do so and let your ghostly contributor know that Lord Treybourne agrees."

Part of him tensed inside, readily acknowledging the stretching of the truth in his words. There would be time to explain that his essay had already been submitted and in print before this discussion. He admitted in that moment that he would have to allow one more contentious exchange before they stopped.

"So, do you return to London now?" Nate asked. The unasked but clearly heard rest of the question was *before anyone realizes you are here under an assumed name.*

David's efforts at remaining undetected and unrecognized had been a success, but the longer he stayed and the more he went about in public, the more the chance that he would be exposed. Still, there was nothing ignoble about discreetly searching out one's foe to assess their strengths and weaknesses. Truly not.

"Actually, Ellerton is waiting for my arrival at our hunting box. I had thought a short holiday would be in order since there is time before Parliament is called to session in October."

"You still run with the same crowd then?" Nate smiled, obviously contemplating some of their more adventurous escapades at the university. "Ellerton and Hillgrove?"

"The same, although we behave in a much more circumspect manner now that we are older and wiser." David laughed now. It had only been seven years since their last meeting, not a lifetime, and yet he'd changed so much he knew Nate would be shocked at the extent of it. "Perhaps we are simply older."

"And none of you have fallen into the parson's mousetrap?" Nate asked. The frown that had lived on his forehead disappeared as their topic turned to something more pleasant.

"The pressure is growing, but none of us have tossed the handkerchief yet. And it would appear that you have not? How does your father abide you remaining in the bachelor status?"

"I confess that there is someone, but the lady shows no sign of accepting my offer."

The frown was back and David suspected that the expression on Nathaniel's face bespoke of his own surprise that he had admitted to such. David held his tongue and did not ask, for he was certain that Miss Fairchild was the object of Nate's affection and intentions. His own surprise was that she would have turned Nate down, for his title and properties alone made him a marriage target. However, knowing almost nothing about her other than her profession and that a connection existed between her and his friend, he hesitated to guess at the reasons.

At that moment, Harley knocked and announced that their meal was ready. It was a welcomed respite for David, for he did not comprehend what to say or how or if he should reveal his plans for the following morning and his visit to the castle with Miss Fairchild. It was a simple sightseeing excursion; one that would be appropriately chaperoned so no question of propriety could be raised.

As the flavor-filled aroma of food drew them into the dining room, David decided that in a matter such as this one, it would be better to beg forgiveness than to ask permission. Ever a careful fellow, he also decided to wait and determine if he needed to do either after his morning with the lovely Miss Fairchild.

Chapter Seven

"Julia, do not make me regret that I have granted you a morning of leisure from your studies."

Anna tried to sound stern, but the effort was lost with one glance at her sister's excited face. Usually at work with her tutor or at some task, Julia met her request to accompany Anna and Mr. Archer to the Castle with an unconcealed enthusiasm. Now, trying to draw some of that excitement under control, Anna frowned and pointed to her sister's gloves on the desk.

"A lady always wears her gloves on an outing, Julia."

Julia's reaction resembled that of a child rather than the young woman she was soon to be. At twelve years of age, she had mastered many social skills but still lacked others. Reaching over and tucking an errant strand of hair under her bonnet, Anna hoped her sister would always keep that bright enthusiasm for life within her.

Something she'd not been able to do since shouldering the burdens of caring for her ailing mother and young sister at the age of eighteen. Something obliterated by the realities she faced, first in service as a governess and tutor and then in dealing with the women so much in need. Anna smiled as Julia pulled on her gloves and adjusted them into place.

The door to the office opened and Anna took a deep breath. What would her sister's reaction to Mr. Archer be? How would the gentleman act in response to her sister's presence as a companion? The usual custom was to have an older woman or family member to oversee such an excursion, but Anna knew that Julia would enjoy the visit to see the Crown Jewels of Scotland…again.

Turning, she faced him. The sunbeams that raced ahead of him into the doorway obscured his face from her, but manifested his muscular build and height. After closing the door, Mr. Archer removed his hat and bowed to her.

"Miss Fairchild, a pleasure to see you this morning."

It was the polite thing to say, however, the words trickled into her heart. Sincerity permeated his voice and it was at moments like this that she wondered how he could be so caustic at other times. Well, the time had arrived to present her sister. Surely, it would reveal his true manners…or not.

"Good morning to you, Mr. Archer. May I present—" Anna stepped aside and allowed Julia to come forward "—my sister, Julia Fairchild."

Pride coursed through her as Julia walked to Mr. Archer and did her prettiest curtsy. Anna could see his face as Julia dipped and it stunned her into speechlessness.

The first sign of any true softness covered it and—surely, she could not be seeing this—his eyes appeared to tear up as he bowed to her sister. His mouth tightened as though he strug-

gled against the words trying to escape and his forehead
gathered above those glistening eyes as he listened to Julia's
greeting.

"It is a pleasure to meet you, sir." Julia's voice still held
the lightness of tone of a girl, but her manners were impec-
cable. "I thank you for including me in your visit to the
Castle."

Crumbling was the word that best described what
happened to his face as she watched him greet Julia. If she
had glanced away at that instant, she would have missed the
entire metamorphosis. His entire countenance seemed to
shatter and then, a moment later, he regained control and the
gentleman was back, securely in place. He cleared his throat
and bowed over her sister's hand. "The pleasure is mine, Miss
Julia."

Mr. Archer nodded at her and tugged on the door's knob
to open it. "The carriage and the Crown Jewels await us,
ladies. If you please."

Anna said nothing but continued to observe his now-
guarded expression as Julia did not cease her chatter—not on
the sidewalk, not as she climbed into the carriage and not even
as the driver guided them into the street and toward Princes
Street. When Mr. Archer did not intervene as they turned
toward Queensferry Road and the alternate route to the
Castle's gate, she took pity on him and interrupted.

"Julia, please sit quietly for now and allow Mr. Archer to
enjoy the ride to the esplanade." Julia slanted her a mutinous
glare, threatening to misbehave, but she must have thought
better of it for she did slide back and sit quietly then.

"It is quite all right, Miss Fairchild. Miss Julia told me

more about the Honours of Scotland in those few minutes than I could have learned with hours of research." She met his gaze and found a warmth there she'd not seen before. "She reminds me in many ways of my own younger sister."

"You have a sister, sir? I did not know. How old is she?"

He looked away for a second, the movement hidden by hitting a bump in the road and the resettling of the carriage. When he next glanced back, Anna could see how affected he was over his admission. But why?

"Amelia would be reaching the thirteenth anniversary of her birth this coming November…if she lived."

His words were halting and rough, the pain in his voice evident to anyone listening. It was apparent now that her idea to bring her sister was clearly not a good one. Her only defense was ignorance and she hated that. Without hesitating, she reached over and placed her fingers on his hand. Even through two layers of gloves, the heat of him seeped into her.

"My apologies, sir. I would not have—" she glanced at Julia and then at him "—done so if I had known it would cause you pain."

Something passed between them in that instant. Something essential and wanting. Something caring and personal. Anna felt it and shivered at the intensity of his gaze. She'd seen that look before, however, this time it was not about bullying or intimidation. This emotion shot through her heart and she fought the urge to take him in her arms and offer him the comfort she knew somehow he'd been denied over his loss.

She lived for her sister. Every decision Anna had faced and made held Julia's survival and well-being as the most important issue. What would her life be like without Julia? How would she have continued without her? Her heart broke over even the contemplation of a loss such as Mr. Archer's. It was only Julia's voice that broke into the silent connection between them, and Anna removed her hand from his.

"Anna, Mr. Archer, look! I read that Robert the Bruce's men climbed that wall to infiltrate the Castle and take control of it."

Julia pointed to the sheer wall of volcanic rock that shot upwards from the side of the road they traversed until the edge of it could not be seen from their position. Craggy, utterly steep and uneven, Anna could not imagine attempting a climb up such a wall and surviving it. Even living in the Castle's very shadow, she was continually amazed over its impressive presence and its breathtaking vistas, both from below and on top of its heights.

"It was the only way into such a fortress," he said. "The Earl of Moray used guile and bribery to find a weakness."

"You know the story then, Mr. Archer?" Julia asked. Although her sister was quite the student of their land's history, sharing that knowledge in too much of an enthusiastic manner could annoy and tire most. "Moray was jealous of the Black Douglas's accomplishments at Roxburgh and vowed to best him in the service of the Bruce," Julia continued.

Was her sister destined to become the confirmed bluestocking as she was? Her education contained too high a concentration on literature and the sciences and not enough on topical issues from the sound of their conversation. About to interrupt again, Anna found herself surprised when Mr.

Archer continued the topic and pointed a few places out on the rocks above them.

"Ah, but love won the day, or rather, the night," he replied. "Can you see that small indentation there, on the right?"

Anna followed the direction of his hand and found the place he indicated by his description. Julia, her eyes alight in wonder that someone else shared her passion for the Castle, turned her whole body and leaned back to look. "I see it," she answered.

"That is where a local young man whose father worked inside hid a rope ladder. When the man wanted to visit the young woman he loved who lived below—" Mr. Archer's hand pointed to the row of streets they approached from the northwest "—he would use the ladder to climb down and then return before dawn." His voice deepened and became more theatrical as he revealed the story to his audience.

A sigh escaped from Julia and Anna did not know if it were one of gratitude for a kindred soul with an avid interest in the history of Scotland or an awakening of some romantic longing in her sister. Either one disturbed Anna for its ramifications it meant.

"Moray's gold incited him to break his vow of secrecy and reveal its existence," he continued. Miss Julia was enthralled, as he had been, on hearing the tale. David realized that she probably knew the details better than him, but she did not interrupt once.

His heart had fallen to pieces at the sight of this girl when presented by her older sister. Of all the possibilities, David never expected this when Miss Fairchild promised a companion for their morning jaunt. One look at Julia's youthful smile, polite manners and exuberance and it was as though his late sister Amelia stood before him once more. Even now, he forced the words out and tried not to stare at her.

Until that moment, he did not comprehend how much he'd missed Amelia. Although much younger than he and separated by their years and gender, he had a great tenderness for her and followed her activities and growth with interest. Her death had been the catalyst for so many family changes, not the least of which was his mother's outlook and behavior and his own. Now, faced with the vitality that mirrored what he remembered of her, David grabbed hold and threw himself into it.

"Thus ensuring the Bruce would win the Castle."

He finished revealing what he knew and watched the differing expressions on both lovely faces—the older sister looked ready to shush the younger, but that one looked enraptured. They had the same eyes, though different shades of brown—one the color of dark amber and the other the hue of rich coffee. Although covered by bonnets, he suspected that their auburn hair would curl around their cheeks in the same manner. Much as it had done when he discovered Miss Fairchild's…Anna's…hand on his in a gesture of sympathy, his heart warmed as he gazed on these two beauties.

"Bravo, Mr. Archer! Scarcely do I know another so well-versed in the story," the younger Miss Fairchild said. "I am surprised, for you are a visitor to the city, yet you know it well."

He laughed in spite of himself, thoroughly enjoying the situation after expecting disaster the first few minutes. Miss Fairchild relaxed back against the cushions and listened as he exchanged more information and tidbits with Miss Julia. Soon, they passed the Grassmarket area and arrived on Castle

Hill. The driver was experienced at the steep climb, and in a short time they alighted at the gate.

After another shorter ride to Crown Square at the top of the Castle in a cart pulled by short, stocky workhorses, David assisted the two women out onto the cobblestones. With the deftness of one who had been there before, Miss Julia guided them to the door of the Crown Room and, with the approval of the guard, led them in.

Although the jeweled crown, scepter and sword were the centerpiece of the display, several other royal emblems and robes were scattered around the chamber for visitors to examine. But Miss Julia wasted no time on those, heading straightaway for the cabinet that held the most important items in the room.

"Have you seen them before, Mr. Archer?" she whispered. Her sister smiled as though amused by the awed tone from someone whom he suspected did not customarily observe silence or even quiet in most circumstances. "Come closer," the little general directed.

David noticed that Miss Fairchild stood back so he approached and offered her his arm, drawing her with him to the display cabinet. "I confess it is my first time, Miss Julia. Although I have read extensively about them and how Mr. Scott discovered them here in a box in February past." Drawing her closer, he led the elder sister to a better viewing position.

In spite of the early hour, the chamber was crowded with others inspecting some of the oldest and most valuable jewels in all the world. David weaved around several people and brought Miss Fairchild to her sister's side.

Impressed as he was by the jewels and their splendor, he

found himself enticed and attracted by the woman at his side. That she cared about her sister was clear to anyone with eyes, but there was so much more to it. And even more he wanted to know about her.

David escorted them to each of the cases and joined in with Miss Julia in exchanging bits of information about each one. She knew why there was a bend in the sword; he knew when it happened. She knew the names of the various jewels in the crown; he knew their weight and size. It became a fun game of tit for tat, and soon they'd exhausted their store on trivial facts.

Through it all, Miss Fairchild laughed and asked questions, goading the two competitors along and making him forget, nearly, about his sister. He could see where Miss Julia got such a quick wit and strong mind. It was as they left the Crown Room and ambled along the path to the overlook with Miss Julia skipping ahead that curiosity finally got the best of him.

"Tell me of your family, Miss Fairchild. Other than Miss Julia, are there more sisters or perhaps a brother?" The hesitation in her step lasted only a second, but he noticed it. "If that is too personal a question, I apologize."

David guided her to the wall so that they could see the expanse of the New Town before them. Construction moved now at an alarming rate after decades of near standstill. Soon, the buildings and homes would spread north of the city to the sea. When they stopped, she turned to him.

"Not too personal, Mr. Archer, just not interesting. There is no one other than Julia and me. My parents died a few years ago—my father, Sir Donald Fairchild, first, then my mother." She paused and glanced at him. "We live with my mother's sister, my dear Aunt Euphemia, across the Water of Leith near the new area in Stockbridge." He followed her arm and finger as she pointed out the new area, north and west of the New Town.

"I thought perhaps there was a family connection with Nathaniel."

"None. My connection to him is through his sister, Clarinda. Do you know her?" She began walking away and he strode along beside her. Miss Julia was still several paces away.

"I do not. Although I have heard that she is in town with her husband for their annual visit."

She sighed then. A simple, soft exhalation of air from the lungs, and yet the sound of it made his nerves sing. He wanted to move closer to feel that breath as it left her mouth. David cleared his throat instead.

"I understand that her visits home since her marriage are limited, but it does not stop me from missing her and her company when she is not here."

She'd gifted him with a confidence, he understood that much. And at the same time, given him much more knowledge and insight into her life and her character. His visit to Edinburgh had been only for seeing to one task, and finding an attractive, unmarried young woman was not it. Given even that admission, David decided that enjoying the company of Miss Fairchild would help him bide the time until his departure. A departure that appeared closer now that an agreement had been reached.

"Why do you not visit her then? Will her husband not permit it?" Nathaniel spoke highly of Lord MacLerie as his sister's husband. He doubted Nate would have approved of a cruel or heartless man.

"I fear that visiting her is not a possibility, Mr. Archer, no matter how much I would desire to do such a thing." A meaningful glance at her younger sister told much about her reasons for not traveling to see her friend.

"Ah, I see. Family responsibilities. A burden many of us carry, Miss Fairchild. But with those added to your teaching duties, I suspect there is not much time for leisure."

From his surveillance as well as the information provided by Keys and his men, David knew her schedule as well as her places of employment. Nothing was amiss in her life, but neither was there time or opportunity to enjoy all the good things life had to offer. Well, life offered it if you had an income that made employment unnecessary and unwanted.

"I am not unfamiliar with the small pleasures in life, sir. I simply plan them ahead and do not shirk my duties to satisfy my own needs."

"Admirable, Miss Fairchild. Truly admirable," he commented as they walked down the steeper part of the lane. He placed his hand over hers, appeasing some of his own baser needs in touching her so, and assisted her in the descent. Her words, which mentioned pleasures and needs, created all sorts of reactions in his body. "I only hope that this morning's excursion has added to those small pleasures."

Damn him! He should not even jest in this manner. She confused him so—with her wit and self-reliance and sense of duty. But she was a gentlewoman and not to be toyed with by someone with no honorable intentions. That was not correct for he did not have dishonorable intentions so much as no intentions other than a pleasant morning outing.

She did it again—she let out a sigh that captured his attention again. Where the first one indicated, at least to him, the occasion of loss, this one whispered of pleasure. Pleasure experienced during their time together. A small measure, but agreeable nonetheless.

"This has been lovely, sir. And you can tell, can you not, how much Julia has enjoyed it? I tend to let her ramble on, but you engaged in such an interested conversation with her over the trivial details that confound me. She will, I am certain, speak of nothing else for days to come."

Their brisk pace and inattention to their path brought them to the portcullis gate much sooner than he expected. Not taking things to chance, he'd arranged for the carriage to be waiting there in front of the Castle for their use. Guiding Miss Fairchild to it, and drawing Miss Julia along as well, he decided to try to prolong their jaunt.

"Would you care to join me for luncheon before you return to your other commitments? I promise to have you and Miss Julia back to the *Gazette* office or your home as soon as we finish eating."

David paused and watched as she considered his invitation. Saying it aloud in front of the younger sister gave him the unfair advantage he wanted. Miss Julia, although not speaking, fairly burst at her seams as she nudged and nodded at her sister. He tried not to laugh, a valiant effort he was certain, but it escaped him and she turned a suspicious eye to him.

Anna wanted to refuse. There were so many reasons to end this visit and run directly home, but it was once again the expression in Julia's gaze that changed her decision. She convinced herself momentarily that the look of anticipation in Mr.

Archer's intent blue eyes did not impact on it at all. But, long ago, she'd learned the difficult lesson that deceiving oneself never ended well.

Anna wanted to remain in the company of Mr. David Archer.

She glanced from one to the other and nodded her head. "I will hold you to your promise, Mr. Archer. I must be at the school by no later than half past one. Julia, if we lunch with Mr. Archer, you must accompany me there."

Now that she'd set the rules of this continued encounter, Anna waited for compliance or some semblance of it from the other two in the carriage. Julia capitulated first.

"Oh, yes, Anna! And I will practice my sums while you teach!" Julia's sudden enthusiasm for learning numbers was suspect of course, but it revealed much to Anna about how tedious and regimented their lives were. A new person, a polite invitation, some lively exchanges of conversation and Julia was halfway to infatuation.

"And I promise as well," Mr. Archer added in a voice that mimicked Julia's in excitement but not in the tone. An undercurrent of maleness permeated his response and the wicked and enticing grin that accompanied the innocent words also told her much. He was a man, a stranger for all intents and purposes, and one from whom she needed to keep a modicum of reserve and space. "Yes, Miss Fairchild, we both promise," he added.

"Very well then, Mr. Archer. However, I do have one more requirement of you. So far, all our talk has been of Edinburgh. Neither Julia nor I have had the opportunity to visit London. Perhaps you could enlighten us about the city while we eat?"

"I am not certain that I know the information pertinent to

your fairer gender, but I will give it my best effort, Miss Fairchild." Julia did let out a squeal at that point, but muffled it by coughing at once.

"Do you have any ideas of where to eat or would you like some suggestions?"

"Actually, there is a place I discovered on the High Street, not far from Holyrood House that has excellent food. Nathaniel took me there just yesterday and I thoroughly enjoyed it. Driver," he called out, "we will make that stop after all."

So, he'd planned this all along. Yet, instead of dreading it, Anna felt exhilarated by the thought of continuing in his company. He'd been attentive and courteous and, more importantly to her, he'd been kind to Julia this morning. Their conversation—once the topic of the Honours of Scotland had been exhausted—included a bit of everything—family, friends, town, Scotland and anything else that could be encountered in a well-mannered conversation.

Soon they were ensconced at a well-worn table before the window at a small pub, eating roasted chicken and turnips and bread steaming hot from the oven. In spite of his assurances to the contrary, Mr. Archer regaled them with tales of balls and assemblies and society gossip. Anna held her tongue and did not ask about the one person she wished to know about most— her competitor for public opinion, Lord Treybourne. Mr. Archer seemed to be at no loss in describing any number of persons of the highest standing, leading her to believe that he must either be related to or work for someone high in His Majesty's standing. Anna did notice that he never once mentioned his own family and did not talk of the sister whom he'd lost.

Anna noticed that he also did not mention any other

women in his life—there was not a word about a betrothed or a wife or even a dead wife. Surely in describing the feminine interests of London, he would have slipped in a mention of such a person, if she existed.

After what seemed to be the passing of only a few minutes, Mr. Archer reached into his waistcoat pocket, checked his watch another time and nodded to her. Their splendid morning excursion was done and it was time to return to her commitments. Julia did not argue, thank goodness, and their host guided them back to the carriage for the short ride to the school farther down the High Street. The carriage clattered to a stop and Mr. Archer climbed out first to assist them.

"I have enjoyed myself immensely this morning, Miss Fairchild. Miss Julia," he said with a bow.

Anna curtsied, as did Julia, and then she smiled. "I believe I can say in all candor that Julia and I have not had such a pleasant outing in many months, sir. Our thanks."

She walked to the door and was surprised as it opened inwardly by itself… Rather with the help of several of the women who now gawked at Mr. Archer where he still stood watching her. Anna tried to shoo them away from the door, and the windows she noticed, but they continued to spy until he turned and strode back to the waiting carriage. It was just as she shut the door and prepared herself to face her pupils that Becky's soft voice whispered across the room.

"Lord a-mercy, ain't he a prime looker?"

Acknowledging silently that yes, Mr. Archer was indeed a handsome and dashing figure of a man, she turned her gaze on the girl. "*Isn't* he, Becky. The correct form is 'isn't he.'"

All the girls who'd been watching out the windows and the door smiled as Becky corrected her words.

"Lord a-mercy, Miss Fairchild. Isn't he a prime looker?" her student asked shamelessly.

"Yes, Becky, that he is," Anna answered with just as little shame.

It took several minutes of giggling and laughter before they could all settle down for their afternoon's work. And if Anna found herself drifting off in thought and remembering how he'd looked at her or what he'd said, she blamed it on the silliness of the girls. She would never have had another second's thought about the time they'd spent together or the way his eyes grew dark when she placed her hand on his.

Never.

Anna blamed it on the girls.

Chapter Eight

"My lord?"

David glanced up from the newspaper he was reading to find Harley looming over him, wearing a dark and serious expression. It did not bode well for the rest of his evening.

"Yes, Harley." Folding the paper back up and placing it on the table beside him, David waited for his valet to explain his dire manner.

"This was just delivered. Keys said it would be all over the streets in the morning."

Held out before him was a copy of *Whiteleaf's Review*—the latest copy of it, which he could tell by the date on it. Nearly three days since its release in London, this month's issue was just arriving in Edinburgh. It would be on Nathaniel's desk in the morning and, now that he thought on it, David knew that Nate would not be especially understanding once he'd read this. David took the magazine from Harley and nodded a dismissal.

Perhaps the essay was not quite as harsh as he remembered

it to be? Perhaps his concern over Nate's response was unnecessary and this would not cause any problems? He opened
the issue and found his writings on page four. A few minutes
later, he laid the magazine on his lap and closed his eyes as
he watched the possible scenes that would occur at the
Gazette's office when the article was read. Wincing as they
played out in his mind, David realized there could be no good
reaction to this. At the same time, he did not remember his
words being quite as vitriolic as he now read. If he wrote them
after his encounter with his father, he could understand the
anger and hostility revealed there. And indeed he had so—
his failing memory aside, there they were for all to see.

The clock on the mantel in the hallway chimed eight. Nate
was most likely at home and finished dinner since this city
kept to an earlier schedule than London, even than most of the
English at their country estates did. He tossed the remaining
whisky down in one gulp and called to Harley.

"Ready a horse for me."

"My lord? A horse?" Harley took the glass and the
magazine from him as he stood.

"Yes, a horse. I must speak to Nate before he sees that."
David glanced around the study for his jacket. He found it
tossed over a chair, as he'd left it on his arrival there.

"My lord, would it not be more appropriate to summon Mr.
Hobbs-Smith to you? You are an earl and he is only a commoner,
after all. It is not meet that you should chase him down."

David smiled. No one protected his importance more than
Harley did. Always cognizant of the right way of doing things,
it took but one look at the disdain on the man's face to know
he thought that David was lowering himself.

"If it were earlier in the day, I would heed your advice, Harley. But as a man of honor I must explain this—" he pointed to the publication "—to Nathaniel before he reads it. I gave my word to him and this would mislead him into believing I was reneging on that pledge."

Duty and honor Harley understood and it won the argument. "Very good, my lord." The man disappeared toward the back of the house and in a short time David found his overcoat tossed over his arm and his hat in his hand as he was guided out to the yard behind the house. A carriage stood waiting.

"A horse would have been sufficient, Harley," he muttered as he tugged on the coat and climbed inside.

"Sir," he said, glancing at the driver who stood nearby listening to every word. "'Tis night and you are not familiar with the area. One wrong turn and you could be in the seediest area of the city. Or go down one of the closes or blasted wynds and find no way out." Harley closed the door. "Or be accosted by hooligans along the way."

Not wanting Harley to continue his diatribe or delay his arrival at Nate's any longer, David rapped on the roof of the carriage. "Go!"

He sat back and began to think on how he could inform his friend of the contents of the essay and still keep his pledge. When they pulled over to the curb in front of the New Town home of the Hobbs-Smith family, he was no closer to finding the right words than when he realized the impact of the release of his essay.

Climbing from the carriage and approaching the door, David was struck by the thought that this would also have some effect on Miss Fairchild. She was involved, though he knew not the complete extent of it, in Nate's publication. She mentioned that she helped him and David suspected that it was to correct the weakness Nate had in the art of composition and grammar. A person with such skills would be an asset in producing a magazine aimed at the more educated and literate classes.

A woman in that position was unusual, bordering on questionable, but with their family connections and functioning as a proofreader, he supposed that it was still acceptable...here in Edinburgh. In London, a woman doing such a thing would most likely be cut from polite society, where women were expected to worry about things like marriage and balls and not their survival, as he deduced Miss Fairchild had to worry over.

Keenly aware from his own interests of the plight of the women outside the polite society in England of the difficulties she would face if unemployed, David expected that that realization was the cause for his discomfort. Although Lord Treybourne needed to appear to be the staunchest of those opposed to social and parliamentary reform, in truth it was what he used the funds from his father to support. Just as he was certain that Nathaniel used some of his profits to fund charities for the causes he favored, his own money had established and continued to maintain two orphanages and a school for those orphans, all out of the sight of his father's scrutiny.

David reached up, but before he could use the knocker, the door opened revealing a footman. "Good evening, sir. How may I assist you?"

"Please tell Mr. Hobbs-Smith that Mr. David Archer is calling, if he is available?"

Following the man into the foyer, David took off his hat and waited as the footman went off to deliver his message. The house was not grand, but stylish and modern in its design. Stairs led up to the first floor and several short halls led off to various rooms on this ground floor. From the snatches of conversation he could hear emanating from a chamber through the nearest doorway, Nate had company and was not done dinner yet. Only a moment later, Nate followed the footman back to the foyer.

"Mr. Archer, is there a problem?"

David met Nate's gaze and decided on the direct approach. "There may be. That's why I am here. We need to talk."

A burst of laughter from the other room reminded David that Nate had company and this might not be the best time to discuss the matter at hand. "Perhaps I could return when your guests have departed?"

"Only Miss Fairchild will depart, for the others are my sister and her husband and they, along with their two children, are my guests. So, if this matter is so important that it brought you to my home at night, let us step into my study and discuss it."

Before either of them moved, the door opened and Miss Fairchild walked toward them. Her face glowed and, instead of the dark-colored day gowns in which he usually saw her dressed, this night found her in a charming, pale yellow dress that showed off her hair and eyes exquisitely. And the gracefulness of her neck. And the swell of her breasts as they pushed against the still-demure edge of that dress. With her hair pulled up and arranged to allow some of the curls the freedom to follow the curves of her cheeks, she looked...delicious. He swallowed deeply and shifted his stance to discreetly accommodate the other part of him that was appreciating her womanly attributes.

Simply delicious.

"Miss Fairchild," he greeted her with a bow. "A pleasure to see you once more this day."

"Mr. Archer, I am glad you are here. I wanted to thank you once more for this morning. It was a lovely diversion for both of us and Julia has not stopped talking of it yet."

"You two spent the morning together?" Nate asked, looking from him to Miss Fairchild and back again.

"We three, for Miss Julia consented to be our companion," he answered, watching her face light up as she smiled and nodded. "Miss Fairchild graciously agreed to accompany me on a tour of the Castle and a visit to the Honours of Scotland. Miss Julia was quite the guide around the castle."

Nate was not happy—David could see the growing frown and the change in his stance that spoke of insult. Tension grew until even the lady noticed it.

"I have interrupted your business with Nathaniel. Forgive me," she said. She curtsied once more and smiled at him.

It was the kind of smile that is innocent and wicked at once. Her lips curved into a bow shape and the fullness of them invited him to touch them…to taste them. He cleared his throat instead. This was not the first time he felt tempted to pursue the lovely Anna Fairchild, but he had nothing to offer her. She would not be a suitable match for Dursby's heir. She would never leave Edinburgh.

From the direction and attitude of their past conversations and from his own sources, David knew that she was not inter-

ested in marriage and he would not offer anything less honorable to her. The incident in his past and its repercussions
taught him at least that. He did not quench his physical needs
without much forethought and caution. He would never again.

"We decided to eat later than custom tonight and are about
to sit for dinner, Mr. Archer. Would you care to join us?" Nate
asked in a clipped voice.

Dare he join them? Nate was already growing hostile.
Would that threaten the false identity he'd assumed for his
time here? After the most agreeable time spent with Miss
Fairchild this morning, the chance to enjoy more of her
company before leaving for London was too strong a pull on
him.

"I would like that, Nathaniel. If you're certain this is not
an inconvenience?"

Nate seemed to think on it and his pause was enough to
draw Miss Fairchild's attention. That was all it took for Nate
to repeat the invitation in a more hospitable tone. "It is not in-
convenient. Come then, dinner is ready to be served."

Nate stalked off, calling out to one of the servants about
the addition of a guest, leaving him to escort Miss Fairchild.
He couldn't have been more pleased, even though he knew
there was bad news yet to deliver to his host. His departure
was set for the day after tomorrow and, chances were, he
would not see Miss Fairchild again. By the time they entered
the dining area, a place had been set for him next to Nate's
sister.

Nate handled the introductions and there was a nervous
moment when Clarinda's husband, Lord MacLerie, gave a
suspicious glance. Worried over the possibility of recognition,

he ignored it and changed the subject immediately to something lighthearted. Miss Julia.

The meal, or what he could remember of it, was tasty and filling, but, seated as he was directly across from Miss Fairchild, David found that the view was much more satisfying. The conversation crossed through many different topics, all with a light touch, and no unpleasantness was shown by any as they ate and drank. He marveled at her wit, both humorous and biting, as she offered a not-so-reticent opinion on the various topics. David took some measure of enjoyment in goading her into speaking her mind a few times just so he could watch those expressive eyes flash and those lips move. Soon, too soon in his opinion, it was done, and Lady MacLerie suggested that they take their tea and dessert in the parlor.

"We are *en famille* this evening, Mr. Archer. I hope you do not find the informality of it disagreeable."

"Not at all, Lady MacLerie. Especially since I was the one who invaded your evening at home."

He followed them through the house, up the stairs to the parlor that looked out over the street. A pianoforte sat by one wall and several bookcases along another. The chairs and couches were large and stood gathered in a grouping near the window. The ladies took seats there while the men stood. David accepted a glass of port and remained with Nate and Lord MacLerie.

"What do you do in London, Mr. Archer?" Lord MacLerie asked as they drank their port in the corner of the room.

Miss Fairchild and Lady MacLerie were engrossed in some conversation with their heads bent together—he hesitated to guess at the content of it. Now how could he phrase his answer?

"I handle several estates as well as business interests for several charities." There. The truth dressed up a bit, but the truth nonetheless.

"In London only or other locations?"

"Both, Lord MacLerie." David chose not to pursue it, fearing that the conversation would lead to exposure.

"I have some interests in London and may have need of a man-of-business. Perhaps we can meet when next I'm there to discuss it?"

"Of course," he said, nodding in agreement. The sooner done this topic the better. "Nate knows how to contact me there. If you send word, I will attend you at your convenience."

He made a great show of looking at the ormolu clock sitting on a shelf above the pianoforte and then at Nathaniel. Drinking the last of the port in his glass, he placed it back on the tray and nodded to Nate.

"My lord, my lady, Miss Fairchild," he said loud enough to include the women, "I did not plan to be so long here. I fear I still have business to see to before I leave Edinburgh. Nathaniel, may I speak with you for a moment in private?"

The women gave their farewells and Miss Fairchild appeared to want to say something, but she did not. In truth, this was not the leavetaking he'd imagined. He would rather remain and let the pleasant evening continue. However, the publication in his coat pocket would bring that to an end.

David walked ahead down the stairs and waited as the footman retrieved his coat before speaking. He waved the man off and then faced Nate. Holding the magazine out to him, he shook his head.

"I would ask that you read this after sending Miss Fairchild home. I will meet you at the *Gazette*'s office early in the morning to discuss it."

Nate glanced from the publication now in his hand to David's face.

"I think I will not be pleased by this." Nate began to leaf through the pages and then must have thought better of it. "Half past eight then?"

"I will be there. Please wait until we speak before making any decisions on what recourses are open to you."

Nate's mouth thinned as he considered his plea. With a curt nod, he reached for the door to open it himself. David walked out onto the granite landing and turned back to say…something to mitigate the circumstances, but could think of nothing. He did not want, and did not believe Nate would want, this to escalate out of control, especially when he believed in the causes espoused by Mr. Goodfellow. He turned back to offer his thanks for the dinner and his farewell when Nate closed the door in his face.

But not before catching a glimpse of yellow silk floating along at the top of the stairs. The yellow silk of Miss Fairchild's gown…above the place where his and Nate's exchange had just occurred.

Bloody hell!

Chapter Nine

Nefarious means were all that was left to her if she were going to discover what was going on between Nathaniel and Mr. Archer. The bit of hushed and angry conversation over-heard last night had kept her awake. Turning the words over and over in her mind, Anna could not understand the cause. Now, standing before the office, she pondered her methods.

The carriage sitting just a few yards away was the one Mr. Archer retained for his use while here in Edinburgh, for it was the same one with the same driver who'd transported them to the Castle and the same one that had carried her from school to office several times. If she had not recognized it, the driver called out a greeting to her, confirming her knowledge. She nodded politely and turned the knob on the door.

Silence greeted her, for the others did not report until nine this morning. Nathaniel requesting a meeting before that was to ensure confidentiality. If something was that important, it must affect the magazine and so it was her concern as well. Unsurprising to her, Nathaniel believed he should handle it

without her and just as expected, Anna believed she should
be involved. Hence, the tendency to eavesdrop last evening
and her early arrival this morning. It was only after closing
the door and blocking out the sounds from outside that she
heard the muffled voices.

She walked over to the office door and waited for a
moment or two, deciding whether or not to interrupt their discussion—their rather lively discussion. After hearing their
voices raise each time the other spoke, Anna cursed her curiosity and leaned closer.

Treybourne… Goodfellow… *Gazette*… *Whiteleaf's*…
London… Essays… Causes… This trip… Agreed…

The words and names she expected to hear went on for a
bit until something on Lesher's desk caught her eye. Could
it be? The newest issue of *Whiteleaf's* had arrived? Anna
walked over, put her reticule down and picked up the publication. The table of contents led her straight to page four,
where his lordship's essay began.

If she thought the opening salvo was bad, the essay became
more and more rancorous with each sentence and paragraph.
She had to lean back on the desk for support as she continued to read. First her mouth dropped open and then she heard
herself gasp loudly several times.

Lord Treybourne's conclusion was a challenge, as clear
as if a glove had been slapped across her, Goodfellow's
face, and seconds had been appointed. Holding the pages
closer, she read:

I believed, when answering the first questions raised in
that other publication, that I was entering, on behalf of

all good-thinking men who support their King and His Government, a discourse worthy of gentlemen of honor. It would appear to this writer that the Enlightenment so highly regarded and reported to have centered in that country to our North, Scotland, has met its demise. Indeed, instead of discussion and assessment, my words and defence of King and Country have been met with demeaning insult and even vile threats.

If men of honor cannot meet and exchange words of political importance and cannot offer their own stance on the situations facing the citizens of this illustrious Kingdom, then more is lost than we know.

One thing that is clear is that my Opponent in this War of Words cannot be a gentleman. A Gentleman would speak his Truth and claim it as his own. A Gentleman would stand tall and not hide behind Anonymity. A Gentleman would use honor as his shield and not skulk about in that so-named "Athens of the North," Unwilling to Reveal his Identity to those he insults with his Accusations of Misappropriation and Disregard for the Common Good.

I did not Choose to Escalate our Political Discussions to a Personal Battle, but I will not Shy away from such a Call. I will Issue one in Return to you—Mr. Goodfellow, I Challenge you to reveal Yourself and Stand in the Light. I would argue that blood will tell and surely yours has Proclaimed you to be a Man Without Honor. Remember, Sir, Blood will Tell.

Yr. Servant,

Treybourne

Anna could not breathe. She could not move. She read the last paragraphs again and still could not believe the rancor and insult contained there. If she were a man, she would call him out and let her weapons answer for her honor. If she were a man… Anna sighed. If she were a man none or little of this would have been necessary.

"Dashed earl!" she muttered and then covered her mouth with her hand. The girls, especially the now-departed Gladys, had a penchant for swearing that was influencing her now, while she was under duress. A regrettable habit indeed, but it felt like a guilty pleasure to say it now when no one else could hear.

This essay was dangerous. Always before, Goodfellow's work had skirted the edges of making his point without making enemies. Opponents, yes, certainly, but now the hostilities were increased and insults led to the impugning of their characters and honor.

This would bring too much attention to the combatants, especially with the earl's demand for disclosure of Goodfellow's identity. The focus needed to stay on the issues or the fight would be lost. And, even more important, if the *Gazette* were forced out of business by the earl's powerful family and political allies, so many lives would be in danger and so much progress would be halted. Anna's financial support of the school, as well as the other smaller charities she funded, would be destroyed. She could not even think about what this would do to her own income and the certain level of comfort which she'd finally be able to afford for her and her sister and aunt.

This no doubt was the issue under discussion inside the office. A discussion that had quieted in the last few seconds. Anna lowered the paper to find both Nathaniel and Mr. Archer staring at her. Perhaps she'd been louder than she thought?

"You have seen this then?" she asked, holding out the magazine in front of her and ignoring that they may have heard her indecorous and inappropriate exclamation.

"Anna," Nathaniel said as he took her by the arm and led her back into the office, "the others will be here shortly. Come inside so we might discuss this."

Something was wrong here. The expressions on their faces spoke of concern for her, yes, but also there was something else there, some emotion that kept flitting across their eyes when they met her gaze.

Guilt.

Anna tried to catch Nathaniel's attention. Then she saw it again. Both of them. As though caught doing something they should not be doing. Guilty as schoolboys.

About what?

She thought back on the snippets of conversation she'd heard last night and then this morning outside the door a few moments ago. Then she considered Mr. Archer's appearance and interest in business matters with Nathaniel and Nathaniel's sullen manners around him. Looking at the publication in her hands, she realized that Nathaniel held a copy last night when she watched him speak to Mr. Archer. Before it was available here in Edinburgh, for she knew it always arrived on the mail coach in the morning.

Mr. Archer had a copy before anyone in Edinburgh received it.

"Mr. Archer…"

The suspicion formed in her mind, but the words would not leave her mouth. Was it possible that Mr. Archer worked for Lord Treybourne? Was he here on the earl's orders? What was his purpose here?

"Miss Fairchild," he said, shaking his head. "I can explain."

She stared at him as the truth struck her. He'd come here to find out about Goodfellow and to prevail on some previous acquaintance with Nathaniel to stop the essays. Apparently Nathaniel had stood his ground, hence the arguments.

"Are you the first round of attack then, Mr. Archer? You come here to undermine the *Gazette*'s commitment to social progress while his lordship continues his assault on Goodfellow from a safer distance in London?"

She did not want to hear his excuses. She did not want to think about his ulterior motives for his attentions. Anna simply did not want to think about all of the ramifications of this revelation. She wanted to leave.

Tossing the magazine at them, she turned and left the office, nearly at a run, nearly knocking over several passersby who had the bad luck to be on their way past the office when she barreled out the door. Clutching her bonnet to her chest, she raced from the corner and down the busy street, weaving around as many people as she could without knocking into any of them. With her head down and ignoring her name being called behind her, she kept moving, turning without looking, until she came to a halt in a small park at the end of a street.

Gasping now because of the strenuous run, she took in a few deep breaths and stumbled over to a bench that sat beneath the grove of trees to the side of a grassy knoll. Sitting down with a thump, Anna gathered her wits and considered what had happened to bring them to this point. Hearing Nathaniel's warnings ringing in her head, she now thought discretion, or at least a bit more tact, might have been in order. Now, all their work, all their dreams, might be in shambles.

How much did Lord Treybourne's man know? If he had targeted Nathaniel for his fury, then perhaps he still did not know the identity of A. J. Goodfellow. Anna did not believe that Nathaniel would willingly expose her, but what threats would be necessary to loosen his tongue? What pressure could Mr. Archer wield on behalf of Lord Treybourne and his powerful family that would weaken Nathaniel in his resolve?

The pain behind her eyes intensified and she closed them and held her hands over them. The sounds of the morning washed over her and she breathed in, trying to release some of the pressure. Anna never did her best thinking under pressure and she needed to be clear-minded about this situation. Lowering her hands, she let the warm breezes pass over her. At that moment she realized her hair was loose and her bonnet was gone.

Could this get any worse? Anna leaned her head down and opened her eyes. A pair of boots positioned before her spoke of much worse. Moving her gaze upward, in spite of fearing who it was that stood before her, she knew before she reached the man's face whom it would be.

"Mr. Archer," she said in an icy tone.

"I can explain this, Miss Fairchild." He stepped closer. "May I sit down?" He nodded at the bench, but she was not feeling charitable or polite enough to offer him its hospitality.

"I would prefer that you did not."

Next he did the one thing guaranteed to get her attention—nothing. He stood there, his gaze filled to overflowing with concern and his manner so completely at ease despite the fact that he had also run more than six blocks in the morning's heat. Not a hair was out of place though hers was in shambles and she was aware that beads of sweat gathered on her forehead, neck and back and trickled down beneath her gown. Then she noticed that he held her bonnet behind his back. She tilted her head to see it more clearly.

"Ah, I found this on my way down the street a few blocks back. I thought you might want it for the walk back?"

Mr. Archer held it out to her and took advantage of that movement to sit beside her. Anna slid to the other end of the seat, as far as she could. Insufferable man! Rearranging her hair behind her head, she placed the bonnet over it and tugged it into position. Until she could redress her hair entirely, the bonnet would not fit. This would have to do for now.

"Miss Fairchild, I admit that my actions might be mistaken for…" He paused and searched for a word. She provided it.

"Deceit, sir? Fraud, perhaps? Or simple misrepresentation?"

"How did I misrepresent myself to you, Miss Fairchild? What have I said that you consider a lie?" He turned now and faced her. Although his expression was fixed, there was not the hardness or haughtiness of their first encounter.

"You did not tell me you represented Lord Treybourne." She used the most obvious, *and the most dangerous one,* first.

"My business was not with you, Miss Fairchild, and I did not know what your association to the *Gazette* or Mr. Hobbs-

Smith might be. Nathaniel knows of my connection to Lord Treybourne."

Of course Nathaniel knew him. She could not lay this sin only at Mr. Archer's feet, for Nathaniel should have told her. As was his custom, Nathaniel tried to protect her from the realities of life. Anna let out a breath.

"Why are you here?" she asked.

"What is your connection to the *Gazette?*" he fired back in response. When she did not reply immediately, Mr. Archer leaned back against the bench and crossed his leg over his knee, exposing the fine figure of his thighs to her view. She blinked and then tried to bring her gaze back to his face.

"You see," he said, "for all intents and purposes and regardless of the time spent together in this last week, we are strangers to each other, Miss Fairchild. And there are limits to how much we reveal of ourselves to strangers."

He was correct after all, and without revealing how involved she truly was in the ownership and management of the *Gazette,* she could say nothing more. And Anna could not reveal the level to which her financial interests and control were invested there. But she could allow him a glimpse at why she did so.

"I support the ideas that the *Gazette* is promoting, sir. Social and parliamentary reform. Assistance to those in less fortunate circumstances. And as a longtime acquaintance and family friend to Nathaniel, I do what I can to assist him in his pursuit of those causes."

"Ah, Miss Fairchild, a bluestocking *and* a liberal?"

She hesitated, for instead of the insult usually meant when those words were spoken, his deep voice made them an appealing combination. Somehow, he imbued those words with respect.

"Yes, sir, both, and inordinately proud to be called either," she replied, lifting her chin and daring him to say they were otherwise.

She was magnificent!

As she sat there challenging him with her chin tilted back and her eyes blazing, he fought the dual urges to smile and to drag her into his arms and kiss her until she was breathless. Not the simpering misses of the *haute ton* in London, Miss Anna Fairchild made her point with intelligence and common sense. She thought about serious matters and did not dwell on those that plagued most single women in his class, such as the weighty issues of which mantua-maker to patronize or which soiree to attend.

For all those details he knew about her and her life, and now these opinions and causes so close to his own true ones, he felt a wave of respect grow inside him. David recognized this feeling, and that it, along with the all too apparent and all too frequent attraction he felt toward her, was dangerous for many, many reasons. David sat up and straightened his waistcoat and jacket.

"In honor of your disclosure, let me tell you this. I am here on Lord Treybourne's behalf. I seek out the identity of the person who is currently publishing essays under the name of Mr. A. J. Goodfellow. And having found myself on the opposite side of the opinions of Lord Treybourne, I came to see if I could negotiate an agreement between both *gentlemen* involved to return to the original level of discourse at which these essays first began."

The lady startled with each revelation and he worried that she would see the whole truth behind his prevarications. Nothing he'd told her was a lie, but nothing he revealed was the complete truth of the matter, either. Caught between his own beliefs and his father's increasing demands, David had thought to find the man and come to some agreement with him. If they each backed down from the height of their arguments, yet each maintained their positions and fought for them in the publications each month, all would win. So, coming to Edinburgh, under the cover of an assumed identity, seemed the thing to do.

Now, looking at her face, watching her eyes darken as she considered what he'd told her, and wanting to know more about her for nothing but his own personal reasons, David knew he'd made several tactical errors. The way that she made his heart beat wildly, he wondered if retreat were even still possible.

"From the essay I just read, it would seem that Lord Treybourne does not value or agree with your efforts in this matter."

"He can be stubborn, Miss Fairchild. One must wear him down in order to gain his compliance." He noticed that her gaze softened then and he smiled back. "Is Mr. Goodfellow as stubborn?"

"I cannot speak for him, sir, but I expect that this newest volley from Lord Treybourne will not go unanswered."

As he suspected, there would be at least one more escalation in their exchanges before they could bring it under control. There were advantages to this, of course, for each essay brought an increase in the sales and subscriptions for their respective magazines, thereby increasing the attention drawn to the issues.

"I thought as much, Miss Fairchild." He stood and offered her his arm. "Nathaniel must be frantic by now and ready to call the city police. May I escort you back to the *Gazette?*"

Although she gave him a glance that spoke of indecision, she rose and slid her hand around his arm, allowing his escort. She also wore no gloves—working around newsprint and ink most likely made that impossible—and so the tips of her fingers lay just past the end of his sleeve, touching his skin directly. Shivers tore through him as he noticed it. He began to walk but he knew not in which direction. After a few aimless blocks, she pointed him in the correct direction but did not remove her hand from his. Just before they'd reached the intersection of the office, she tugged him to stop.

"What are your plans now, Mr. Archer, if I might inquire?"

Leave Edinburgh while I still can were the words that came to mind, but facing her on the busy street, all he could think about was finding reasons to stay longer.

"I will finish the business I have to accomplish and then go back to London."

"And report to his lordship?" she asked. Her eyes narrowed and he could hear the suspicion in her voice.

"Yes."

"Do you think his lordship will seek to destroy Nathaniel's publishing business?" She lowered her voice and leaned closer. "That is my greatest fear, Mr. Archer."

Stunned at the private revelation she'd shared with him, he searched her face for some sign of falseness. Convinced that her concern was honest and personal, too, he offered frankness in his answer.

"I do not believe that Lord Treybourne would do any such thing, but I cannot speak for those around him." David stepped back.

He'd spoken the truth of the matter for he was truly alarmed over what he thought his father had already done, or had done on his behalf—altered the text he had written for the essay before it was published. His missive, though strongly worded, did not include the venomous insult that the one published contained. For now, from here, he could do nothing but wait for Mr. Goodfellow's response. Certainly, there was another thing he could do while waiting.

"His father, the marquess?"

"Just so, Miss Fairchild. I cannot vouch for the lordship's actions." She thought on his words and nodded at him. "And now, Miss Fairchild? What will you do now?"

"I will continue as I did before you arrived in Edinburgh, sir. Seeing to things that are important and living one day at a time."

"The causes you favor?"

"Yes, Mr. Archer, and my sister's well-being and future."

"And your own future, Miss Fairchild? Who will see to that?"

The words spilled out before he could stop them. It was a completely inappropriate and impolite question, made even more so since it came from a stranger. The expected answer came in a soft whisper, filled with an air of quiet desperation and loss. And when it came, it nearly knocked the stuffing out of him with its simplicity and loneliness.

"As before, sir, I will see to it."

* * *

Anna crossed the street and approached the office…and Nathaniel, with some amount of trepidation. Their relationship was a strange mix of personal, family and friendship, with a botched attempt at romantic thrown in as well. By all rights, she should be furious now at him. Upon her arrival, Lesher, who stood near his desk reading the copy of *Whiteleaf's* she'd dropped there as Nathaniel had pulled her into his office, nodded a greeting and returned to reading. By the manner in which he shook his head and tsked, Anna could tell he was reading Lord Treybourne's piece.

She approached the doorway and took a deep breath, pushing the door open to discover the office was empty and Nathaniel was gone. She heard Lesher approach from behind.

"I saw him going out on my way in, miss."

"Did he say where he was going?" Had he followed her? Had he gone out for some other reason?

"He, I, went looking for you, Anna," Nathaniel said as he entered and walked up to where she stood. "I feared you would be upset by the disclosure made here." He stepped into the office and closed the door behind them. "Come. Sit. We have much to discuss."

His manner was different somehow, but she joined him inside and sat by the desk. Anna untied her bonnet and removed it; she would repair the damage done to her hair when they finished. Once seated, she waited for him to begin.

"I was not truthful with you, Anna, and I sincerely apologize." He met her gaze and she saw the regret there. "I blame it on simply trying to protect you."

"Would not the truth have been better? Why did you not

just admit you knew Mr. Archer because of his connection to Lord Treybourne?"

"I believed I could handle him and he would be gone before you knew. I was only trying to…" he stuttered along.

"Nathaniel, you have been a dear friend and have been my stalwart in this endeavor. Mr. Archer explained that you have been negotiating a truce of sorts in this matter." Anna leaned in and watched his reaction at her next question. "Does he know the truth about our situation?"

"Anna, I would never do anything to endanger you. I did not tell him anything that is not public already."

"Did he ask about Mr. Goodfellow?" She continued her observations as he answered.

"He did and I told him that I did not know the identity or anything about the man. Mr. Archer only asked that I negotiate with the writer to cool the fires created by the heightening of tensions between the dueling essayists."

Anna rested back in the chair and considered their options. When she realized there was a spy in their midst, the terror overwhelmed her and she'd run. Now, after comprehending Mr. Archer's involvement and his obvious displeasure with his employer's actions, she thought there might be a solution to their dilemma.

"Mr. Archer shared with me that he is not in complete agreement with Lord Treybourne's opinions in this."

"What?" Nathaniel asked, startled by the revelation.

"I believe that we can sway him to our cause and he can use his influence over the earl. If not to change his position, and I understand how that may not be possible, then to keep him from any drastic measures that might influence our solvency here."

"Sway the earl?" Nathaniel had a blank look on his face, but since he did not object, she explained more.

"I do not think that Mr. Archer would stand by and watch as the earl destroys this publication if he knew what the money from our endeavors supported. I think we should tell him." She paused, for Nathaniel made the most distressing sound at her suggestion. He tugged at the neckline of his shirt and tried to loosen his cravat.

"Anna," he whispered.

She shook her head. "Do not misunderstand my intentions in this. I simply think that Mr. Archer has a conscience and if he sees the people dependent on our success, especially on our financial success, he will attempt to mitigate matters with the earl on our behalf."

In spite of the still early hour of the day, she watched as Nathaniel reached into the bottom drawer of the desk and lifted out a bottle and a glass. Without ever looking at her, he poured several ounces of whisky into the glass and drank it straight down without pause or hesitation. Anna intervened when he tilted the bottle to fill the glass once more.

"Nathaniel, I will show him the school. I will inform him as to its funding and how it is dependent on this publishing endeavor. How the other charities are as well. I will show him the conditions that the poor live in here and around the city and how we are trying to help."

Anna stood at his side and lifted the bottle and glass from his grasp. This was not the time to lose control of his sensibilities. She needed him to continue in his role as she would in hers, at least until Mr. Archer could be convinced. At least until the next Goodfellow essay came out. Two weeks at the longest.

"Stay the course for two more weeks, three at the most, Nathaniel. In the meantime, meet with the Whig ministers who are here for the August break in Parliament, or on their way to their hunting boxes, and solidify your position amongst them. If something untoward should happen, you will still have a future with them."

"Untoward?" he asked. "Untoward?" he moaned, lowering his head in his hands and shaking it side to side.

When he began to argue, she sat down again and made her case with him point by point. Strong spirits had their place it seemed in the negotiating process for a wee dram with each point appeared to make the discussion go smoothly. By mid-morning, she had a plan of attack and he was in his cups.

David bided his time by carrying out some errands and visiting his banker before going back to the *Gazette*'s office. Almost two hours had passed since he'd left Miss Fairchild there and he needed to find out if she suspected that he'd not been completely truthful with her. Or if Nate had revealed the truth to her? Opening the door and nodding to the men working there, he strode down the corridor toward Nate's office and reached for the door.

"'E's no' to be disturbed, sir," Lesher said from behind him.

"He's expecting me, Mr. Lesher," David lied with confidence, and did not wait for any further objections.

Turning the knob, he entered the office to find Nate asleep and drooling, with his head resting on the desk at an awkward angle. The odor of strong spirits filled the air. A loud snore echoed through the office and Nate shifted, now slobbering on his arm. When his first three efforts to rouse him were un-successful, David realized his friend was drunk as an Emperor. Finally, the fourth vigorous shake seemed to wake Nate from his whisky-induced stupor.

"Let me be!" he moaned.

"Nate, wake up!" David shook him by the shoulders and waited for his eyes to open. One did.

"It's you!" Nate moaned as he pulled from David's grasp.

"Yes, it is me. Now, Nate, I need you to concentrate on my words. Did you talk to Miss Fairchild about me?"

"Yessss," he slurred. "She only wanted to talk about you." Nate kept closing one eye and opening the other, as though it were difficult to see with both eyes at the same time.

"You are cupshot!"

"It was Anna who did it. She plied me with whisky, she did." A loud belch emanated from him and then another groan. "She is a devil!"

"What did she say about me?" David asked.

"She said…" He paused, leaning back and, this time, managing to open both eyes at the same time. "She thinks you have a conscience…." His words drifted off as he fell back asleep once more.

"She does? Miss Fairchild does?" he asked, shaking his drunken friend to rouse him. "What did the lady say, Nate?"

Nate raised his head and his eyes opened at an unusual pace—first one, then the other, then neither, then both. David knew from past experience that there would be suffering for his friend after this kind of overindulgence.

"You were speaking of my conscience," David repeated.

"She only said that because…" He paused and looked

around as if confirming that they were alone. In a lower voice, he continued, "Because she does not know that you are *you*."

The next question came out before he could stop it. In spite of knowing it was not a good thing to press his luck, he asked, "Why did you not tell her the truth then?"

Nate sat up straight in the chair and for a moment, David thought that his drunkenness was all an act. Pulling back his shoulders and clearing his throat, Nate squinted and then stared at him with only one eye.

"It would break her heart, Trey, and that is something I will not do to her."

A reply stuck in his throat and he recognized the true emotion behind Nate's actions—he loved her. Well, that certainly explained several things and answered a few of his own questions.

"So, worry not, *the earl's* secret is safe."

Without warning, his friend fell onto the surface of the desk and began to snore. This time, David did nothing to awaken Nate, allowing him to sleep as he stepped away. He knew well the desire to protect the young woman in question. For, despite knowing all the reasons why he should not feel it, he shared the need to protect her.

It had begun during their outing to the Castle and continued to increase even today as he watched her reaction to learning of his assumed identity and the possible threats it posed to those people and causes she held dear. He could feel himself falling into the same trap as Nate—since the woman worried about everyone but herself, he worried over her.

He shuddered at the realization. David could not afford such an entanglement. He was here for a purpose and, once completed, he would return to his life and continue his work. He did not toy with innocents. He did not break hearts. If he'd learned nothing else from the debacle of his past, it was to avoid young, unattached women who carried unblemished reputations and eager eyes. Miss Anna Fairchild certainly fit that description.

David positioned his hat and opened the door of the office, resolved now to finish his quest and leave Edinburgh behind as planned. Closing the door quietly so as not to wake Nate, he made his way down the corridor, nodded at Mr. Lesher and left. As he climbed into his waiting carriage, he understood that caution must be exercised, for Miss Fairchild was an intelligent woman and would not miss careless mistakes made on his part upholding his false identity.

Chapter Ten

~~~

"Did he respond, Clarinda?"

"No. As you requested, I sent the invitation purposely late so that he would not have time to beg off."

Anna turned in her seat and looked around the seating area of the Theatre Royal for any sign of Mr. Archer. The show would start at any moment and she did not see him. Of course, Clarinda's box opened to the back and he could enter through there without walking up the aisle. She sat back and shook her head.

"Perhaps I did not plan this well after all?" she mumbled as a stirring began outside the curtained box.

"Did not plan what well, Miss Fairchild?"

She would recognize his voice even in the dark. Mr. Archer had accepted the invitation after all. He held the curtain back and entered the small enclosure with six seats. Anna glared at Clarinda and touched her handkerchief to her forehead with a great amount of dramatic exaggeration.

"To be inside the theater on such a heated evening, sir. I

should have planned my wardrobe with more thought to the weather and the heat."

A quick glance at Clarinda showed that her friend was going to laugh, so Anna lowered her handkerchief and turned back to Mr. Archer, who apparently had just noticed that he was the only male present there.

"I assume that Lord MacLerie and Nathaniel had other plans," he said. "I cannot believe my good fortune then to be left in the company of three lovely women."

Clarinda was familiar with the compliments of flirting men, as was Anna, who'd received her own share of them over the years. But Aunt Euphemia giggled much in the way Julia did when she was feeling silly. Peering across Clarinda, Anna wondered which of her relatives was teaching the other the trait.

Mr. Archer greeted each one individually, speaking kindly to her aunt and inquiring about her various complaints before thanking Lady MacLerie for inviting him to this evening's entertainment. When he stood behind her, Anna found herself nervous with anticipation over what he would say.

It had been just over a week since she'd seen him last. The morning that had brought about the revelation of his identity also brought his absence from the city. Anna discovered that she had grown to expect his presence outside the house where she taught or in front of the *Gazette*'s office. And Julia spoke incessantly of their trip to the Castle.

Nathaniel informed her of his note about leaving to go north to one of Lord Treybourne's family properties and, at the time, she thought it a superb idea and excellent timing. As was her custom, she used the first few days after receiving

Lord Treybourne's latest essay to sketch out her immediate reactions and initial thoughts on addressing his arguments. Then Anna planned several "occasions" when she would lead Mr. Archer to various places in Edinburgh where the unfortunates lived and struggled to survive. This evening's invitation was not one of those, but would be the beginning of her plan.

Those activities had taken all of one day and then she waited. When she found herself staring out the window of the office, she stopped herself. When she discovered she stood, on the sidewalk outside the school, watching the street for some sign of that carriage he'd hired, she berated herself for such foolishness. When she maneuvered Clarinda into this invitation tonight, Anna acknowledged one unavoidable fact: despite his association with the dreaded Lord Treybourne, she found Mr. Archer exceedingly appealing. Now, as the houselights dimmed and the crowd focused its attention toward the stage, he chose the chair behind hers and sat down.

The first part of tonight's entertainment consisted of a humorous skit about a local fishwife, and soon the entire audience shook with laughter over the woman's antics. Mr. Archer's deep rumbles of laughter from behind her caught her attention. Then, a few minutes later, it was his breath against her neck and ear that nearly sent her off the edge of her seat.

"I have heard rumors that Rob Roy is being produced for the stage, Miss Fairchild."

A simple statement, a respectable piece of theater gossip considering that the story had been first published here, but the feel of his heated breath on her skin sent chills down her back and raised gooseflesh on her arms. Yet, in spite of the strange and somewhat forbidden feelings it engendered within her, she hoped he would whisper again.

He did.

"It is said that the author even now works on the play in his estate by the Borders."

Again, an innocently whispered comment with devastating results. This time, when she pressed her handkerchief to her forehead, she really was perspiring and overheated. Yet, she did not move herself farther away from his tempting behavior. Clarinda tapped lightly on Anna's hand with her fan, warning her that they were being noticed. The skit finished and, as the stage was being set up for the next performers, Mr. Archer stood.

"Would you ladies care for something chilled to drink?"

At their nod, he turned to leave and Anna decided she would give him assistance in his errand. "Clarinda, I will show Mr. Archer the way."

Since several of Clarinda's acquaintances were heading up the aisle to their box and calling to her, Lady MacLerie was soon distracted. Aunt Euphemia was likewise engaged, so Anna followed Mr. Archer out into the corridor. The crush of people seeking refreshments carried them down the stairs to the place where the establishment sold cups of punch or lemonade as well as something stronger for the gentlemen.

He surprised her when, instead of waiting in the lines, he pulled a footman aside and whispered something to him. Anna noticed a few coins exchanging hands and knew what he'd done.

"If I might prevail upon you, Miss Fairchild? I feel the need to take a brief respite from this heat. Would you care to step outside for a moment?"

There were sufficient crowds around that she did not think this completely inappropriate. Indeed, many of those in attendance were heading out of doors during this brief intermission. They walked a few paces out the door and Mr. Archer led her to a small open space not far from the sidewalks. Then he stepped back and took a place at the edge of the shadows, one that obscured his face. Anna glanced around to see if they were being watched.

"Are you hiding, Mr. Archer?"

"You noticed, then?" His voice held amusement.

"Whatever for, sir? Are you not permitted an evening of leisure?" Anna laughed softly and looked around again. "No one seems to have taken an interest in your presence here." He did not step out of the shadows. "Is Lord Treybourne such a hard taskmaster that he never permits you to seek entertainment on your own?"

"I simply do not wish to defend or uphold his latest position on his behalf, Miss Fairchild."

"Ah, so you know that the furor still rages here over his words? There does seem to be something of a battle brewing."

He reached out and used a single finger to lift her chin. The movement so surprised her that she stayed within his touch.

"You do not seem displeased by such a reaction. Do you think this will help Mr. Goodfellow's arguments then?"

"I think," she said, "that it will help bring attention to the issues. Lord Treybourne's arrogance and unfeeling nature will demonstrate the shortcomings of his party's beliefs and approach to the poor."

He moved his hand so that his fingers slipped around her chin and the back of his hand caressed her cheek for a scant moment. "Do you never think of anything but the serious matters of society?" His smile was enigmatic for a second and then broader and more open. "Do you never have an evening of leisure for yourself?"

"We were speaking of Lord Treybourne's demands on your time, Mr. Archer." Anna pulled away then, afraid of how much she enjoyed his touch. Delicious shivers raced through her after only the slightest of caresses.

"Ah, so it is the mere mention of Lord Treybourne that sends you into this righteous anger? You give his lordship great power in your life."

Anna wanted to argue and point out the many faults of the man that she—no—that Goodfellow battled, but the thought of that touch of his hand silenced her. She remembered back to the first time she saw him in Nathaniel's office and realized that her first impression was true—he was the devil incarnate tempting her with the worldly things she'd ignored and never thought to have in her life.

He reached up once more, but this time he simply replaced a curl that had fallen in her face. Did he know the power *he had* right now? If Anna were some innocent just out of the schoolroom, she might be lured into something quite dangerous with this man, his connection to Lord Treybourne be damned!

"You gasped. Are you well, Miss Fairchild?"

Her lack of control brought him closer now and Anna found herself tugged a step or two into those shadows where he stood. Now next to her, she had to tilt her head back to look at his face. Another mistake, for he leaned his head down and for a moment, a very long moment, she thought he might try to kiss her.

She thought.

She hoped.

She prayed.

She repented and tried to clear her mind of whatever bewitching spell he was placing on her better judgment. It didn't work, for she found herself watching his lips as he spoke to her.

"If you are to swoon, Miss Fairchild, let it be over something pleasant like this and not over that boring old Lord Treybourne."

She began to laugh, but his kiss covered the sound of it. He touched his lips to hers softly at first and then with a bit more persistence. Only his mouth greeted hers, and when she started to ask him about his insult, he took advantage of her distraction to slip his tongue inside. He tasted of something minty and something else unknown to her. Then, as quickly as it had begun, Mr. Archer stepped away and took a breath.

She could not breathe, it was as simple as that. He had mentioned swooning and although never having done it before in her life, no matter the circumstances, Anna felt ready to now. Even worse, she could form no words to speak after the experience. She was fully aware that his behavior had been too forward and that she should reprimand him and warn him of the consequences of another attempt. The problem was that in her heart of hearts she would welcome his mouth on hers again.

And again.

The world around her that had faded away at his first touch and disappeared during his kiss now intruded. The movement of those who'd sought a cooler respite outside between performances and were now moving back inside drew their attention. Mr. Archer held out his arm to her and it was a trembling hand she placed there. If he had said something then, something amusing or irritating, she could have found a voice, but instead he led her back into the theatre, up the stairs and to the back of Clarinda's box without a word.

The footman he'd spoken to near the line to buy refreshments stood there and nodded as they approached. In his hands he held a tray of five glasses of lemonade, which Mr. Archer lifted and carried in as the footman now held the curtain back. Anna was left to follow.

"Ah, Mr. Archer! I was beginning to despair of something to drink." Aunt Euphemia smiled at him and looked past to Anna. Her eyes narrowed and Anna wondered if everyone would see some mark on her that exposed their scandalous moment outside. "Anna, help Mr. Archer with those glasses, if you please."

Mr. Archer stepped into the back row of seats and allowed Anna to move past him to hand both her aunt and Clarinda a glass. The audience had quieted and the second performance was about to begin.

"Anna, pray be seated!" Aunt Euphemia whispered loudly.

With no alternative, Anna sat in the chair behind Clarinda and Mr. Archer took the last seat next to her. Her cheeks felt heated now more than before and Anna touched them to see if it was an illusion. How did she proceed now?

The musical introduction to the "drama in two acts" began and Anna sipped at her lemonade. Downing it in two mouthfuls, it proved no success in helping her to cool from the heat and from the kiss that had occurred. Tempted now to press the empty glass to her forehead and cheeks to use its chill to ease the heat in her skin, she could not, for Mr. Archer lifted it from her grasp and placed the other filled one there.

"You appear to need this more than I, Miss Fairchild."

She glanced at him and noticed that he, too, had finished his drink. For the first time since *it* happened, Anna allowed herself to meet his gaze and found some evidence that he had been just as affected by that kiss as she.

"My thanks, sir. You have, it seems, thought of everything this evening."

Not everything he wanted to reply to her. Instead, he took her now-empty second glass and placed it with his on the tray held next to him by the footman. Once he'd gone and the curtain fell back into place, David tried to determine what the devil had made him be so forward with Miss Fairchild.

Try as he might, he could not fathom the reasons for breaking from all of his plans and indulging in a familiarity with this young woman. That was not being honest with himself, for one look at that face and those lips now swollen from only one kiss and there was no doubt that, given the opportunity, he would attempt to repeat the sin again.

He was not an untried lad when it came to women and the pleasurable arts, but the innocent kiss allowed him by Miss Fairchild moved him far more than he'd like to admit. She tempted him to ignore some of the promises he kept to himself and others in a way that no other woman had.

"I do try, Miss Fairchild," he whispered.

David leaned against the back of the chair and watched her profile as she watched the actors on stage. He had indeed made arrangements with the footman to meet them here with the beverages so that he could escape with her for a few moments. The kiss, well, the kiss had happened all on its own.

She turned to him, their eyes meeting for only an instant, but the emotions he saw there overwhelmed him. She broke the encounter and glanced back at the stage. Surely, this could not have been her first kiss? Surely not. However, the innocence he tasted suggested it could be.

How had this woman escaped marriage? Quite the bluestocking, it was true, but she used that intelligence to help others. And she was caring and thoughtful. And protective of those she loved. And graceful and…

This was going in a direction he could not follow, but David refused to think about simply leaving Edinburgh and not seeing her again. He'd tried that. Spending the week fishing and shooting with Ellerton and Hillgrove held little appeal once he arrived at the Dursby hunting box. He saw her everywhere he looked and she even invaded his dreams. The kiss he'd just shared with her paled in comparison with those they shared in the dark of night when Miss Fairchild haunted his sleep.

He could call her Anna there. He did not have to be polite and reserved toward her in his dreams and she screamed out his name, not his title, when he made love to her thoroughly, showing her the passion she had yet to discover. He shifted in his seat as his body reacted again to his thoughts and desires about her.

"Pardon me, Mr. Archer. Did you say something?" she whispered now. Not his name as he'd like, but he must have spoken without realizing it.

"No, Miss Fairchild. Did I disturb your enjoyment of the performance?"

She sighed then, a light airy noise that set him straight into even worse shape than he had been. "No, Mr. Archer. I am enjoying this evening immensely."

She turned and gazed at him then, giving him some hope that she was as truly affected by their breach in behavior as he was. David swallowed and then again, his mouth drier now than before. He'd drank the lemonade in one gulp and now he was definitely in need of something much, much stronger. Miss Fairchild had picked up her fan and began using it. Had she any idea of how much he needed one of those fripperies right at this moment?

David forced his urges back under control and tried to center his attentions on the actors parading across the stage instead of the young woman at his side. Only a few more days here until he was certain that Goodfellow had turned in his next essay, and then he could leave. He planned to use a bit of arm-twisting if need be on Nate to get an advanced look at it before he left for London and his own next article.

It was as he was glancing around the theater that he thought he saw a familiar face in the audience. In the low light, David could not be certain that it was the man he thought, but he could really not take any chances of being recognized. He needed to avoid even a chance of being recognized until he completed his task. It would be abrupt, but he leaned forward and spoke in a low voice to Lady MacLerie.

"Do you have a carriage waiting, or is Nathaniel returning for you?"

"We have a carriage waiting, Mr. Archer," she replied. At once, she glanced over her shoulder at Miss Fairchild. "Is there some problem?"

"None at all, Lady MacLerie. I have just remembered a previous commitment which cannot be avoided, even if I would rather remain here. If you are certain that you do not need my escort, I will take my leave of you. You have my thanks for including me in this evening." When it could not be delayed any longer, he turned to Miss Fairchild to give his regrets as well. She was quicker than him.

"Mr. Archer, it was good of you to join us, in spite of our late invitation."

Still wearing an inscrutable expression, one that had graced her face since their kiss, she nodded. David wished he knew what she was thinking, what she thought of the kiss—had it been addlebrained familiarity or something else?—but she said nothing. "Miss Fairchild, a pleasure as always."

With a hurried bow, he left the box and then took the back stairs down and out of the theater. A double line of private carriages and coaches stood at the ready in the street outside the building and extended up Princes Street while the hired hackneys stood along the North Bridge waiting their turn. David pulled his hat down and walked the several blocks to where he'd left his own hired coach, and climbed in.

Although no closer to finding Mr. Goodfellow than when he first arrived in Edinburgh, David knew with certainty that he was much closer to trouble.

"Anna," Clarinda whispered. "Come and sit by me now."

Anna stood and stepped around the chair in front of her and sat down then next to Clarinda. "Not so engrossing a plot?" she asked as she nodded past Clarinda to where Aunt Euphemia now sat, head bowed, sleeping.

Clarinda reached over and touched Anna's cheek. Anna knew it was still hot and doubted that it would ever cool. Each new thought about Mr. Archer and his kiss created a new wave of heat that poured through her. Her cheeks simply gave the condition away.

"He kissed you!" Clarinda whispered, and then in a lower voice she asked it. "He kissed you?"

Anna could not deny it, but did not want this to be the center of some conversation that could be overheard. "Please, Clarinda. Keep your voice down. There is no reason to make this the new topic of gossip."

"That bounder! I thought him a person of some manners. Just wait until Nathaniel…"

Anna stopped her by grasping her hand and squeezing it tightly. "Mr. Archer did not offend me. He simply kissed me," she whispered back. "It is not the first stolen kiss in history, not even my own first stolen kiss, so be at ease with this." She looked at her friend for acceptance of her words. "And say nothing of this to Nathaniel."

"So, you enjoyed it then?" Clarinda asked, now she had hold of Anna's hand and would not relinquish it. Aunt Euphemia shifted in her seat then and they both watched her until she settled back to sleep. "Well?"

Clarinda could be relentless and creative in her efforts to discover any tidbits of information or, in their younger years, secrets Anna carried, so Anna decided to give her the truth.

"Yes," she said quietly.

And she had. Even when she comprehended what his intentions were, she did not stop him. Simply stepping away from where he stood in the shadows, even before that—not allowing him to pull her there—would have prevented it. Clarinda let her hand go and then patted it as she placed it on her lap.

"I had all but given up on you, Anna. Perhaps there is hope after all."

"Whatever do you mean?"

"With all of your—" she paused and threw a glance at Aunt Euphemia "—with all of your interests and causes and your work with Nathaniel, I had all but despaired of you ever finding an acceptable man and settling to the idea of marriage."

"Clarinda, this was only a kiss. A simple kiss," she replied. As she uttered the words, her heart gave lie to them. There was more than that, but she did not want to think on it.

"Ah. Much more than a kiss, Anna. It is a sign that there is hope for you yet."

"Not all women want to settle into marriage, Clarinda."

How could she even have spoken those words? Of course, most, all women wanted marriage. That was the way of things. Anna found that she wanted other things first and if it meant postponing her own personal happiness for a bit, well, that was fine with her.

"It is a sign, Anna, and I will not hear otherwise. I suppose I should reexamine Robert's staff and the local gentry for suitable matches for you."

Anna closed her eyes and prayed that the drama, both the one onstage and this one in the boxes, would soon be over. It only became worse.

"Perhaps Mr. Archer could be brought up to scratch? He seems like an amenable man, high in the esteem of his employer from the look of him. Intelligent. More than passing good looks."

Anna opened her eyes and stared at her friend. This was moving too fast and in too dangerous a direction.

"And from the calf-eyed look on your face when you came back in here, a more than passing good kisser as well."

Could someone swallow their own tongue if they were not in the middle of a fit? Anna wished that Clarinda would do so in that moment, but instead she herself began choking and Clarinda was patting her on the back to help her recover her breath.

"Come now, Anna, you are not some squeamish girl. We have spoken most candidly about the physical pleasures to be had in marriage. It is part of that estate. And Robert, well, Robert is…"

Anna lifted her hand to Clarinda's mouth to stop this conversation. "I only need to know that you are happy in your marriage. I need no more details that will make it difficult to meet the man's gaze when next he speaks to me." She leaned closer, for Aunt Euphemia seemed restless and about to wake from her nap. "And about Mr. Archer."

"Yes?"

"He works for a man who seeks to destroy everything that I believe is important, everything that Nathaniel and I have worked so hard for. It would be complicated to look past that fact."

"Ah, complicated. Life is complicated, Anna, as is love."

"Clarinda! It was only a kiss! Do not make more out of it than that, I beg you."

The audience began to applaud, marking the end of the production on stage and waking Aunt Euphemia from her sleep.

"Very good! Very good!" she called out without hesitation and disregarding the fact that she had missed most of the show. "Too bad that Mr. Archer had to leave early, for he missed a wonderful performance."

Clarinda and Anna shared a dubious glance at her and then stood, straightening their gowns and collecting their accoutrements. Anna knew from the frown on her friend's face that their private discussion was not over, just postponed to a different time and place. A time and place preferably without the presence of her dear aunt.

As they made their way to the MacLerie coach, through the crowds, greeting this neighbor or that acquaintance, Anna feared that Clarinda had the truth of it.

It was more than just a kiss.

Chapter Eleven

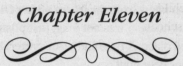

"What do you mean she was not there?"

"The driver said he waited two hours and the young woman never left the building."

"That's damned strange, Harley," David said. He closed the book he was reading and straightened in his chair. "She is nothing if not a creature of habit. He went to the correct place?"

"My lord, he said he waited in the place where you have waited and Miss Fairchild did not leave."

The rain poured outside and David watched it streaking down the windowpanes. Dark clouds tumbled across the sky and covered any hopes of a pleasant day in Edinburgh. Although the driver assured him that these late-summer storms passed quickly, he could only think of Miss Fairchild making her way along the slick cobblestones as she walked from one of her "commitments," as she called them, to the next.

The daft woman would be carrying that large umbrella he'd seen, the one big and sturdy enough to drag her for blocks if the wind got caught under its frame of canvas and wood. And she'd be wearing that large dark canvas overcoat to keep the rain from her. He'd laughed the first time he saw her walking by in it, but realized it was her way of avoiding the use, and cost, of hackneys or sedan chairs.

"Should I tell him to return and wait longer?"

Miss Fairchild—Anna, as he now thought of her—had changed her schedule. This was Tuesday morning and she should be at her teaching duties there on the High Street. Nathaniel sent word late yesterday that he was called to his family's estate south of Edinburgh and would be gone several days. His absence was part of the reason David had returned to the city after losing all patience with Ellerton and Hillgrove and their leisure activities.

"No. I will be going out after all, Harley."

Harley let out a loud, irritated sigh, which David refused to acknowledge or answer, and turned to leave. "Very good, my lord."

Tensions were growing and he could not imagine Nate making himself scarce this close to the next issue of the *Gazette* coming out. Keys had discovered that Mr. Lesher was the managing editor of the magazine, handling the day-to-day duties and overseeing the others who worked for the publication. But, with so much importance now on each issue and on each essay in the battle between the earl and Mr. Good-fellow, David did not understand how Nate could leave for the country now. And, at present, Miss Fairchild seemed to be missing or, at the least, not where her usual habits would have her.

Within minutes, the hired carriage traveled up Nicolson

Street, over the South and North Bridges toward New Town. On the chance that the driver had missed her, David directed him to circle around past the building and then on to the *Gazette* office. Satisfied that she was not walking in the almost constant morning showers, they proceeded to Frederick Street where he entered the offices to find only Lesher and another man peering at sheets and sheets of paper on the desk.

"Ah, good morning, Mr. Archer," Lesher said as he came around the desk and greeted him.

"Is—" he began.

"Mr. Hobbs-Smith isna yet returned from his trip, sir."

The man was efficient, if nothing else, responding before he could even ask the question. David glanced over and noticed that the other man watched him with thinly veiled curiosity.

"And Miss—"

"I couldna say, sir."

The stiff lip and set of his face spoke more than words. The man would offer no information on the whereabouts or business of the young woman…at least not to him.

"Is that next week's issue?" David asked, taking a few steps toward the desk. "Is it complete?"

Lesher moved to block his progress, waving him off as he did. "Mr. Hobbs-Smith said to tell ye that the essay has no' yet arrived so no' to bother searching the office or harassing the staff."

David laughed. Certainly not what he expected to hear from an underling. "He said that, did he?"

Lesher, surprised by his reaction, stepped into his path

and positioned himself between David and the desk. "Truly, sir, it isna here."

"I intend no bodily harm, Lesher. You can stand down."

Although Lesher relaxed his stance, a wary watchfulness still remained. "Yes, sir."

"Have you any notion of when Mr. Hobbs-Smith or Miss Fairchild will return?" A safe question, less personal than querying the man over their whereabouts.

"I canna speak for the young lady, but Mr. Hobbs-Smith expects to return by Friday."

"So late then? I thought he would be here to finalize the edition." David paused, hoping that Lesher would offer some bit of information. Tight-lipped did not begin to describe the man's ability to keep his mouth shut.

Now what? His prey eluded him and his resources for finding her diminished with each stop. Then it struck him. Nate's sister, Lady MacLerie, would know. If she would share her knowledge with him was another question, but he was willing to try. On the short ride over to Nate's house, he realized that his reasons for seeking about Anna had changed.

At first, he simply wished to be assured of her safety and comfort when she faced the elements outside, but he recognized that his true intent was to discover if the kiss they'd shared had affected her as much as it had him. Days had passed and still the thought of her sweet mouth on his was as fresh in his mind as when it had happened days, and nights, before.

Seeing her standing there, moonbeams surrounding her in her righteous indignation over him, even though she did not know it was him, with fire in her eyes and temptation on her lips, he was lost. Tugging her closer and kissing her was not a good idea. Spending time with her certainly wasn't, either. Even thinking about her was a dangerous pastime, and yet here he was searching for her all over Edinburgh.

Still, and he knew the words for the lie they were even as he thought them, he needed to make certain that she had not been insulted by his actions. When he left, he did not want bad feelings between them. For if—or, more likely, when— she found out that he was the arrogant, unfeeling Lord Trey-bourne of their discussions, loathing and betrayal would be the result. Something deep within forced him to continue to try to keep that day as far off as possible.

The carriage pulled up in front of Nate's house and he climbed out. The same footman opened the door as he approached.

"Is Lady MacLerie receiving?"

"I will see, sir."

Apparently he was remembered from his last visit here, for the servant did not ask his name. David watched as the man climbed the stairs to the drawing room and waited. The squeal that erupted inside the room informed him of Miss Julia's presence here. But, was Anna?

The footman reappeared, took his hat and gloves and directed him to the drawing room, where he also announced him. Miss Julia was certainly present and excited, and she looked as though she had a very tenuous hold on her control. David bowed to the women and greeted them.

"Lady MacLerie. Miss Erskine. Miss Julia. It is a pleasure to see you again." He peered around the room hoping that Anna was present but out of view, however she was not there.

"Mr. Archer, how nice of you to visit us. Would you care for some tea?" Lady MacLerie greeted him and pointed to a chair.

"I was hoping to catch Miss Fairchild. Is she here?"

"She's at the school," Miss Julia blurted out.

"She keeps quite busy, you know," Miss Erskine announced. "Her days are her own."

Lady MacLerie simply glanced at him. "Anna is not here, as you can see."

"I wanted to offer an apology," he began. In spite of their lovely and genteel appearance, and their manners, David felt sweat gathering on his forehead. And the summer heat had nothing to do with it. "About the evening at the theater."

"Why, Mr. Archer! Did you do something that requires some request for forgiveness?"

From the lady's tone and arched eyebrow, he suspected she knew exactly what had passed between him and her friend.

"For abandoning you at the theater without an escort home, Lady MacLerie. Why ever else?" he asked, knowing well that she would not speak of anything she knew, if indeed she knew of the kiss, with Anna's aunt and sister present. He returned her glance with one of his own. "After your kind invitation, I should have stayed to ascertain that you did have someone watching out for your safety."

"Lord MacLerie sent the coach around for us, although Anna suggested walking." Miss Erskine's voice revealed how she thought about the prospect of walking.

"Mr. Archer?" Miss Julia interrupted and received a stern look from her aunt, one which did not slow her down at all. "Have you visited anywhere else in Edinburgh since our visit to the Castle?"

"I fear that my business has kept me quite busy, Miss Julia. And after our visit to the Honours of Scotland, what can compare?"

"The Libraries of the Advocates and Writers to the Signet in Parliament Square are worth a visit, Mr. Archer. Of course, you need to know someone who is a member to gain entry."

He laughed out loud at her advice. A girl of her tender years who would suggest such a place was extraordinary. But, of course, she was her sister's sister and he was learning that extraordinary seemed almost commonplace in their family.

"I will take your recommendation under consideration, Miss Julia."

"Julia!" Miss Erskine called. "There are more appropriate things to visit in Edinburgh than a library for solicitors. You must pardon her, Mr. Archer. Her education is a bit unorthodox."

"Fear not, Miss Erskine. I am certain that Miss Julia spends as much time on her needlework and watercolors as she does reading educational tomes."

Miss Erskine grumbled something under her breath that sounded like "from your mouth to God Almighty's ears," but he could not be certain. Laughing was out of the question, so he winked at Anna's sister. Julia leaned back and grimaced at him. Apparently the womanly arts did not appeal to her, either. Evidence of the influence exerted by her unconventional sister whom he could not imagine sitting with needle and threads or a paintbrush and watercolors.

Teaching indigent children. Helping to edit a magazine. Kissing him in the moonlight.

"I will not keep you from the rest of your day. Please give Miss Fairchild my regards when you see her." David stood, and bowed to the women.

Lady MacLerie rose as well and walked with him to the door of the drawing room where the footman stood waiting to escort him downstairs. "Go ahead, Ian. Gather Mr. Archer's belongings and we will be right down." The footman went off to do the lady's bidding.

"Mr. Archer, Anna sometimes stays behind at the *school* to work on her own projects. You can probably still find her there," she whispered as they walked down the stairs to the entryway. "Tell Mrs. Dobbs that I sent you."

Startled by her cooperation, he looked at her and shook his head. "Lady MacLerie," he began, not sure of what was to follow.

"I think that Anna becomes too deeply engrossed in the problems of others and does not see her own, Mr. Archer. A bit of a look-around never hurts."

"A look-around?"

"At life, as it passes by so quickly that it will be missed by those who need it most. Unless, of course, friends and those who care intervene." They reached the doorway and she patted his arm. "Her office is at the top of the stairs, first door on the right. You may tell her I expect her for dinner and that Julia and Miss Erskine are already present if you need a message to deliver."

What could he say when she offered him the excuse he needed to barge in on whatever occupied Anna's time? "My thanks."

Soon David found himself back in the carriage and on his way to the school. And Anna.

* * *

Anna pulled her sketchbook out of the desk drawer and opened it to the last unfinished page. The actress playing the wife in the drama-in-two-acts. The outlandish costume had drawn her attention and Anna thought she had captured it well in her sketch. The feathers stood at attention above the garish stage cosmetics and wig. The shocked expression in the woman's eyes at finding the truth. A few more strokes to complete the mouth and it was done.

Usually, drawing soothed her rattled nerves and helped her concentrate on the words she needed to use in the essay. Now, though, her thoughts jumbled in her mind and would not organize as she needed them to. Lord Treybourne's essay also lay there in front of her, goading her to answer in the same harsh tones he had used. And would that not be the way a man would answer such slurs cast upon his reputation?

Anna put the sketchbook aside and studied the paragraphs she'd written so far and found she was neither pleased nor satisfied with their construction or content. This was not going well at all. Especially when this essay needed to be completed and in Lesher's hands by the day after tomorrow. She leaned back against the hard wooden back of the chair and tried to pull her thoughts together about this.

Now that Lord Treybourne had raised the stakes, how did she respond? A man would strike back, matching the threats and insults and making new ones. Could he, er, she afford to do that? More than anything, Anna wished to keep this about the issues and not the personalities involved. Could she, though, now?

The words flew around inside her thoughts once more.

After a few more minutes of frustration, Anna picked up the sketches again. This time she turned to a new page and simply let her hand move at its own pace and direction. The outline of the face that appeared on the page should not surprise her, for he had filled her thoughts for days and days.

The details surprised her, for she did not realize that there was a slight crook in the bridge of his nose until she saw it there on the page. His mouth was full and his strong chin had the most appealing dimple when he smiled. However, no amount of skill or practice could get the intensity of his eyes correctly. Or how they made a person melt under their scrutiny. Or how blue they were. Her charcoal pencil would never capture the color.

This woolgathering would get her nowhere. "Inappropriate," Aunt Euphemia would say. Wasting time thinking about a man who would never be anything more to her than her enemy's messenger. But was he only that?

Mr. Archer could be exasperatingly discreet or exceedingly kind. Dashing and handsome or heedless of his appearance. Arrogant or earthy. He was a wild combination of extremes all at once. Anna knew that she was attracted to him in an unseemly manner and amount for a single woman with no connections or expectations other than those she made for herself.

True, she needed him to intercede on her, or rather the magazine's, behalf with Lord Treybourne, and soft or personal feelings would simply muddy the already murky waters that swirled around this endeavor. He needed to see the good that the profits enabled but not all the connections involved. And she needed to be clear-minded in order to accomplish it.

Anna glanced once more at the sketch, intent on putting it

aside. With a sigh, she closed the sketchbook and closed her eyes for a moment. She could see his face there before her. He'd had an unexpected effect on her life and she wondered how she would go back to the normalcy when he left for London. A noise in the corridor outside her office caught her attention and she opened her eyes. The strange thing was that she could still see his face.

"Miss Fairchild?"

And hear his voice.

Anna shook herself from her reverie and discovered Mr. Archer standing before her. With his hat in his hand, he stepped closer to the desk…and to seeing the papers on which she worked. A. J. Goodfellow's next essay. She met his gaze as she scooped the papers into her satchel, hoping and praying he had not seen them.

"Mr. Archer, forgive me," she said, standing and offering a polite curtsy. "I did not hear you enter."

"Most likely the weather covered my approach," he offered.

Anna glanced at the window to discover that it was raining. In concentrating on both writing the essay and on some questions about the financial backing for the school, she admitted to herself that she had not looked out the window in hours. "Ah, the weather."

She had not noticed how strong the storms had become, but the bolt of lightning and crash of thunder made it clear. Now she realized that he stood dripping on the floor. Before she could offer assistance, one of the younger girls knocked behind him.

"Yes, Molly?"

"Mrs. Dobbs would like to know if you want tea for your visitor, miss." Molly's eyes became as wide as her belly when Mr. Archer turned and smiled at her.

"Yes, Molly, please," he replied, and then he turned to face Anna. "If Miss Fairchild permits it, that is."

"Of course, Mr. Archer. Molly, please tell Mrs. Dobbs to send tea."

The girl still appeared dazed by his attention, and knowing well that feeling, Anna cleared her throat to get the girl's attention. With a curtsy and another glance at Mr. Archer, Molly left.

"She is new here and learning to serve as a housemaid."

"So your school teaches its pupils more than adding their sums and writing their letters?" He walked to the desk, and nodded at the chair. "If I may?"

"Of course, Mr. Archer. And to answer your question, this school teaches the girls many skills they will need later…when they leave." She found it difficult to speak of that, so she took her seat as well. Anna noticed the copy of *Whiteleaf's* still on the desk at just the same moment that her visitor did.

"Ah, so you are still bothered over Lord Treybourne's article, then? Even now, more than a week later?" He reached over and picked up the copy, reading it silently. Anna could not help but notice that his lips tightened into a thin line of disapproval as he continued reading.

"His words are hateful and unnecessarily provocative. Surely you see that? Instead of discussing the issues raised by Mr. Goodfellow, he had resorted to personal attacks."

"If my memory serves me, it was the last essay by Mr. Goodfellow that began that attack. He specifically called

Lord Treybourne the 'representative of an unfeeling and un-responsive government' and accused him of—what were the words?—ah, 'making money off the backs of the poor and un-fortunates in our society.'" Mr. Archer sat up in his chair and leaned forward, placing his elbows on his knees. "Wouldn't you call that the first assault?"

When he turned his gaze on her, she lost the ability to remember all the facets of her arguments. Anna could discuss society's ills for hours with Nathaniel and his business asso-ciates. Even Lord MacLerie engaged in lively debate with her, and she could make logical, rational points for her position. Now, though, sitting just a yard or so from Mr. Archer, she dis-covered that she could not put more than a few words together.

"Perhaps, sir, but—"

"Perhaps? Come, Miss Fairchild, I gave you more credit for your knowledge and intelligence that that. Lord Trey-bourne did not—"

"Did not what, sir? Did not use his power and connec-tions and those in his employ to undermine Mr. Goodfel-low's position? Your presence here in Edinburgh speaks to that, Mr. Archer."

"I am here of my own accord, Miss Fairchild, as I believed I explained to Nathaniel." His calm demeanor was beginning to falter. She could see him searching for his words, too.

"Ah, looking for property to buy here in the New Town was the reason you gave for your business."

He stopped then, and a slight smile lifted the corners of his mouth. "In spite of my use of that as an excuse to keep you from knowing my true purpose, I have bought several of the building sites in the new area in the eastern approaches."

"For Lord Treybourne?"

"Yes, for his and for my own uses. I have discovered much to like about your city and decided that property here would be of value to me."

Somehow, even though she knew he most likely spoke of the business possibilities here, a part of her thought she might play a part in his liking of Edinburgh. And another part, the shameless romantic that lived within her regardless of how many times she learned the hard lessons of life, hoped that she did.

"Miss?" Molly's voice broke into a discussion that had somehow become much too intimate.

"Yes, Molly. Please come in."

Molly carried a small tray with a teapot and two cups on it, as well as a sugar bowl and some cream in a small pitcher. The pieces did not match, but that was not important. Molly handled it smoothly, placing the tray on her desk and then standing back and waiting further instructions about whether or not to serve it.

Anna saw Mr. Archer's expression as he caught sight of Molly's belly. He could have missed it before, but now, standing this close, he would have to be blind not to see that the girl was "in a delicate condition," as they would say in polite households. In the very same polite households responsible for getting the girl into that condition.

"Thank you, Molly. I will serve Mr. Archer." Unsure of his reaction, she wanted to shield the girl from any disdain he might show. Molly curtsied again and turned to leave.

"Molly," he said. When the girl turned back to face him, his face was troubled. "How old are you?"

"I'll be sixteen on my next birthday, sir."

He seemed to want to ask something else, but only nodded to the girl. "Thank you for bringing the tea, Molly."

"Ain't nothing…" She paused and looked at Anna before saying more. "My pleasure, sir, miss." At Anna's nod, Molly left and Anna noticed the satisfied smile on the girl's face as she completed her task successfully.

He said nothing as Anna poured the tea, offered him sugar and cream and placed the cup before him. She preferred hers plain and lifted the cup to her lips. Over the rim, she noticed he stared into his.

"Is there something wrong with the tea, Mr. Archer?"

"Are all of your pupils in the same condition, Miss Fairchild?"

Here was the opportunity she'd hoped for. A chance to explain some of the good that the profits from the *Gazette* accomplished. So far, he had demonstrated a kind and tolerant attitude toward others. Would it continue when he knew of her involvement?

"Yes, Mr. Archer, they are. Although in various stages of that condition."

His expression took on a new aspect now. A haunted, bleak look entered his eyes, and for a moment, she felt the need to offer him some comfort. "And you teach them?"

"Although many would shun them, sir, I do teach them. Is it not our Christian duty to care for those who cannot care for themselves?" She did not wait for him to answer, for it was a rhetorical question. "They did not choose to be in this condition. In most of these situations, it was thrust on them by someone to whom they could not raise an objection."

When his eyes widened for a scant second, Anna knew he

understood her reference and just who would be forcing women into private relations. "I believe you are an honorable man, sir, and I wish to share some private information with you in the hopes that you can convey the spirit of it, without the details, to your employer."

He regained some measure of control and looked at her now. "Please go on, Miss Fairchild."

"I…own…hold…an interest in the *Gazette* and use my profits to maintain this school."

Would he be shocked, as most would, to learn this? It was the truth—well, part of the truth—of the situation. She could never reveal the whole truth without threatening all of those involved.

"You do not cease to amaze me, Miss Fairchild."

She watched him speak, afraid to see the censure that most of society would feel toward her in this situation. A gentlewoman of good breeding did not associate with the lower classes. A gentlewoman from a good family did not engage in business. A gentlewoman who hoped to marry well did not besmirch her reputation by spending her days teaching girls who would bear illegitimate babies.

His gaze held only respect when she finally gained enough courage to meet it. Respect and a strange sadness that disappeared as soon as she thought she glimpsed it again.

"So, the popularity of Mr. Goodfellow's battle with Lord Treybourne and the resultant increase in subscriptions have increased your charity here?"

"Yes!" He did understand. "I am hopeful that if the magazine continues to grow and the focus on this problem does as well, we will gain enough donations and will be able to open a second house. There is such a need among these young women. But if this becomes a personal disagreement and draws attention away from the needs of those less fortunate, this endeavor will fail."

He lifted his cup and drank the tea without pause. "And how did you develop such a conscience about matters so grave as these?"

"When my father passed away, I worked in the places where these women did. My situation as a governess or tutor was somewhat different—" she paused and swallowed, trying to make the words come out smoothly "—but I was witness to some despicable behavior by those in the noble class."

There was a hardness about him now and she feared that she had revealed too much to him. If he told Lord Treybourne the whole of the matter, it would take no large effort on his part to undermine their work here. If Lord Treybourne discovered the names of those who donated funding, he could, with nothing more than a discreet word whispered in the right ear, shut that funding off as quickly as it started. Unfortunately, from his expression now, Anna could not tell what Mr. Archer's intentions were.

"I will consider this matter, Miss Fairchild." He stood and took his hat from the desk. "I interrupted your work and will let you return to it. Good day to you."

The man who was turning to leave was a far different one from the man who entered her office a short time ago and she was not certain how or why he had changed before her eyes. A chill passed through her and she feared that Nathaniel's warnings would have been better heeded than ignored.

"Mr. Archer, did something bring you here today?"

"Ah, yes. I was bringing a message from Lady MacLerie."

"Clarinda? When did you see her?"

"I was completing some errands of my own when I met up with her. Lady MacLerie wanted me to remind you of your dinner engagement at her home this evening."

"She did?" Anna rose and walked to the door. "I appreciate you acting as messenger, Mr. Archer."

"Good day, Miss Fairchild," he said once more as he strode through the doorway, and down the hallway and stairs. She heard Mrs. Dobbs herself let him out the front door.

Resisting the urge to look out the window, Anna lasted only a moment or two before she crossed to it and peered out into the Edinburgh rain. Mr. Archer waved off the hired carriage he used and stalked up the High Street toward the South Bridge. It wouldn't take long before he would be soaked through to the skin in the torrents of rain that fell from the sky. She watched his progress for as long as she could see him and then turned away.

Had she misjudged him after all? His manner and attitude during their conversation had turned completely around and she wondered what had done it. Although clearly bothered by some part of it, he had not been unkind to Molly—indeed, his behavior could have been described as concerned or even solicitous toward the unfortunate girl. However, something had caused the change.

Would everything she and Nathaniel had worked for end in destruction for her misstep? As the thunder rumbled through the sky, she worried that it would. And with Nathaniel out of town, there was no one to talk to about this dilemma.

Chapter Twelve

He wanted to break something, but the glass, as it shattered against the back wall of the fireplace, was not nearly as satisfying as he'd hoped it would be. David thought to throw another, but knew it would not settle the anger and frustration within him.

When Lady MacLerie told him Anna's whereabouts, he thought to have a bit of light conversation and apologize for being forward outside the theater. And perhaps to entice her to another outing before the next essay was published and hostilities increased. But from the moment he entered the room and saw her at work on some task or another, he wanted to remove the frown from her forehead and put the sparkle back in her eyes.

The sight of his article there, and knowing that she worried over it, took his breath away. David wanted to take her in his embrace and soothe all her concerns. He wanted to make promises to her that he had not thought to offer a woman before.

Bloody hell!

Every promise he'd made to himself about not being drawn into anything more than a gentlemanly concern for her was blown apart at the very sight of her in distress. As she opened herself to him, offering an explanation of her noble actions and intentions, David realized that the woman who so affected him would be horrified by the sins of his past.

The irony of it was not lost on him. The Earl of Treybourne, one of the most eligible marriage catches in all of society, one of the wealthiest men in His Majesty's kingdom, had committed the one sin that the courageous Miss Fairchild would condemn him for out of hand, and even worse, he conjectured, it would be a far more grave offense in her view than the charade he was performing.

He had taken advantage of a housemaid.

A housemaid who became pregnant and was turned out for doing so.

A girl who then died giving birth to his child.

David reached for the whisky and filled another glass to near the rim. He drank almost all of it down in two gulps, letting the powerful brew burn a path to his gut. Penance, if nothing else, for his sins.

In spite of his efforts since then, in spite of the good he tried to accomplish, he could still feel the shame when the extent of his actions and their terrible repercussions finally sunk into his brain. Even now, with the whisky pulsing through his veins, he could not delude himself into thinking that Sarah had truly had any choice. As Anna had pointed out, girls like her would hardly be able to raise any objection without losing their position. Their living.

He'd liked Sarah. It wasn't all about taking advantage, he

could now think to himself. David enjoyed every moment he spent with her, whether enjoying her favors or her quick wit and humor. Perhaps that was what saved him and allowed him to realize the wrongness of his actions when he discovered her fate.

A knock on the door interrupted his thoughts.

"My lord, Mr. Forge has arrived and waits upon your convenience."

Thomas Forge was the man-of-business who handled his more personal matters, the ones he kept out of his father's sight.

"Get him settled in his room and give him something to eat, Harley. I will meet with him after that."

"Is there anything else you need, my lord?"

The ultimate in efficiency and discretion, he knew Harley had heard the glass shatter. "Absolution?"

The word came forth on its own. Harley had been the one who found out where Sarah went and had been with him when he'd discovered his infant daughter. He, more than anyone, knew his master's sins.

"That is out of my hands, my lord."

His valet quietly closed the door and David knew that no matter what he had accomplished since discovering Sarah's fate, his guilt would never be extinguished. Sometimes he could only sleep at night by reminding himself of the countless others in Sarah's situation and worse, whom he had helped. His daughter was one of them.

David emptied the glass and placed it on the table at his side. There was business to discuss and arrangements to be made with Thomas, and the man had traveled hundreds of miles to handle his affairs. Standing, he stretched before the fire that Harley had stoked into a blaze on his soaking return from seeing Anna.

Irony, he continued to discover, was a harsh mistress. In attempting to meet his father's demands and gain the financial support he needed to fund his own charities, orphanages and school, he now endangered those established and supported by his opponent. If his stomach were not rolling, he would have laughed at the absurdity of it.

His deepest fear was that Anna's concern about his father destroying all she held dear was a valid one and one worth worrying over. Now that Thomas was here, he could set him off to get a better estimation of just what Anna's interest in the *Gazette* was and an assessment of the financial stability of the school. And how she had managed to keep it secret, for, in spite of his man's investigations and inquiries, her connection had never been revealed.

Once he had a clearer idea of her involvement, he could develop a contingency plan for some of the possibilities if things went awry.

When things went awry.

"No, Clarinda."

"Anna, he seems quite nice after all."

"No, Clarinda."

"Anna…"

Anna finally resorted to action and stamped her foot down in front of her like a recalcitrant child. "You should not have sent him to the school and you should not invite him to dinner."

Clarinda closed her mouth and thought on Anna's words, but

Anna knew her friend was not done. Once a topic appealed to her, she clung to it incessantly. Now, apparently, that topic was one Mr. Archer. "I am certain you are misreading his reaction."

"Did I misread Lord MacLerie's when we first met?"

Although Clarinda would like to argue the point, Anna knew she would lose, for Clarinda's husband was not so accepting of Anna's "eccentricities" as he called them as Clarinda was. Lord MacLerie had made his concerns known and did not wish his wife's reputation stained by association with someone who stood just beyond the pale. Her friend had other ideas and it took only a few exchanges to disabuse him of such "folderol" as Clarinda liked to call it. Now, they both knew of most of her activities, most of them, and politely ignored them.

"But that has changed, Anna," she replied. "Perhaps your plan to expose him to the good that is undertaken due to the success of the magazine is the right path? Perhaps he simply needs to be brought a bit further down it?"

"Nathaniel told you, did he?" Anna sat down on the couch and looked at her friend. How much did she know? Would Nathaniel have revealed it all?

Clarinda followed her and took her hand. "He confides in me because I am his sister and he trusts my judgment." She patted Anna's hand. "And my discretion, Anna. As you know well that you can."

It would feel good to share some of the burden with someone who knew the details and who would keep them in confidence. When she had shared with Mr. Archer her concern over Lord Treybourne's possible retaliation against their endeavor, she felt lighter inside. When she revealed the true nature of the school and the students she taught and her interest in the magazine, Anna understood Clarinda's comments about her husband's ability to be her helpmate. Not that such a thing was possible between her and Mr. Archer, but the appeal of such a relationship was intriguing.

"We are so close to success now, Clarinda. I am just not certain of how to get there."

"You know, inviting Mr. Archer, as I suggested, may be just the thing. You could speak with him about Lord Treybourne and share that information with Goodfellow for his essay. If you knew more about your opponent and understood his motives, you may be able to plan a strategy that will gain you the success you need."

As she thought on Clarinda's suggestion, she chose to avoid for the time being the possibility that Nathaniel had shared Goodfellow's identity with his sister.

"You may be correct, Clarinda. Although Goodfellow's next piece is due in the day after tomorrow, there would still be time for Nathaniel to edit in anything we discover that could support our position."

"There, you see? I can be of help to you."

Anna began to stand, but Clarinda pulled her back down with the hand she still held.

"He fancies himself in love with you, you know?" she whispered in spite of them being alone in Clarinda's chambers.

"Mr. Archer?" Anna lost her breath at such a thought.

"Nathaniel, silly gel! My brother has been in love with you for years." Clarinda laughed and leaned over closer. "But he is not the right one for you."

"Clarinda!" Anna whispered back, feeling the heat in her cheeks from even thinking that Mr. Archer might be attracted to her. "Nathaniel and I have an understanding."

"As in the way of men and women, my dear Anna, what we understand and what they think they understand are two completely different matters." Anna laughed at Clarinda's interpretation of the issue of men and women, which only seemed to encourage her to more outlandish observations.

"I would wish nothing so much as I do wish that you were my sister-by-marriage, but I realize through my own experience with Robert that a woman needs to have other suitors to know she is making the correct choice."

Anna shook her head, disbelieving that Clarinda could be so wrong about the situation between her and Nathaniel and additionally between her and Mr. Archer.

"Although I do think your idea of gaining details about Lord Treybourne's motives from Mr. Archer has merit, I think that to consider anything else about him, especially to use him in some way to compare his attributes to Nathaniel's, is unfair." A pang of guilt struck her as she remembered doing exactly the very thing from the first time she saw the man in Nathaniel's office. Not only his attributes but now also his position with Lord Treybourne.

"So, dinner tomorrow night. Nathaniel promised to return by noon, so let's plan for an early meal and perhaps some music afterward."

"Clarinda, you are getting carried away by some strange notions about this situation. And we have no way of knowing if he will even accept the invitation. If the manner in which he left the school today is any indication, you may receive his regrets in the morning instead of the acceptance you seem fixed upon receiving."

"It is you, dear Anna, who will not see the truth when it sits before your very eyes. The man ran today, most likely overwhelmed by the feelings that he is developing for you. Now, all we must do is determine if he was indeed running away and how to make him run toward."

Anna let out an exasperated breath. Clarinda was like a hound on the trail of a fox and God help the fox, or in this case, Mr. Archer. It was best at times like this to agree with her and then find a way around her. The dinner would offer many such opportunities.

She nodded her faux assent to Clarinda. Anna knew only that she would have to work long into the night if she were to finish the essay she'd planned. After Mr. Archer left today—stalking off in the rain, daft man!—she got no further along in its outline or completion. And, if she need wait for any tidbits or insight from him before writing it, she would barely have enough time to finish it. Still, Clarinda's idea was a good one. Changing the subject, Anna rose now and walked to the door. "Should I invite Aunt Euphemia?"

Clarinda thought on it for a moment and then shook her head. "No, I have some others in mind. A younger set."

"Please do not go out of your way on this, Clarinda."

"Nathaniel does not entertain enough, so I must do so while in town if for nothing else but appearance and the family reputation. If I can have a bit of fun as I do it, so much the better."

"If you need any help, please call on me."

"I have everything under control, Anna."

And that was what worried Anna the most as she went through the rest of her day. She tossed in her bed that night, words and phrases ringing in her ears and in her thoughts as she tried to at least plan the best approach and attitude for Goodfellow's answer to Lord Treybourne. A man of honor would answer the insult. A man of honor would take his lordship to task for raising the very issue.

Anger, but restrained, would be the approach. Acknowledge his lordship's insults, but do not escalate the battle with more of her...*his* own. At least that would be her framework unless Mr. Archer revealed something useful in their discussions.

Chapter Thirteen

"I told you he would attend!" Clarinda whispered as the footman announced his arrival.

Anna did not have time to reply, for Mr. Archer came immediately to greet the host and hostess of the evening. He wore a black jacket and pantaloons with a deep rose-colored waistcoat and looked completely fashionable for an evening in London and interestingly, his choice of clothing nearly mirrored the black-and-pale-rose silk gown she wore. She would be the first to admit that he presented a dashing figure of a man, with his broad shoulders that did not appear to need padding to enhance them.

"Lady MacLerie, Lord MacLerie, good evening. Miss Fairchild." He bowed to the group and smiled. "My thanks for including me yet again in one of your entertainments."

"We will be leaving for home soon and I did so want to further our acquaintance, Mr. Archer," Clarinda said, fanning herself as she spoke. "Nathaniel does so little entertaining without us and since you seemed to enjoy our outing last week, it seemed just the thing to include you this evening."

"Well, whatever the reason, I am pleased to be here."

"Anna, would you be so kind as to introduce Mr. Archer to our other guests? I need to speak to Cook about the timing of the courses this evening."

Anna knew a deception when she saw it and this was one of the best. Cook knew very well when the courses should be served, but this was Clarinda's way of beginning the subterfuge against him. With her not-so-veiled comments about their encounter at the theater, Anna could not be certain that he would not bolt right now. When he offered her his arm to escort her to the others, Anna accepted it and guided him to the small group standing near the pianoforte.

"Mr. Archer, may I make you known to Mr. and Mrs. Robertson of Aberdeen and Mr. and Mrs. Campbell and Miss Campbell, Mr. Campbell's sister, from Glasgow? They are distant cousins of Lord MacLerie."

A few minutes later and they were conversing politely. Nathaniel arrived, late for some unknown reason, and joined the group just in time for dinner to be announced. Lord MacLerie claimed his wife's arm and led everyone else down to the dining room, which was elegantly appointed for the dinner—candles in the chandeliers and set high in wall sconces gave light to the room and was reflected off the crystal and silver in the table settings. Anna was not surprised to find Mr. Archer holding her chair when they found their places.

Between the soup course and the next, Lord MacLerie finally turned to Mrs. Campbell for a quiet question. Mr. Archer leaned over to her at the same moment.

"I confess, Miss Fairchild, that I was not certain I would

be welcomed by you tonight." His voice was low in volume, the comment directed only to her ears.

"Why ever not, sir?" She leaned over and caught his gaze. Would that piercing stare ever not affect her?

"The last two times we have been in each other's company, I have behaved rudely. At your school the other day and at the theater last week." He leaned away to allow one of the footman to place a platter of roasted pheasant near their places, and then leaned in closer again. "I would plead that you so completely surprised me in each incident that I was not thinking straight."

Anna was startled herself by his assessment. "*I* surprised *you,* Mr. Archer? How so?" Was he horrified that she accepted his kiss and did not slap him for his impertinence?

"I did not understand the depth of your commitment to your cause, Miss Fairchild. I underestimated you and discovered that your resolve in the matter of..." He paused and looked around to see if their conversation was drawing attention. "In the matters you shared with me was admirable and worthy of respect."

Could everyone see her blush? She could feel the heat climb into her cheeks at his words. She lifted a goblet of cider to her lips and sipped it, hoping it would cool her. "You are too kind, sir," she whispered. "I would confess to you that I thought perhaps you were shocked by my association with such women."

"Startled and surprised but not shocked, Miss Fairchild. With each encounter, I learn something more about you," he said, glancing at her. "And then the evening at the theater..."

His words drifted off and she found herself staring at his

mouth, remembering the feel and the taste and the heat of it against hers that night. Her breath caught in her chest and Anna felt as though she would beg him to kiss her again in that moment.

"As I said to Lady MacLerie—"

"Lady MacLerie?" What did Clarinda have to do with his kiss, their kiss?

"I spoke to her and offered my apologies for not seeing Lady MacLerie, you and your aunt home safely. I would offer them to you now. I should have sent word of my delay to my later commitment and taken you home first."

It took a few seconds for her to realize that he was teasing her. He did not speak of their kiss directly, instead he spoke of something quite acceptable and all the while he stared at her mouth. Exhilarated that he teased her instead of apologizing for it, Anna nodded her acceptance of the other and took another drink of the cider. She leaned away as more dishes were placed before them—from the aromas, one was fricassee of rabbit, another was a whole stuffed salmon. However, as the servants were taking away and placing new ones, and despite the evidence on her plate, she could not even remember tasting the ones being removed.

Mr. Archer turned to Mrs. Robertson on his left and exchanged some words before facing her for a moment. A moment just long enough to shatter any control or reserve that she was maintaining.

"I will not, however, apologize for kissing you, Miss Fairchild. And I cannot promise that it will not happen again if the opportunity arises."

"Oh my!" she exclaimed, gaining the attention of the whole

table. Wishing for a cold Edinburgh rainshower to cover her, she coughed strenuously and lifted the goblet again. "I think that this cider is a bit strong for my tastes tonight."

A footman took the glass from her and brought a clean one and a pitcher of lemonade. She did not partake often of spirits, and from the topic being discussed with Mr. Archer, she knew she must keep her wits about her. After a sip, she dared a glance in his direction.

He did not look away when she met his eyes and for a moment the rest of the guests, the table, the candles and every single other person and item in the room faded away into darkness. Anna could only see him and could feel and hear the promise and expectation in his words about kissing her again. She felt something pulse deep within her as her body reacted to him as a woman to a man. Her breasts seemed to swell against her stays and a tingling grew in her belly. Being honest with herself, she dared to hope it would happen soon. For once the essay came out, everything between them would shift and unsettle.

A cough and then another brought her back to the reality of the dining room and she broke away and looked across the table at Clarinda. A suspicious glimmer in her friend's eyes warned her of something coming. It was not long before Lord MacLerie raised his voice and spoke to everyone at table.

"Mr. Archer, I understand that you work for Lord Trey-bourne."

"I do," he answered, glancing across at Nathaniel and then at her.

"All we know of his lordship is the view of him presented

in his opinion pieces in *Whiteleaf's*. Surely there is more to the man than rage and insult?"

Oh, good Lord! Had Clarinda or Nathaniel put him up to this? Anna tried to remain calm and to take note of any important facets of Lord Treybourne that Mr. Archer revealed.

"I find him to be a fair employer, Lord MacLerie. And although he favors remaining loyal and constant to those institutions that have made His Majesty's kingdom strong, he is not oblivious to the problems facing it."

"He owns lands here in Scotland, yet he doesna come here?" Mr. Campbell asked now.

"I believe there is a hunting box and a property or two here in Edinburgh. His lordship manages several of the large estates for his family and cannot always find time to spend on each of their properties." Mr. Archer faced Robert now. "As the owner of about the same amount of land and properties, Lord MacLerie, how often do you find yourself in London?"

"Your point is well taken, sir, but even you must admit that his position in the forefront of the Tory party has become a rallying point."

"As has Mr. Goodfellow's with the Whigs."

Anna listened as the discussion continued and soon realized that Mr. Archer was presenting the clear, rational and logical method in which Lord Treybourne made his points. If she could strip away the rhetoric, argue the points and then apply her own style back to it, she—or rather, Goodfellow—could tear his position apart. Part of her wanted to laugh aloud at the prospect, but another part was cognizant that she was taking advantage of the man beside her to accomplish that aim.

She shifted in her seat and looked at Clarinda, only to discover her friend watching her. At her raised eyebrow, Anna shook her head slightly. It felt dishonest to handle it this way. She would rather fight his lordship outright than win by this underhanded method.

"Gentlemen, if I might suggest that you join us in the drawing room after your port?"

Clarinda understood her message and interrupted the discussion as a hostess could. The men stood as she did and waited for the women to leave before sitting back and drinking their port. Anna followed down the stairs, uncomfortable with the thought that Mr. Archer was still the target.

"My wife was unhappy with our line of questioning, sir," Lord MacLerie announced as they enjoyed their first glass of the deep red liquor. "She thought to call an end to the inquisition."

"Although I cannot speak for his lordship, I will field any questions you care to ask."

David understood exactly what was happening during dinner. He suspected that the elusive Mr. Goodfellow was present here tonight and using this as a way to gain information to be used against him in the next essay. It was what David would have done, use subterfuge to understand his opponent. What he *had* done by coming to Edinburgh. Now, excited by the very thought that the man was here in the room, he waited for the next round to begin.

The discussion continued through three bottles of port, and several of the men lit cheroots. David found himself enjoying it, for it gave him the chance to work out some of the flaws in his logic so that he would be ready for the next article. At one point, using the arguments he put forth in a previous essay, he nearly swayed Mr. Robertson to his—or rather to the official—position espoused by Lord Treybourne. With the man's thick Scottish brogue and rolled inflections, it was difficult to tell at times.

Although he continued to suspect Nathaniel, David wondered if Lord MacLerie could be the writer. He was educated, opinionated, well-spoken and articulate in his position on the various topics of parliamentary reform, social improvements and commerce. With his money and power, although centered in the western Highlands, Lord MacLerie would be able to financially back the magazine to keep it on its feet until it was a success. The family connections to Nathaniel made it a perfect fit. So, was he A. J. Goodfellow then?

Before he could pursue his own questions, a footman arrived with a request from the ladies for the gentlemen to join them for entertainment in the drawing room. Sensing that the questions were at an end, David now looked forward to spending some time with Anna. He walked with the men downstairs and the topic of their discussions changed to horses and even harvests among their distant farmlands, both subjects that interested him.

As they entered the drawing room, a trio of musicians were tuning their instruments, and the furniture had been cleared to the perimeter of the room, all indications that dancing was in order. Anna would never attend a social event in London, or at least one at which the high and mighty Lord Treybourne attended, so he relished the thought of guiding her through a dance here in this informal setting.

Lady MacLerie claimed him to start the set and he smiled

and watched as Anna took Nathaniel's hand. It wasn't until a country dance, the third of the evening, that he could get her as his partner. And, frustrating him even more, it was a new dance to him and he needed to pay heed to the movements to avoid tripping himself or the others dancing. When one of the dances called for four couples, he bowed out and walked to the table where refreshments were offered. His wish was answered as Anna walked to his side there.

"I remember that the cider gave you some problems at dinner, Miss Fairchild. May I get you something else to drink?"

"Tea would be pleasing right now, sir."

The blush on her cheeks could be from the exertion of the dancing, but he hoped it was for the same reason as the one at dinner. David had been thinking of their kiss and had been watching her mouth as she spoke. His promise to repeat it was bold and risked impertinence, but once he said it, he knew it to be true. Her eyes betrayed her thoughts as well, for her cheeks colored then and her gaze went to his mouth.

She'd been remembering it, too, for her breathing became erratic and David's body reacted in the normal way. But, he was not a man ruled by his baser instincts, not in many years, and assuredly not where someone like Anna was involved. Not any woman who could not be his wife.

He waited as the footman poured for both of them and then led her to the sitting area, where she took a place on one of the long couches. Instead of sitting beside her, he sat in the chair next to it and turned it slightly so he could face her better while they talked. "Should you like to ask more questions about his lordship, please do so now so we can move onto more pleasant topics before the night is done."

"Your directness is refreshing, Mr. Archer," she said, laughing softly. "Would it offend you if I asked?"

When her brown eyes shimmered with glee and turned the shade of warm brandy, she could ask him anything. He cleared his throat. "Not at all."

"What is he like? I do not mean his political views, but his person. Nathaniel revealed that they were at school together so I know their ages are near, but his attitudes seem so much…"

"Stodgier?"

"Older, I was going to say."

He laughed, but considered carefully his choice of words and how to answer her. He wanted to somehow redeem Lord Treybourne, himself, in her eyes once she inevitably learned the truth. David was not a fool and realized that Anna would discover the truth. Bloody hell! Why had he ever thought this was a good plan?

"He is subject to all the same pressures as those in positions of authority and who own land or businesses or estates, Miss Fairchild. The welfare of those in his service is utmost in his concerns."

"So, are you saying that his personal opinions and those put forth in his public statements differ?"

Now he was caught, for to admit to such a thing would give away too much. He could not betray the arrangements he had with his father or all of his interests would be in jeopardy. "I would hazard a guess that in some cases, yes, that happens. There are, after all, many reasons to support a cause."

He drank his tea and decided to ask his own question. "So, should I be prepared for the worst possible scenario when the

Gazette is published in two days? I would prevail upon our acquaintance for some warning of what to expect."

"Have you spoken to Nathaniel?" she asked. At his response, she continued, "He has the last look and makes any last-minute changes before it goes to press."

"So, you have not seen Goodfellow's essay?"

"No, Mr. Archer, I have not."

"Will you? Before it is published?"

He would wager his yearly income that she would, but would she admit to it? She lifted her cup and drank down the contents before answering.

"Yes, Mr. Archer, I will."

Now it was time to gamble whatever this was between them. "Could I ask the same courtesy of seeing it before its general release that I afforded Nate?"

"So you can send it by messenger to your employer?" she asked, her voice devoid of warmth now. Had he pushed too far too fast?

"Candidly, yes. It is something I promised to do." She did not know that he was thinking of his father and the arrangements with him for the prompt delivery of the new issue.

"Since it will change nothing, I will ask Nathaniel if he will allow it. It is, after all, his decision."

"What is my decision?" Nate asked as he approached them. David stood and faced him.

"I asked Miss Fairchild if I might receive a copy of the *Gazette* before it is distributed. Call it an advanced warning."

Lady MacLerie interrupted them and called everyone back to the entertainment. "All this talk of Lord Treybourne has brought the feel of doom and gloom to our gathering of family and friends. I forbid the mention of his name for the rest of the evening."

She raised her own glass of wine and encouraged the rest to follow her example. Apparently hunting season was over.

"Here, here!" called out Mr. Campbell and Mr. Robertson.

"Yes! More dancing!" exclaimed the other single woman there, Miss Campbell.

"Very well," Nathaniel said. David knew it was the answer to his request and not that of his sister.

Standing now, he held out his hand to Anna, who did not hesitate to join him. The rest of the evening passed quickly, too quickly if he had his choice, and at times, he felt very much like the condemned man having his last meal.

The new issue would increase the pressure on him from his father, for he did not doubt that Goodfellow would rise to the bait. Moreover, each faction would press for their own position and the result would be more division, not less. David knew that neither party would move from their stated platforms and that left only those few important moderates or undeclared members in Commons or Lords to be swayed by these arguments.

But, for the rest of the night, he would push all of that— all the matters that weighed heavily on his conscience, all the questions of his path and his decisions—aside and concentrate on the lovely young woman who graced his arm now. If there were any doubt he could do so, all he had to do was look at her and remember the kiss.

Then, early by London standards, but late for Edinburgh, the clock struck one in the morning and the gathering drew to a close. Although he would like nothing more than to escort

Anna home, he could not and he watched as the Robertsons promised her safe conveyance. His coach was announced from the doorway downstairs and he took leave of the group. To his delight, Anna suggested that she see him to the door. He walked ahead of her down the stairs and waited for his hat. Once delivered, the footman stood discreetly aside.

"Other than the inquisition you suffered, I hope you found some pleasure in the evening, Mr. Archer."

"Other than the inquisition, I can assure you that I found much enjoyment in the evening and, most especially—" he paused and lifted her hand to his mouth, touching it in the polite fashion "—in seeing you again, Miss Fairchild."

He did not let go and she did not remove her hand from his. So many questions and considerations raced through his mind all at once, and no satisfying resolution was present. Damn tomorrow to hell, he thought as he turned her hand over and kissed the inside of her wrist.

David could feel her pulse just beneath her skin there, and smell the scent of roses. Her indrawn breath spoke of her reaction to his intimate kiss and he repeated it just to hear her gasp. This time though, he stared into her eyes as he did it. And he spoke the only words he could at that moment.

"I wish…I wish…" he whispered with each touch of his lips to her skin. He knew though that to voice the wishes now swelling in his heart would create more problems, insurmountable ones, than they currently faced. As a man of honor, despite the less than honorable desires flooding him at this moment, he could offer her nothing.

Only his heart, and that would accomplish nothing for her or the life she led. Certainly nothing for the life he must lead as well.

Her gaze moved to a spot just over his head and David knew they were being observed. The urge to pull her close and kiss her as he needed to almost overwhelmed him, but he did not know who stood above them. He had his suspicions, though. David released her hand and bowed. "Please convey my thanks once more to Lady MacLerie for including me in this evening's plans, Miss Fairchild."

"I will, sir."

The quiver in her voice and the trembling of her hand as he released it demonstrated the extent of how affected she'd been by his touch, something that made him inordinately happy.

"Clarinda is waiting for you, Anna."

Just as he thought. Lord MacLerie stood on the landing above them. Now he began walking down the steps and Anna went up. The moment when they met and the glances exchanged spoke of caring and concern. Anna did that to men— brought out any protective elements in them. He felt it, he knew that Nate did as well and apparently others did, too. She met his gaze for a scant second before proceeding down the corridor to the drawing room.

The irony was that she was the most self-sufficient woman he'd ever met or known and the one least in need of a man's protection. And yet, she drew them to her and something about her nature provoked that response. In Nate's case, and he was coming to recognize it in his case, there were other, stronger feelings at work, but he could swear in Lord MacLerie's situation it involved nothing like it.

"Might I have a word with you, Mr. Archer?" Lord MacLerie reached the bottom and walked to the door, waving off the footman. "A breath of fresh air perhaps?"

MacLerie knew.

They walked outside and down the steps. Standing on the sidewalk, MacLerie led him to a spot where they could not be overheard before speaking.

"I do not know what your game is, Treybourne, but do not think to include Anna in your sordid charade."

"How long have you known?" he asked.

"Just after the first dinner here. We met some years ago in London on one of my infrequent trips there." David shrugged, not remembering the meeting. "It was something you said that made the connection for me."

"Does Lady MacLerie know?" He wanted to know how far the news had spread.

"No. I would spare her any worry over her dearest friend. I went to Nathaniel, who assured me that you two had an agreement about your presence here."

"We do," he replied, not certain he wanted to share more than that. Both men protecting the women they loved. Irony raised its ugly head again in his life.

"I wanted you to know that despite her lack of family, Anna is not without friends. Friends who would do what must be done to protect her. Keep your focus on your opponent, Treybourne, and leave her out of your sights."

"I came here only to discover the identity of my adversary and to gain a truce of sorts in the attacks, MacLerie. Nothing more, nothing less."

"And what have you learned?"

The Scottish lord crossed his arms over his chest, looking very much like a Highland warrior of old, missing only a kilt and a broadsword to complete the image. Miss Julia would have noticed the resemblance immediately and that thought made him smile. Coming back to the topic under discussion, he watched the man's expression as he voiced his suspicion.

"Tonight, I began to suspect that you might be the man I am searching for." There. The accusation was out now.

A robust laughter escaped from MacLerie. "Do you now? Well, I will neither deny nor confirm such speculation."

David shook his head. What a waste of time that had been. Had he really expected the man to confess to him?

"Goodfellow aside, I want you to know that Miss Fairchild is not to be part of whatever you are doing. The lass is a woman of honor and does not deserve to be played in your game."

Before he could assure Anna's friend that whatever he felt for her was honest emotions, MacLerie leaned in closer. "Our estates and wealth are about equal by my estimates. Although your father chooses to exercise his power through politics, mine does so in commerce and shipping. As enemies we could each inflict considerable damage to the other. I would prefer you as a friend."

"As I would you."

"Then complete your task and go back to London."

His steadfast friendship, or rather his wife's, with the woman in question did not give MacLerie the right to order him about and David bristled at being made to feel like an errand boy.

"I have commitments to honor and when I have fulfilled those obligations, I will return home."

"Just so," MacLerie said, stepping away and waiting obviously for David's departure from there in his position on the sidewalk.

David could tell their conversation was at an end, so he nodded and walked toward his carriage. As the coach soon clattered down the cobblestones, away from New Town, David knew that it would be a long night. He only wondered if it would be so for Goodfellow, whoever he was.

Anna stumbled back and leaned against the wall for support. Her lungs refused to draw a breath as the words she'd heard echoed through her head. Listening to the hushed conversation outside the door through the hole used by the doormen and footmen to hear their approaching masters, she'd heard enough of the shocking words to know the danger that truly existed for her.

Lord Treybourne!

David Archer was Lord Treybourne.

The man she was coming to like and who had just kissed her so intimately was the very man she hated above all others. How could she have been such an empty-headed ninny?

Her head began to spin as she considered every word he'd said and every deed he'd committed since their meeting. Lies, lies and more lies. Anna lifted her hand to her forehead and dabbed at the perspiration now gathering there. Snippets of conversation flashed through her memory and she realized that, worse than being attracted to this man, she had endangered exactly what she'd hoped to protect by revealing so much to him.

The footsteps on the stairs told her that the servant was returning to his post and she knew that Lord MacLerie would come back inside in another moment or two. She needed to pull herself together and get home where she could consider

all the ramifications of her lapse in judg-ment. Anna stepped
out of the alcove and passed the footman on her way to the
stairs. Only by placing one foot before the other could she
continue up to the drawing room where the others waited.

Oh, no! She realized that not only would she face the dis-
cerning gaze of her friend, but she would also have to look
Nathaniel in the eyes and not let on that she knew the truth now.
Her heart pounded in her chest and the pain of his betrayal
twisted like a blade, making it difficult to breathe. Why would
he have done such a thing? He'd apologized when they let out
their lie about Mr. Archer being Lord Treybourne's man and
she'd accepted it as truth. Making her even more the fool.

And now? What did she do now?

She reached the door, but shook her head at the footman sta-
tioned there. Anna needed another moment to gather her wits.
She would go in, make her farewells and escape to her own
room, where she could mull this over and decide what to do.

What to do? Tears threatened, so she cleared her throat and
nodded to the footman who opened the door. The sooner
started, the sooner finished and then there would be time to
sort through all of her missteps and even to mourn her foolishness and naiveté. The thought occurred just as she caught
Clarinda's gaze.

And the sooner to plan her own revenge for his dishonorable
actions. Goodfellow would come in handy in that regard.

Robert returned inside to offer his farewells to the rest of
the guests. With a look, he told Nathaniel to wait up for him.
Clarinda was all aflutter after the party and she chatted on
and on about how the dinner went and how the guests were

pleased and about all those details about which women cared so much. It was only his mouth kissing hers and a strenuous and always pleasurable bout of marital intimacy that finally stopped her long enough for the fatigue to catch up with her.

He waited for her to fall asleep in his arms and when she did, he slid from the bed. Robert tugged on the dressing gown and tied it as he walked down to the study. Nathaniel sat nursing a glass of whisky, his current favorite drink. From his appearance, Robert did not think it was the first such glass.

"Is my sister asleep?"

"Sleeping like a weel-fed bairn," he replied, allowing his accent to leak through. He seemed to fall back into it while on his estates in the Highlands and lose it when here in the city or in England. An attempt at civility, he supposed, in the face of such prejudice against native Scots.

"So you spoke to him?"

"Yes, and I warned him off."

"Do you think it will work? Did he say when he was leaving?"

Robert walked to the sideboard and poured his own glass. "He is frustrated over not being able to find Goodfellow. Once this issue is out, he will go back to London to write his reply." He drank some down and then looked at Nathaniel. "The bigger concern must be An— Goodfellow's essay. Will it be toned down and less inflammatory?"

"I doubt it," Nathaniel admitted. "She understands the need, but was incensed by the last one. She said a man of honor would not back down from the insults."

"That, Nathaniel, is the problem. The lass has more

honor than most of the nobility in Scotland and England combined. It is difficult to believe she does not hail from the Highlands."

He thought back on Treybourne's leaving this evening and realized that something else was happening as well. "I have often thought that Anna would be led by her sense of honor until her heart was engaged."

"You think they are involved?" Nathaniel shifted in his chair, clearly uncomfortable with the thought of a formidable adversary for Anna's heart. Robert hesitated to reveal the complete threat as he saw it.

"I think that there are some tender feelings between them…." He stopped and thought about the scene he'd witnessed in the entryway as Treybourne was leaving. Robert did not ever remember seeing such an expression on Anna's face before. He should have intervened, but it was only a kiss on her wrist. Then, after he saw the effect it had on her, Robert wished he had stopped it.

"If there is something between them, why does Treybourne not make an offer of marriage for her? Although gentry, her father was a baronet, a respectable title. With the wealth of his grandfather's estates and those held in trust for the titles he will inherit from his father, he does not need to marry for money."

"She would refuse him as soon as he revealed his identity, of course," Nathaniel argued.

Robert thought about it more and shook his head. "I think, that with the correct amount of remorse and apology, Treybourne could make his case. So, what is it then that keeps him from doing so? Why did he need to come here under a false identity?"

Nathaniel considered his words and nodded again. "He has something to hide. Something that will keep them apart."

"He sent investigators here to find Goodfellow. I think we should do the same and discover what else Dursby's heir is hiding."

"Do you have someone in mind?" Nathaniel asked. "There is some need for haste with the way this is going."

"My father has a man-of-business in London who I trust with something this personal. I will send word tomorrow and see what he can find."

"Anna—" Nathaniel began.

"We need not hurt her with anything we find. If he is the man of honor that you believe him to be, he will not take advantage of her. We need not besmirch his reputation to her or anyone as long as he does what he said he would and leaves when finished."

Nathaniel poured another two fingers of whisky in both glasses and handed his to him. Robert drank it down, deciding that it was the last one. He stood and looked at his brother by marriage.

"Will Treybourne discover the truth here?"

"Robbie, we have done everything we can to make that impossible. The arrangements have withstood other inquiries."

The words did not reassure him. The whisky now swirling in his gut did not help, either.

Chapter Fourteen

The words would not come out, but the tears did.

Her candles had long since burned down to stubs and still she struggled to accept the truth of Lord Treybourne's presence and betrayal and to find Goodfellow's next message. Anna picked up the slate and rubbed the second passage into oblivion. Again.

Paper was too precious a cost to waste on her drafts, especially when any one essay went through three or four or five versions before she was happy with the tone and the content. This one had passed five versions about the time when she should have retired for the night. Admittedly, there were other reasons this night for her inability to concentrate on her task.

His face invaded her thoughts once more. The memory of the intensity of his blue gaze as he lifted her hand to his mouth and the heat as he touched his lips to her wrist sent shivers through her body even now. His words had sounded so sincere, passionate even, as he stared into her eyes at that moment.

Damn the man!

Regret at her lack of control, over her use of inappropriate words and her stupidity in not having seen through the deception filled her.

A part of her wished she'd not learned the truth until after
Goodfellow's message was complete. The task was difficult
enough without adding the emotional upheaval in which she
found herself. Try as she might to convince herself to the
contrary, she had let her enemy too close and now feared all
of the possible outcomes.

Now, as she tried to sort through her confusion and hurt,
Anna was afraid to sleep before she organized her thoughts
and used what Mr. Archer, or Lord Treybourne, had told her
about himself and his position. Considering the way he spoke
of "Lord Treybourne" as a separate person, she wondered
where the truth of his words began and ended. Pulling her
robe tighter around her, she turned the remaining lamp up a
bit so she could see how bad, or possibly good, her last efforts
were.

The slate hit the desk with a thump. It was bad.

None of the specifics fit her arguments. The tone and
attitude was wrong. When Nathaniel had returned from the
country and his meeting with his father, they had discussed
at length the need to appease Mr. Archer. Not exactly that, for
she agreed that the essay needed to be centered on the topic
and not the person. After all Mr. Archer had allowed, the cad!
She thought in retrospect that Goodfellow could certainly
answer the insult. Despite the truth of his identity, it was still
the answer to their shared problem and she tried to seize on
the idea now.

Again.

But, the words would not come.

Anna lifted the teapot and discovered it empty. It was too late to brew more, or to even heat the necessary water, so she poured some water from her bedside pitcher and sipped that. The sleeve of her robe slid down her arm, exposing her wrists. She feared that this was the cause of her inability to write.

Overstimulation of the inappropriate kind, considering the truth she now knew.

Overstimulation of the most exciting and appealing type, regardless of the truth. Lord Treybourne was the most handsome man she'd met and with all honesty she could admit that it was true even when she thought him to be only Mr. Archer.

She closed her eyes and rubbed her forehead, seeking clarity, and all she could see there was his gaze as he lifted her hand to his mouth. The heat of his lips and their teasingly soft touch against her pulse came alive and she peered at her wrist to see if some mark remained. Instead her pulse quickened and more shudders tore through her, leaving her breathless and in awe that such a small thing could cause such a large disturbance in her.

Scandalous sensations that made her toes curl.

Scandalous sensations brought on by the very man she loathed and one who was behaving in the most awful way possible for someone of good breeding and noble rank. Just like all those years ago…

Shaking herself, she gulped down the remaining water in her cup, hoping it would help to cool down from the improper emotions racing through her body.

The worst part was that she recognized these erratic and pleasurable feelings as the reason why so many good, God-fearing women fell into sin. Many of the girls in her school reported that they participated in their own downfall and, after experiencing the passion of just two of the diabolical kisses of her adversary, Anna could well understand why.

The truly startling revelation to her, for the short time that his deception had lasted, had been that for once she might understand the appeal of marriage. For so long she'd opposed even the thought of that institution, but she'd let down her guard with this one and the idea had crept inside her heart, even as he had.

The thought of marriage to someone like "Mr. Archer," who believed in what she believed, who seemed to like her sister, who worked for a living and did not live off the work of others, who stirred feelings within her that she'd long denied even existed… Well, marriage to him would be different.

Anna laughed softly and with derision at her contemptible lack of awareness and at the sad way she was willing to change her whole perspective because of a few kisses.

A few kisses by a man who lied at every encounter between them.

Exhaustion covered her and threatened to send her sprawling to the surface of the desk. Anna looked at the too-empty slate on the desk before her. Morning raced at her and Lord Treybourne and his latest essay must be answered. Then she would worry about the weaknesses in her defenses concerning men like him. Surely she could come with a plan that would allow her, at some advantageous point, to reveal his identity and spurn his questionable efforts to gain some measure of personal involvement with her.

Her conscience flared and reminded her that he had not truly taken any steps toward her—no offer had been made nor any words of affection exchanged. Indeed, even recognizing that no offer could be made or accepted in their current circumstances did not put an end to the confusing and haunting feelings of passion stirring within her at just the thought of his nearness or his touch or his kiss.

Whatever the connection between them, it was at an end. She and the causes and people she supported could not afford the risk of such a relationship with a man capable of destroying everything. And Anna could not allow herself to lose control over her words, thoughts or her actions. Not now when her goals were in sight.

She picked up the slate and leaned back in her chair, reading the words aloud. Originally, she planned to accept "Mr. Archer's" offer of a truce, but with his perfidy known to her, Anna found it difficult to be so agreeable. No, she shook her head, she would not be so soft now. The phrasing still did not convey her thoughts and, more importantly, did not make Mr. Goodfellow's points.

Still, thoughts of the man and his appeal clamored within her. Anna realized that what they had shared could be the first steps in an honorable relationship or a seduction. But, now that she knew the truth behind the façade, she wondered which was his aim. The Mr. Archer she thought she knew would not be of a mind to seduce an "innocent" young woman.

And Lord Treybourne's true purpose? Well, she had little

to go by other than his words and his essays. Could she believe that he was there only to find Goodfellow? Why did he feel it necessary to hide behind a false personality?

This was far too confusing and she needed to write this essay now. She would put off all other thoughts and uncertainty until it was finished and published. She would have to face Nathaniel over this, too, and feared the repercussions of such a confrontation. Their friendship was long-standing and Anna felt certain that Nathaniel's cooperation in any subterfuge was his attempt to protect her. Lord MacLerie could be forgiven, for the same excuse could be claimed by him as well.

Anna placed the slate on the desk and rolled her shoulders to loosen the growing tension there. Taking in and letting out a few deep breaths, she thought back to the conversations from dinner tonight and tried to pick out a few snippets of Lord Treybourne's words that could be used...against him.

The clock below the stairs chimed softly, announcing that the hour of four in the morning had been reached and reminding her of her continuing failure. Holding her head in her hands, Anna searched for something that "Mr. Archer" had said tonight. Something about rules of rhetoric, a topic lacking in hers or any other woman of quality's education for it was thought to be both unnecessary and inadvisable to teach women.

His words teased her for a while longer until she finally grasped the missing element of her argument. Then, first with chalk and slate and then in a finer hand with pen on paper, the essay flowed out from her, making her points and making infinite sense while treading the fine line between goading and appeasing. Her other concerns faded into the night as she wrote…and wrote.

It was nearly noon when Anna declared it satisfactory to her and had it sent over to the *Gazette* office their usual way—two different boys with it changing hands in the Old Town before landing on Nathaniel's desk at the office. Exhausted by the overnight writing session and all the strain and worry from these last days of preparation, Anna fell into bed and slept.

Nathaniel's reaction would arrive on her doorstep soon enough, but more important to her in that last moment of wakefulness was, what would "Mr. Archer" think of it?

He opened the wrapping and spread the page out before him on the desk. Taking a deep breath, he read from beginning to end without pause as was his usual custom. Then he read each paragraph separately and evaluated the tone and phrasing. Last, he took each point made and assessed its clarity of purpose.

Astounding! She was truly an incredible woman, able to produce something like this, an essay of substance, and yet she followed his instructions over the lengths to which she could go to make her points. Stunning!

Nathaniel read it once more before handing it to Lesher for typesetting within the issue. As Trey had said, some retaliation would be expected, but Anna had used just a touch of sarcasm and enough emotion without the essay sounding too soft after the attack leveled by his lordship. After thinking on it, he scratched out the word "scurrilous." Other than that, it was perfect.

The issue was ready except for this one piece and would be printed in the next two days and hit the streets the day after that. He debated on when to forward a copy of it to Trey as he'd agreed to do and decided to wait until the issue was complete so the essay could be read in the context of the other pieces.

Now, all he could do was sit back and wait—wait for the issue's release and the reaction to it, wait for Trey to hie himself back to London as promised and wait for Anna to come to her senses. Oh, and wait for any information about Trey's past to arrive from the man Robert had commissioned to seek it out.

And with the usual storminess and heat of Edinburgh at the end of August, waiting was something he could do. There was little else of interest in the city at this time. Except Anna, of course.

The waiting was interminable. Letters came from Ellerton and Hillgrove at the hunting box asking for his return, but David dare not leave yet. Neither man seemed in a hurry to return to London or even to visit Edinburgh, so he wrote of his arrival soon and sent it off.

The marquess's missives found their way to him and those demands were not so amiable. This summer break from sessions was a time to shore up support for several bills his father planned on introducing in Lords and he ordered his return to London to participate, *as agreed*. David felt the chain tightening around his neck and being yanked across several hundred miles.

Thomas had not yet discovered the depth of the links

between Anna and the *Gazette,* but he continued to ply financiers and banks across Edinburgh to free up someone's tongue. Their contingency plans were also vague at this point, for David's request to be able to continue maintaining his current commitments without additional funding made the usually calm Mr. Forge lose his composure and pound on the desk in protest. David did not doubt the man's resourcefulness, if given time, so he urged him on in both tasks.

And he waited.

The three days until the expected release of Goodfellow's latest passed more slowly than many years of his life to date. Would the writer follow Nathaniel's request? Would he strike out with words and make the situation worse? If that were the sorry case, would Nathaniel have the backbone to intervene and make the changes necessary to quell the hostilities?

He was tired. He was cross and short-tempered. He missed Anna. And the thought that he would be leaving Edinburgh and her did not sit well with him. He needed to get back and handle all the business in his control and, for the first time in the years since hatching these plans, he did not look forward to it. Now, he would return knowing that there was a woman out there who was perfect for him, who agreed with his politics, who would support those endeavors he did and one who he could not have.

David looked over at the cabinet and noticed that the decanter of whisky was gone. Damn Harley! His valet was much too efficient to miss such a thing, so David knew he'd done it on purpose. A message that he was drinking too much these last few days. He rubbed the ache in his head and wondered if Harley was too smart for his own good.

He paced over to the window and peered out. In anticipation of the next edition of the *Scottish Monthly Gazette,* Edinburgh was drawing all sorts of visitors from the south. Too many who knew him on sight. Too many acquaintances who would question his presence there. So, he was banished to this house to wait.

Finally, a messenger arrived from Nathaniel with a portfolio and a brief scribbled note. "As promised." David slammed the door of the study behind him and opened the magazine. Searching through it, he found the essay and began to read it. Shorter than most of the others in the ongoing series, this was more to the point.

Blood will Tell, My Lord?
It Certainly will and it Certainly has in this Series of Exchanges. But it has also Spoken Most Eloquently in many Matters that the King and His Government seem Eager to Ignore. Allow me to Remind His Lordship about Blood that will tell—
The Blood of those who Honored the King and this Country with their Lives fighting against the tyrant on the Continent. The Blood of Those Loyal Soldiers who Returned to find only Poverty, Death and Disregard as Their Reward for such Service.
The Blood of the Innocent Children of the poor and unfortunate who ask for Nothing More Than Bread to Eat and Water to Drink.
The Blood of Those Killed in Riots over the Price of Food, the Price of Farmed Goods, even the very Price of Living in His Majesty's Kingdom.

Blood Will Tell, My Lord, and the Needless Spilling of Blood will not be Washed away or Ignored so easily.

Instead of Demonstrating your Righteous Indignation at my Challenges to your Sensibilities and Accusing Me of Having No Honor—an Accusation which I will hold him Accountable for—I would urge My Lord Treybourne and Those with Whom he holds sway to Consider what must be done to Stop the Bloodletting and to proceed in this Prematurely Bemoaned, but not yet lost Age of Enlightenment so that King and Country may Benefit.

Bring your Attention back to the issues at hand—parliamentary and social reform—and leave the name-calling to Lesser Men. The good People of our Country would be better served if we did not allow such Distractions to pull us from our discourse. So, I urge you, My Lord Treybourne, be the Better Man and put forward ideas and not insults, suggest Enhancements not Hindrances to the common good and Promote Progress and not Stagnation.

His Majesty's and Yr. Servant,

A. J. Goodfellow

He read it again to make certain he'd not missed a word, just as, he suspected, everyone would do so in the coming days across Britain. Then he read it for the subtleties and nuances not apparent in simply reading the words, but there in the context of the essay.

Simply put, it was brilliant! Goodfellow had done it! Exactly as they needed. Exactly as he'd asked. Exactly what all parties concerned needed to get back to the substance and away from the distractions.

David read once more to be certain he'd not missed anything and then let out some of the tension that he'd been holding inside. The loud yell brought Harley and Thomas to his study.

"My lord?"

"This might work, Harley. It just might work out after all."

"Very good, my lord. Does this mean I should begin packing for our return to London?" he asked.

"And civilization, Harley?"

"Just so, my lord." Harley had made no secret that living here was like living in some foreign land. His valet could not understand the other servants they'd hired, nor the tradesmen they dealt with.

"Soon, I think, but not just yet."

"My lord?"

"Thomas, are you any closer to finding anything about what I asked you to look into?" He turned and faced the man. "That is most important to me."

"I have made some progress, but it will take another few days before I have it complete, my lord."

Harley let out a loud, exasperated sigh, letting him know that every day here was a trial to his patience. At his look, Harley nodded and bowed. "Very good, my lord."

David was restless now that he knew what was coming. Something bothered him though and after he dismissed Thomas and Harley, he picked up the *Gazette* again.

The first thing he recognized were his comments about the soldiers who'd returned from the war on the continent to no place and few jobs to employ them. Then he saw his own observations about the price of goods and food staples. David had made both of those comments during discussions at Lady MacLerie's dinner and Goodfellow had used them against him in the essay!

As he suspected, Goodfellow had been present and listening—it was the only explanation. So close to his quarry and not successful yet at flushing him out of the bushes!

Turning back to the wording and the content, he noticed that Goodfellow had chosen a key phrase from the last one of his to use as the centerpiece around which he built his article.

"Blood will tell" was the telling one. The problem was that he'd never used those words.

Raking his hand through his hair, he closed his eyes and thought back to the original essay. Going over it in his mind, David knew that his father had altered his words. And, if he sent his next essay ahead of his return and lingered a bit longer here as he'd been toying with the idea of doing, his father would turn that one into something guaranteed to begin the personal conflict anew.

His return to London must indeed be soon. He shook his head. Regret over so many things filled him, but the one most in his mind was Anna. Regret over all the things that could have been for them and yet could not be.

If he could find a way to free himself from the devil's bargain with his father. If he could convince her that his charade had been the only way he could handle the situation. If he could allow Anna to know that the real Lord Treybourne was him and not the man she thought him to be.

He threw himself back into the chair, knowing the foolishness of such wishes. His personal wealth could not be touched until he gained control of his inheritance from his grandfather on his thirtieth birthday, another year away. Ending the bargain with his father was not possible until then.

Well, his time here was nearly over, so David decided that he would see her as many times as he could arrange before leaving. Although he was certain she would be angry and hurt when she found out his identity, he would remember her spirit and her beauty always. And most likely, he'd long for what could have been between them.

Chapter Fifteen

Nathaniel had not shown up on her doorstep after all. Neither had "Mr. Archer." Instead, the two nemeses to her peace of mind had absented themselves for several days after she'd turned the essay in to Nathaniel. Anna went about her various duties and did not seek either man out, waiting for one or the other to reveal their hand first. Her strategy worked, for Nathaniel appeared without warning at her front door just two mornings after the newest issue of the *Gazette* arrived in the hands of anxious readers across Edinburgh. Londoners would be receiving their copies this morning.

"Anna!" he said as he entered, and hugged her. "Goodfellow's latest is a smashing success!" He lifted her from her feet and twirled around with her in his arms as though doing a waltz in her drawing room.

As difficult as it was not to join him in his excitement, Anna waited for him to notice that something might be awry. She closed her eyes and did allow a moment of weakness as she floated in his arms and felt his support around her. Then, she took a deep breath and pushed out of his embrace.

"Is something wrong, Anna?" he asked. Nathaniel took a step or two back and, still holding on to her shoulders, examined her stance. "Something *is* wrong."

She offered a smile, a weak one that did not sit comfortably on her face. "Will it satisfy Mr. Archer?"

"Absolutely it will. Have no fear on that account, Anna. You, er…Goodfellow walked the very fine line as *he* needed to, neither capitulating nor antagonizing Lord Treybourne personally. This skirmish belongs to Goodfellow."

Anna backed out of his grasp and it was she who walked a few paces away now. Grasping the back of a chair, she met his gaze and waited for him to understand. When his eyes widened and the smile he wore froze in place on his face, she knew he'd comprehended the situation.

"Anna," he stuttered, reaching out toward her. "I…"

"You can explain, Nathaniel? I am certain you can and I am simply holding my breath in anticipation of it."

Anna evaded his grasp as he strode to the front of the chair and reached for her hand. He took a step to the side and she countered with a step away. She shook her head at him.

"Stay there. I have no wish for you to touch me while you explain the reasons behind your betrayal." It was how she felt about his compliance with Lord Treybourne's obvious plan to keep the truth from her.

"I was attempting to protect you until he left. Nothing more than that. I saw no reason—"

"No reason to enlighten me to his true identity? No reason to share this valuable information with me? No reason to tell me the truth when I stumbled near it?" Her voice rose and Anna trembled at the strength of her anger. "I thought that this was a partnership, Nathaniel. I expected better of you than this."

Now it was her turn to stalk him, taking several steps closer until she could poke her finger in his chest. "You took a stranger's side in this over mine. What did he promise you? What did he threaten you with?" Then she stopped and considered the worst of it. "What did you tell him?"

"Sit, please. Can we not talk about this calmly?" Nathaniel asked as he pointed to the chair they circled. He walked to the couch and waited for her to move. "There is much to say."

Anna debated for a few minutes and thought about everything that existed between them. As angry as she felt, she would not turn her back on their years of friendship. She nodded and slid onto the chair, arranging her skirts while gathering her thoughts and letting her anger calm.

"I have told him nothing of our arrangements. Indeed, his interest in you lies in a completely different area."

Startled at the implication, she frowned. "What does that mean, Nathaniel? What interest does he have in me?"

Could it be that he was planning on using the information she revealed about the connections between the charitable endeavors and the magazine? Now, thinking back to Nathaniel's objection over that course of action, it made sense. And she'd given the very man who could harm them the most the weapon with which to do it.

"Come now, Anna. He is attracted to you as any man with eyes and a brain would be. You are a lovely young woman, in spite of your attempts to ignore it, and one who has the appealing ability to carry on conversations that are not about gowns and balls."

She felt the hot blush move up on her cheeks. He did not compliment her often and now, with Lord Treybourne in the mix, she felt embarrassed by it.

"So intelligent that I could not see through this deception or yours," she muttered.

Nathaniel stepped over to where she sat and knelt before her, lifting her chin with his fingers. It reminded her of another's touch. Now, she saw only her dear friend.

"I beg your forgiveness for not disclosing his identity. I took his word as a gentleman that he had only one task and then he would leave. Since we have worked so long to cover Goodfellow's tracks, I saw no reason why that task would take more than a few days or a week."

Torn between her anger and his words, Anna considered them for a moment. Nathaniel then added the maddening words that always made it impossible for her to refuse him.

"You know my feelings toward you, Anna. I did it only to protect you in the best way I could. At the time, when he first arrived, I thought it best to go along with Lord Treybourne to get rid of him sooner rather than later."

This time, she could hear Clarinda's words in her head about Nathaniel's true feelings about their relationship. Although it faded into more a familial one for her, from the soulful expression in his eyes and the soft caress now of her face, he still thought and expected more.

"Nathaniel, I have been honest with you about our relationship," she began. He dropped his hand, drew back a bit and narrowed his eyes.

"Then…you are taken with him?"

"Taken with? Whatever do you mean? Surely you do not refer to Lord Treybourne?" Anna pushed past him and walked to the window. Peering out, she took a deep breath and tried to refute the feelings she knew to be true. "Is a woman not permitted to appreciate the handsome visage or fine figure of a man? Or to enjoy a few meaningless conversations with the old acquaintance of a trusted friend?" Turning back, she cleared her throat and offered the last lie. "That is all that happened."

Whether it was the tone of her voice or the unfamiliar quality that entered her gaze, Nathaniel knew her words for the lies that they were. Treybourne had made more than a passing effect on Anna and an unusual jealousy tore through him at the realization of it. But, before he could act on the impulse, the true affection between them flared as well.

He stood and straightened his waistcoat. "There could be no more between you and him than that, Anna. Surely, you understand?"

It would not do to get her hopes raised, if she had succumbed to those customary feminine ones regarding men and marriage, for Treybourne's position as earl now and marquess later put him far above her in social status and expectations.

"Oh, I understand my standing completely, Nathaniel, and I would not have presumed otherwise if I had known his identity."

Had she even noticed the slip? Did she realize the truth she'd just exposed to him? Damn! She did have tender feelings toward the blighter!

"Anna," he said as he approached her, "Treybourne will be

gone soon, for his every effort to discover Goodfellow's identity is without success. In spite of my failure to grasp the danger of his presence at the first, I will not fail to protect you now."

"Actually, the truth would have offered me any protection I needed from him, Nathaniel. As it will now that I know."

The steely glint that foretold trouble entered her gaze now and Nathaniel shook his head. "Anna, you cannot mean to engage him now that you know? Now that Goodfellow's essay is published, his return to London is imminent."

He watched as the hurt young woman turned into the warrior before his eyes. When her chin lifted and she placed her hands on her hips, he knew nothing good could be heading his, or Treybourne's, way.

"Other than Lord MacLerie, with whom have you shared Lord Treybourne's secret?" she asked, her voice deceptively low and even. "Clarinda?"

He knew she could be more determined when she was calm. Perhaps he should have tried to make her angry? When she raised her voice, it did not signify imminent danger for anyone, especially not the target of her ire.

"I did not tell Robert or Clarinda."

"Ah, so Lord MacLerie had met him previously, too. I thought I noticed a look between them at the dinner, before their outside conversation."

He laughed then, in spite of his concerns. Anna continued to do somewhat inappropriate things even as she tried to be the consummate lady and teach her sister the manners and comportment of polite society. Listening at open doors and occasionally using an unsuitable expletive were her two biggest faults and not acceptable even in the more relaxed world of Edinburgh.

"Your ear was not positioned correctly to hear all the details, then?" Nathaniel tried to look stern, but failed in his attempt.

"The noise of the coaches rolling by in the street made clarity more difficult," she replied dryly. "I missed most of their conversation due to the noise and simply getting the doorman away so I could move closer."

They both laughed then and Nathaniel realized that, in spite of disagreements and momentarily lapses, they still shared a common bond between them. They knew each other's shortcomings, strengths and secrets, and would protect them.

"You may not find my plan as humorous as my inadequacies, dear friend," she warned. "I will use his presence here to gain information, much as he planned to do so against us."

"Anna. Please do not consider such an undertaking."

He would drop back to his knees if he thought it would work. One look at the wicked expression now planted firmly on her face and he knew his efforts to turn her from her plan would fail.

"I have been thinking back on what I have revealed to him in our conversations. If I rely on 'Mr. Archer's' words, which is all I am left with, I do not believe that Lord Treybourne will use the school as a target. He seemed quite undone by his visit there when he realized what our goals were and who our students were."

"Undone?" He did not ever remember seeing Trey "undone" by anything. "How did he respond?"

"He was completely the gentleman to the girls, especially when Molly served us tea. Then, a short time later, he withdrew."

A frown rested on Anna's forehead as she contemplated the visit. Nathaniel wondered at the significance, if any, for any member of the peerage would be outraged to be served by a maid so visibly *in the family way* and to be handed the knowledge that there was no legitimate union behind the condition. It would be unthinkable to put a member of polite society in that situation. She shook her head and did not speak for a moment.

"He apologized at the dinner for his impolite reaction."

"Anna, please let this go. Let him go without pursuing any action that might endanger our activities. We know the Tories' aims and their plans are no secret."

"I cannot, Nathaniel. If I were a man, I would have called him out long before this, but that is not an option open to the fairer sex. If he came to use you to find Goodfellow, I intend to return the favor."

"Anna…" he moaned, leaning his head into his hands and feeling the strong urge to find a bottle of whisky. "Now that you know, you should be going as far away from him in the other direction as possible."

"Discovering the specifics of Lord Treybourne and his party's aims and intentions can only help our cause…and Goodfellow's arguments, Nathaniel. Surely you see that?"

Actually, no matter how he thought on this, he could only see death and destruction. Well, not that dire of an outcome, but Anna would be hurt, again. She could not survive another debacle.

"If you choose to follow this path of folly, Robert and I may not be able to protect you, Anna."

"You and Robert? How is he involved?" She stepped closer

and he sank onto the couch to avoid her. "What did Lord MacLerie tell you?" she demanded.

"Anna, he came to me when he thought he recognized Trey. Robert only spoke directly to him when his attraction to you became apparent. Warned the man off from doing anything untoward."

Instead of angering her as he thought it would, Anna simply nodded and smiled. Her words revealed the worst of it.

"Since you and Lord MacLerie are so intent on keeping Lord Treybourne's secret, then I hope you will offer me the same courtesy and support as you give our enemy."

"Anna—"

"I do not intend to encourage him to linger here, but I will seek out anything that will help our fight. And I expect you to remain silent, as silent as the grave, about my intentions and my other identity. For all Lord Treybourne knows, I still believe him to be his own not-so-humble lackey."

Her directness and lack of dissembling unnerved him. Part of him would love to have her enthusiasm and drive, in his home and in his bed, but the larger part of him wondered if he could marry such a woman. No matter the number of years they'd been acquainted, no matter the successes and failures behind them, he could do nothing to control her actions when it became her wishes against his. She believed herself an equal in their dealings and, in many ways, they were, but he wanted a wife he could control. A marriage as it should be.

With that realization, his burden lightened and he laughed aloud. Grasping her hand, he tugged her down to sit next to him. Once there, he lifted their clasped hands and kissed the back of hers.

"I will always love you, Anna, and I think you know that already. Know also that I will always be here if you need me." He watched as her eyes filled with tears at his declaration. "But I must say that I pity poor Trey now that you have set your sights on him. The *puir mon* has no idea of what he has done or what you can do when you set your mind to a task."

"The *puir mon* indeed!" she said. With a brisk rub at her eyes, she stood and smiled at him.

Nathaniel stood and took his leave then, knowing that they were still in each other's good graces. And knowing that Trey stood no chance of completing his task now that Anna knew the truth.

Three days after the article was published, David sent word around to the school saying he would arrive at noon. Even watching the messenger leave with it in his hand brought about such a feeling of anticipation in him that he berated himself for being foolish. But, fool he was in wanting to enjoy her company before he finished everything here and left. Forge gave him every expectation that the end of their quest—both to find Goodfellow and now to discover the links between Miss Fairchild—would be successful very, very soon.

The invitation for him to join them at the Assembly Rooms several days hence, which had arrived on his desk from Lady MacLerie this morning, surprised him. David didn't think that MacLerie would allow his wife to extend such a request after their conversation. Even so, he should decline it, considering that Edinburgh was crawling now with people he knew. The time to leave was quickly approaching.

His plan to have Harley pack a basket for a meal al fresco, perhaps in the small park near Holyrood Palace, was dashed by the arrival of the now usual thunderstorms. Blasted weather! Did it never stop raining here?

If it was not the rain, it was the *haar,* the inhabitants' name for the sea fog that could roll out of the firth and cover the city in minutes and without warning. Once gone from here, he would surely not miss the dampness, for at least the south of England had days of glorious sunshine and warm breezes to offer between bouts of wet and wild weather.

Now, he sat in the carriage, at the side of the High Street, its hood raised against the weather, waiting for noon to arrive. David lifted his watch from his waistcoat pocket and checked it again. Only five minutes had passed, making him twenty minutes early. He lifted the cover from the window just in time to see lightning slash across the sky, unnerving the horses and most of those on the street around him. The crash of thunder that followed rumbled through the streets and echoed down the closes and wynds of the Old Town. The carriage jostled then; the horses were becoming difficult to calm in this weather. David climbed out and yelled to the driver. "Take the horses and seek shelter from this." The wind picked up in strength, so he called out louder. "Return for me in an hour or when it is safe."

He did not stand to watch them leave, for he could feel the rain pelting him. David ran up the steps and knocked on the door of the school. He tucked himself in the doorway and out of the storm while he waited for someone to answer.

"Mr. Archer?" Mrs. Dobbs opened the door and peeked out. "Come in out of this rain." Once she moved back, he entered and waited for some of the water to drip off. Removing his hat, he placed it on a table near the door.

"I sent the carriage for shelter," he said. "The lightning—" a flash lit up the shadowed room as he mentioned it "—is spooking the horses."

"It isna doing much for my nerves, either," Mrs. Dobbs replied.

"This is my first time here in Edinburgh in the late summer. Are these storms a common occurrence?" David stepped away from the door, moving toward the larger room off the entryway and expecting Anna's arrival at any moment.

"Weel, they dinna happen every August, but every couple of years they seem to blow in. Aboot five years or so ago, the lightning was so fierce it caused fires. And if my memory serves me, the storm started just as this one did, building with the heat of the day." The housekeeper shuddered as yet another bolt lit up the sky outside and shook the house with its accompanying thunder.

"Hopefully, this will not follow that pattern."

Although when he compared today's with the previous storms this week, he recognized that this one had a dangerous feel to it. Even just standing in it for a few moments, he could smell something in the air that made the hairs on the back of his neck tingle. The storm pulsed with an angry power.

"I have arrived a bit early for my appointment with Miss Fairchild." The housekeeper stammered and glanced toward the door and then back at him. Something about this was not right. "Isn't she here?"

"Weel, Mr. Archer, the lass didna ken of yer visit for yer note arrived after she'd left on her errands. But, Miss Anna said she would return by now." Another glance at the darkened windows. "But she hasna. I am worried about her being oot in the storm alone."

He could not have heard her correctly. "Out? Alone? In this storm? Please tell me you are jesting?"

From the sheepish expression and the nervous way she twisted the long white apron over her dress, he knew it was as bad as that. "I told her no' to go, but the lass can be stubborn when it involves one of the gels. I am sure she wi' be back in a scant bit."

David looked at the windows shuttered against the rains and winds, listened to the sound of the powerful storm and considered the options for a moment. He had to find her and make certain she was safe. "Where did she go? Did she have a carriage or chair?"

"Wait. One of the gels gave her the message. Molly!" she called out, running to the farthest door. "Molly!"

The young girl he'd met waddled into the room and whispered to Mrs. Dobbs while peeking at him around the housekeeper's stout form. Then with a quick curtsy, the girl ran from the room.

"Molly said she went to Lochlend Close to meet with a girl who might need help."

A pregnant servant girl, in other words.

"Where is Lochlend Close?" He already had his hand on the doorknob by the time she reached him. "Which direction and where on the close did she go?"

"Go down past Canongate Kirk. It is three or four closes past the kirk. The one on the north side of High Street. Molly did not know more than that."

Bloody hell, would he ever find her with such scarce directions? He would have to, it was as simple as that. He turned the knob and was nearly knocked down by the strong winds buffeting against the door. With Mrs. Dobbs's help, he pulled it closed. At the last moment, she thrust something into his hands and the door closed with a bang.

He spared a glance down to discover one of the long coats made from canvas that many here wore as protection against the frequent rains. All it took to convince him of the need for it was a burst of wind against him, and David tugged it on and hooked the latches across the front. It would not cover his head, but the water ran off it and would make it easier to move.

With his hand and arm blocking some of the downpour and wind from his eyes, he ran down High Street toward Holyrood Palace until he found Canongate Church on his left. Continuing on, he counted three and looked for the wall plaque with the street name on it. It did not match the name given him so he ran on to the next, and then the next, until he found Lochlend Close. Turning in, he stumbled down the close and looked for Anna.

Closes in Edinburgh were usually closed-in spaces, but this one seemed to go as far as the next street over from the High Street, and open there. Tall, stone buildings towered over the narrow, open space. Although some of Edinburgh's most fashionable addresses and personages were housed along the closes of High Street, this close was a more humble one. The houses and other buildings were in disrepair and showed signs of neglect and abandonment. Some tenants, no doubt those who could afford to, moved to the New Town to escape the decay bound to happen.

David searched for some sign of her along the cobble-stoned path, but no one was out in this storm but he. He could not go door to door, so he did the most obvious thing…

"Anna!" he called out as loud as he could. Walking a few paces down the path, he yelled again, "Anna!" He moved away from the buildings to see farther down the close, but the torrents forced him to take cover. He waited for a pause in it and called out again.

Lightning shot through the sky, over and over, almost tearing the sky in two and making the dark day like the brightest morning he'd seen. This time, it had a target, for he heard and felt the force of it hitting somewhere close by. The thunder that followed was joined by the crash of whatever it had hit. Sweet Jesus! He had to find her.

Calling out her name, he scrambled from building to building, and just when he thought he was in the wrong place, he saw her off in the distance, leaning against the side of a three-story tenement. Was she hurt? Did she not hear him?

"Anna! Stay there," he called out.

When lightning flashed above him again, he waited until the noise passed before calling again. He was only a building away when the next burst of lightning struck. Drawn by the brilliant burst of light above him, he watched as it hit the roof of the building and shattered the stone gable on the front. In horror, he realized that the falling chunks of stone would fall close to Anna.

With a speed he would have thought impossible, he ran along the front of the building, grabbed her as he moved past and dragged her out of the way. The debris landed only seconds, and a few feet, behind them. Out of breath, he pressed her against the side of the building until he could be certain nothing more fell from above them. When he turned her to face him, her eyes were wide with fear and her hair tumbled loose from its usual well-kept state. She clutched at him as the reaction caused a panic in her.

"Are you hurt?" he asked, searching her face for any sign of injury. His heart raced inside his chest, the sight of the stones tumbling to the ground heading toward her still fresh in his mind,

"No, only frightened," she said.

He fought the urge for a moment and then gave in. David tilted his head and took her mouth in a kiss that spoke clearly of concern and desire, but even more about possession. She clung to him and then, a scant moment later, she returned his passion, touching her tongue to his as he tasted her deeply. Lost to everything but her kiss, he continued to claim her mouth over and over until the crash of another lightning strike broke into their dreamlike moment.

The storm poured down around them and Anna was shaking. Leaning back with an eye toward the perilous old building, he looked around to see if there was shelter nearby. The lightning continued, so he did not think it prudent to chance a run all the way back to the school from here. Realizing that the same overhang of stone that had broken apart on the front of the building was actually their best protection on the side, he took her hand and guided her to the side of stone tenement away from the gusts of wind and slicing rains. David was not completely at ease with their location, but it should shield them from the worst of the weather. Once there he gave her some room and tried to catch his own breath, labored now due to his own fear for her, running from the school and the desire that surged through him even now.

"I thought…I thought you…" he whispered. "I saw the bolt knock the stones free and thought you would be hit." He lifted her sodden hair from her face and brushed it back, touching her cheeks now, and when she lifted her face to look at him, he kissed her.

This kiss was different from their first one. Not as frantic, but just as much about claiming, and as she leaned into his arms, he wrapped his around her and held her closer. Covering her mouth and touching her lips with his tongue, he teased her until she opened once more and allowed him entrance. The noise of the storm faded once more and he savored the feel and taste of her until she drew back. She could not move far from him before she touched the wall, but he felt it and released her. She gazed up at him, her eyes awash in a confused blend of fear, desire, anger and sadness.

"Thank you for saving me from the stones," she whispered.

"Your servant always, madam," he said with a nod, trying to make light of his actions. "But what could have been so important that it brought you out into this storm?"

She stiffened in his embrace at his words and he realized that she took them as a rebuke. Well, they were, but he had no standing in her life to issue such a reprimand. David remained close to keep the rain from hitting her, but let his hands fall to his sides, no longer touching her.

"I was looking for someone who needed help. She told one of the girls that she was increasing and would be turned out and had no place to go."

"So you risked your safety to find her?" He would never forget the sight of those stones falling toward her from the rooftop above.

"It was only raining when I left and I thought I had adequate time to meet her and return to the school before you arrived."

"Did you find her?"

"No, I went to the address and no one lives there. Many of these buildings are being abandoned or are falling into ruin as families and businesses take up quarters in the New Town."

He laughed then, the absurdity of the situation striking him. "It is astounding to me that you can calmly discuss the problems of urban development when you were just nearly killed by part of that very problem."

She nodded, still seeming to watch him with suspicion, and said, "I have been told often that I am different, Mr. Archer."

"Now that I have saved your life, do you think it permissible for you to address me by my given name?"

Her expression turned into one of disdain and he was stunned by it. Certainly they had experienced enough of an acquaintance to allow it? Perhaps not in London, where no one, not even his mother, called him by it, but here where no one knew him, could it not be permitted?

"I did not take you for such a stickler of conventional behavior, Miss Fairchild."

From the anger flashing in her gaze that turned her usually warm brown eyes into the hue of molten copper, he expected an angry retort. She appeared ready to deliver one until another bolt cut through the sky above them, so strong it blinded him for a moment. When he looked into her eyes, the anger was gone. He would blame her changeable mood on her close call with danger.

"I cannot believe that I am going to admit this to you, Mr....Mr. Archer, but I fear I am overwhelmed by the events here today. I must go now," she said in a rapid sentence as she tried to step around him. The booming thunder as it filled the close and echoed around them seemed to change her mind on the matter of leaving.

Anna took a deep breath and tried to focus on anything, anything but the man before her. Her shock at seeing him running toward her, screaming out her name and then pulling her to safety would explain her reaction. Surely, someone who had faced certain death could be forgiven for not remembering that she hated the man who saved her life?

The same excuse could be given for her lapse of judgment in allowing that same hated man to kiss her...and kiss her...and again until she was so breathless she could not then think clearly.

Now, even as she tried to blame the storm for keeping them in such close proximity, Anna knew that her plan to approach him logically and coolly at their next meeting was in complete shambles. The second part of her plan was to keep things impersonal and social and never to allow him close enough to engage her emotions. Her failure to adjust and regroup as things went from bad to worse at this first encounter since learning the truth spoke more to her inexperience than to her intentions. She'd almost convinced herself that she could flee him now and put her plan back into action when he blocked her escape from the close.

Candidly, she did not think he did it for a purpose other

than the honorable one of her protection—well, at least until he pulled her back into his strong embrace and lowered his mouth to hers. She could think of no explanation for this incessant need of his to kiss her. Her thoughts were scattering as she realized that he, Mr. Archer or Lord Treybourne, had not changed since their last meeting. The person who had changed was her.

But, if she had changed with the knowledge of his true identity and his deception, why did his kisses still thrill her? Why did she wish to push herself farther into his embrace and allow him to continue to hold her and protect her against the wild storm blowing around them? Why did she not denounce him for the scoundrel he was?

Anna intended to do just that until his hands moved up to cradle her face and to hold her still during his sensual assault. She did, truly, plan to pull away and reveal that she knew his name, and the charade would reach its end. Then his tongue dipped inside her mouth and touched hers and all rational thoughts fled in the swirl of desire that grew deep inside her.

How could she explain this? She, the liberal, reformist bluestocking, kissing the very lord of the peerage who defended everything she opposed? And with such abandonment of proper behavior?

The only thing she could consider was that her heart was finally overruling her mind. Concentrating, she tried to pull away from whatever control he was exerting, but he did the one thing she did not expect. He moaned out her name.

"Anna," he whispered against her mouth.

She did not hear it so much as feel it reverberate through

her. Anna's heart and body reacted before her mind could stop them. She did the only thing worse.

"David," she whispered back.

Neither of them noticed for several minutes that the rain had stopped.

Chapter Sixteen

Noises around them, the kind that said the city and people were stirring and coming out to survey the damage from the storm, finally drew their attention. The voices grew closer and louder. There were several people calling out her name. David released her and watched with consummate male pride as she touched her mouth and then looked at his.

As they stepped out away from the building and into the street of the close, Anna took a moment to right her appearance as best she could. Her long coat hung loose due to his most recent attentions and, its usefulness done, David helped her to remove it even as he slipped his off as well. The showers left a humid pall over the city and the heaviness of the canvas increased the discomfort caused by wearing wet clothes under it.

It took but a moment for his driver and Mrs. Dobbs's son to see them and call to them. David managed to wave them off and escort Anna to the school himself, but nowhere along the walk there did he find the words he wanted to say. Truth be told, he was completely undone by what had happened between them. Such innocent passion given to him by a rare woman. It was more than he ever expected and absolutely more than he deserved.

And she deserved better than he could give her.

The stone segments of the building could have hit him and it would have been with less force than did that realization as it struck him.

Anna deserved better than he could ever offer her.

The streets became crowded as befit the early afternoon in the city and any sounds of torment he might have made were covered by the sounds of workmen, coaches and horses and other beasts of burden around them. A glance at the woman at his side showed her to be wholly focused on the cobblestones and bricks of the sidewalks and street as they walked up the High Street toward the school.

Honor demanded that he cease his attentions toward her. More than that, the affection that was growing between them made his discomfort rise. If he cared, and the way his heart pounded and his breath stopped at the sight of her in danger told him he did, then he must stop escalating a situation he knew could never work.

Any thoughts he had of expressing his affection or his concerns over his behavior toward her ceased when they approached the school. Mrs. Dobbs, like a watchman on duty, called out at the first sight of them. Then, surrounded by some of the girls who lived there, she climbed down the steps and waddled toward them not unlike a mother duck leading a pack of ducklings. Once they reached Anna, he did not signify at all, and was lost among all the caring and concern expressed loudly and with vigor for the one who did.

His driver now stood by the carriage waiting on him, so

David watched as Mrs. Dobbs drew Anna close and put her arm around her shoulder, guiding her up the steps and through the doorway. It was just as the door was closing, with him standing like a forgotten beggar on the sidewalk, that she turned back to him for a moment.

Their eyes met and, in that scant second, it was only the two of them again. He recognized a question there in her gaze, but she did not ask it and he did wonder if she could see the way he felt about her in his eyes. Then her lips moved and she said the words without speaking them.

Thank you, she mouthed.

Mrs. Dobbs bustled her in and the door slammed behind the group, leaving him to consider her words. The driver called to him, rousing him from his thoughts, and David climbed into the carriage at the edge of the street. For now, he would return to his house, change his now-soaked clothes and begin to make his plans for answering Goodfellow's latest volley and returning to London. As much as he wanted to stay, the truth had fallen on him many ways this day.

First, he learned that a man could find a woman who was right for him in every essential way and fall in love with her. Then, he ascertained that he could indeed fall in love with a young woman who was wrong for him in every way possible.

Finally, he discovered that hell was realizing both of those things at the same time and knowing that honor demanded a certain outcome that carried a high price to pay—his heart.

He arrived back at the house and discovered three people waiting for him. The first, Thomas, he expected. Ellerton and Hillgrove were the surprises.

"I have some news, my lord," Thomas began when David motioned for him to speak. "About Miss Fairchild."

As expected, Hillgrove and Ellerton quieted and turned their attentions to the discussion. He'd rather hear it all in private, but his two closest friends were involved already and would be drawn into his plans more in the near future.

"She owns the magazine." Thomas, excited by his discovery, stammered out the words. "And her involvement with the school is far more substantial than I...we first thought."

"She? There is a woman involved in this?" Ellerton asked.

"From the look on his face," Hillgrove replied, nodding his head in David's direction, "there is definitely a woman involved, and in more than some school or magazine." Walking closer and laying his arm over Ellerton's shoulder, he nodded at David. "And from the painful expression on Trey's face, I would make a wager on another involvement with the woman under discussion, as well."

"Damn you, Hillgrove! This is not the time to make light of the situation. Thomas, go on."

When the two men looked as though they might interrupt with more unsuitable merriment, he quelled them with a look. Pointing at two chairs near his desk, he said, "Sit there and listen. There will be time enough for your comments after you realize the depth of this."

David took the chair behind the desk and nodded to Thomas, who held piles of papers and portfolios in his hands. He held them out to David, who now suspected he knew what was revealed inside.

"Apparently, after securing a modest investment from an

unnamed source, Miss Fairchild started up the magazine. After several years of careful stewardship, she has paid back the original investor and owns it totally today."

Ellerton's loud gasp covered his own surprise. "A woman owns the *Scottish Monthly Gazette?*" He glanced over at Hillgrove and then at David. "I thought that your old schoolmate, that Hobbs-Smith chap, owned it."

"As did I," he said, unable to stop the heaping measure of respect from flooding his soul at her success. "As does Edinburgh and London and anyone who reads it."

The room quieted as the other, more complicated, possibly even dangerous implications sunk in

"No one can know these things," David warned. "Your reaction is mild compared to that which would happen if Edinburgh discovered that a woman was running the magazine and using it to support unfortunate women."

David knew exactly what would happen—investors and advertisers would run in the other direction, the targets of their editorials would attack once they knew they'd been embarrassed by a woman's publication, and subscriptions, the other lifeblood of financial success, would dry up immediately.

Yet she held it all together admirably. Not many men could have put this scheme together and pulled it off as well or for as long as she had.

"So, Hobbs-Smith works for her? And Goodfellow? They're working for a woman?" Ellerton asked. At Thomas's nod, he continued with his questions. "What did you mean, she supports unfortunate women?" Turning to Hillgrove, he shook his head. "Dear God, do not say she is one of those reformers?"

"Apparently, she is that, too," David said dryly. In spite of his friends having somewhat more liberal views on some topics, even they had their limits.

"One can only hope that the marquess does not learn of this. I fear his opinion of reformers is not nearly as accepting as mine might be," Hillgrove offered.

If his father discovered that the publication making a mockery of his beliefs was owned by a woman, he would destroy it without compunction or any measure of indecision. Then something else occurred to him, but he hesitated before asking. "Thomas, there is more about Miss Fairchild, is there not?"

The young man shuffled his feet a bit and then placed the records and such on the desk. "There is, my lord."

Thomas searched through the papers, pulled out a small portfolio and handed it to David. Before he could review the contents, Thomas explained. "Although some rather substantial donations come in from other 'sources,' Miss Fairchild is the main financial support for the Kirkhill School and Home for Women."

Ellerton whistled low and long at the disclosure. "A reformer and a bluestocking and the owner of a charity school. Could she be any more of a target for the marquess and his Tories?"

"Only if she were Goodfellow himself!" Hillgrove exclaimed and laughed.

David laughed, too, but something about the notion unsettled him. He shook his head as he realized that, in spite of MacLerie's refusal to confirm it, he still believed it was Robert MacLerie who held that position.

Ellerton laughed now. "No, for no solitary woman could

pull off each of those things. I believe that Hobbs-Smith handles the magazine for her, in return, no doubt, for the public exposure it gives him and his hopes for a seat in Commons. I read his name in several newspapers and publications recently."

So had David, and Nate had not denied such aspirations when faced with the question. It would behoove him to publicly support the ideals of the Whigs and to manage one of its clearest voices.

"As for the school, well, that is at least more fitting for a woman's involvement. But has she no father or brother to guide her in the proper behavior expected of women today?" Hillgrove asked. "It is simply not acceptable for a woman to take a place of authority in such endeavors, though. No matter her family situation."

Now it was David's turn to laugh, and he did. If Ellerton or Hillgrove met and had a chance to know Anna, they would understand how foolish the question was.

"Miss Fairchild has had to support her sister and aunt and has done an admirable job of it."

His friends turned as one and stared at him. He'd shocked them now, for their mouths hung open and they shook their heads. Thomas simply watched and said nothing.

"It sounds as though you are quite taken with the young woman, Trey. Is there more going on here that should be made known to us?"

"Ellerton! Look at his face!" Hillgrove said, rising from his seat and approaching the desk. "Look there."

Hillgrove pointed at his face and David could not stop himself—he reached up and touched it, searching for whatever Hillgrove referred to. He could find nothing out of sorts there, and shrugged.

"That is the expression of a man besotted over a woman."

"Bloody hell!" David replied.

His harsh expletive drove Thomas back a step and his nod sent the man out of the study. Once the door was closed, David turned to his friends. This kind of speculation must not be allowed to get out of control.

"Imagine it, Ellerton. The earl and the bluestocking," Hillgrove chortled after offering his assessment.

"The marquess's heir and the reformer." Ellerton now offered his own witticism. "It has the sound of one of those *dreadfuls* that my sister sneaks away to read."

"This is precisely why I did not invite you here to assist me in my efforts. The two of you are like old matchmaking mothers who have nothing else to do but seek amusement at a dear price to those involved."

David closed his eyes, not believing his loss of control—indeed, not believing how much he had just revealed to his companions. The silence grew, filling the room and all the space between them as he tried to figure out a way out of this uncomfortable situation. Finally, giving in to the inevitable embarrassment to follow, he took a breath and opened his eyes.

Hillgrove and Ellerton were staring at him once more, but at least they were not speaking. David cleared his throat to say something, anything, however Ellerton held up his hand to forestall it.

"We have been in each other's pockets these last few weeks without much for entertainment, Trey, and I fear that Hillgrove and I forget ourselves sometimes. My apologies," he said, nodding at David.

"Apologies," mumbled Hillgrove as he turned his gaze to the ceiling.

"To clarify my predicament to you both, Miss Fairchild has no idea of who I am and does not realize the severity of the problems that she will face if the marquess discovers her connections to the magazine. He holds a grudging respect for a gentleman or nobleman who steps forward and involves themself in political discourse, but a woman would earn his scorn and retribution."

"Just so," Ellerton agreed.

Standing and walking to the window, David looked out at the deceptive clear skies and then back to Ellerton and Hillgrove. "And I am experiencing a certain modicum of chagrin knowing that a woman is running the very publication responsible for my public downfall as successful spokesman for the Tory party."

"How have you kept your presence a secret here? Surely the city is alight with talk of the battle between you and Goodfellow," Hillgrove asked as he rose from his chair and lounged against the desk's edge.

"As you can see, I have used Dursby House not at all. I have my man-of-business handling most of my daily tasks and am carrying out everything else by correspondence."

"Speaking of correspondence, have you written your reply to the latest essay? Goodfellow certainly made some advances in the Whigs' position in his recent article."

"Ah, so you have seen that?" David asked. News traveled on fleet feet, he knew, and bad or embarrassing news apparently moved with even more haste. "Are you truly just arrived from the north?"

Ellerton faced him now, too, and nodded. "We are just arrived. However, since your servants are the consummate staff you expect them to be, one of your coachmen brought a copy back with him yesterday on his return from here. So, here we are to offer what support we can in your attempts to flush out this Goodfellow scoundrel…and to return directly to London and all the pleasures it has to offer."

He watched as Ellerton circled the desk and shifted a few of the papers, uncovering the as-yet-unanswered invitation to a ball to be held in the Assembly Rooms. Ellerton's face lit when he realized what it was.

"So! There is entertainment here after all." He held the parchment up so Hillgrove could see it. "You see, he has been here enjoying the cultural life of Edinburgh while we have been sitting in the mountains hunting and fishing wild game."

"I think it might have been safer to seek the refuge of the mountains," David muttered under his breath. He pointed at the invitation and raised his voice to be heard. "I am not attending and will send my regrets. It is too much a risk to go to a party where the leading members of Scottish and any English society in the city will show up in droves." The two men nodded in understanding.

"So, what is your plan, then, Trey? Do you leave for London soon? Or return to the hunting box?" The grimace on Ellerton's face when he mentioned the Dursby's mountain retreat spoke eloquently of his lack of tolerating the box's distant location and spartan living conditions.

"I have a few bits of business and the like to finish here and expect to leave for London in a few days," he answered. He crossed the study in a few paces and lifted the invitation out of Ellerton's hand. As nonchalantly as possible, he slid it back into a pile of other correspondence there. "There is no need for you two to be cramped into this house until then. I will send word to Dursby House and you can enjoy the comforts there."

"Excellent!" said Hillgrove. "I for one am pleased to accept the hospitality of your family's establishment on the other side of town."

Ellerton glanced down at the desk once more and then met his gaze. David recognized the glint in his friend's eyes as the perception of the situation as it was. Despite Ellerton's occasional lapses into ridiculousness, he was a thorough and insightful judge of character. "It is not far if you have need of us, Trey."

"I, too, am anxious to be on my way home." He clapped Hillgrove on the shoulder and nodded to Ellerton. "Now, if I can confirm Goodfellow's identity while I am here, well then, it is all the better."

"The marquess expects nothing less," Hillgrove replied. "Have you any ideas about how to do that?"

"There are two people who know my true identity here in Edinburgh and I plan to avoid them. It is those of the fairer gender who I think can be persuaded into revealing some details about the elusive Mr. Goodfellow."

"Is Miss Fairchild one of those you hope to convince to reveal her truths?" Ellerton asked quietly. David did not sense teasing in the question, only concern.

"Much as I would hope so, I fear she does not trust me enough to share her truths with me."

"And should the lady do so when you do not trust her with your own?"

David met his friend's gaze and shook his head in answer. *No.*

"Is this woman the one, or of the many?" Ellerton asked, his scrutiny intensifying. The question, developed through their years of friendship, was their private assessment of the importance of a particular woman, or relationship, to their lives.

David cleared his throat, giving himself a moment before making a declaration that he had only just stumbled upon himself. "In spite of my wishes in this, she cannot be."

His avoidance of saying it outright was more telling than any declaration he could have made. Ellerton nodded and walked to the door.

"Then perhaps it is a good thing to be leaving soon."

David watched as Harley showed them out to the waiting carriage. When the house was once more drenched in silence as the city was smothered in the heat and humidity of a late summer afternoon, David allowed himself to contemplate the truth he would rather not face—that Anna Fairchild was the perfect woman for the man known as David Archer and the most impossible choice of a wife for the Earl of Treybourne.

Chapter Seventeen

Anna turned in her bed and pulled one of the pillows over her head. Even tugging the bedcovers over the pillow, she discovered, did nothing to block out the light of day. The terrible storms of yesterday had given way to an apparently glorious today and all Anna wanted to do was avoid it. The continued knocking on the door of her bedchamber spoke of Aunt Euphemia's dedication and endurance to her chosen course of action which was, in this instance, forcing Anna from her seclusion.

"Anna, dear, you must get dressed," she called from the other side of the door.

More banging followed and then her aunt gave up her efforts. At least the ones from outside the room. Now, the door opened and Anna peered out through a small opening in her fortress to see Aunt Euphemia, Julia and the maid enter. In spite of being completely garbed in a walking dress with matching bonnet and gloves, Julia immediately climbed into the bed and burrowed her way under the covers until Anna realized there was no hope of a quiet, private day to spend

soothing her nerves and sorting her feelings. Her aunt's pro-
testations went ignored until Anna pushed the covers aside
and gave Julia a playful shove to get her to her feet.

"Lady MacLerie's coach will arrive shortly for us, my
dear. The storms have washed out to sea and a magnificent
day has dawned. Come quickly now, for we do not have much
time."

"Time for what?" Anna asked as her aunt and the maid
each took an arm and tugged her from the bed.

Fighting them off was not a viable choice, so she allowed
them to guide her from the bed. At least they allowed her a
moment of privacy as they chose her dress and accessories.
As she washed her face over the basin of cool water, she
repeated her unanswered query.

"Time for what, Aunt Euphemia?"

Her aunt shooed away the maid and walked over to Anna,
taking hold of her hand.

"I know that your experience yesterday was terrifying and
you would like to do nothing more than to hide away from
the world for a bit. But, Anna dear, you know that you always
face life and its challenges straight on. I think Clarinda's idea
of a short excursion and a brief period of relaxation is just the
thing for you to recuperate from your traumatic event."

Anna tried to smile at her friend's and her aunt's attempts
to help, but they did not know half the trauma of what had
occurred yesterday. And the near-death episode of the falling
stones was the least of it.

Anna had fallen in love with the enemy.

Worse, when she finally realized that she was prey to the
same emotional weakness of all women, it was with the one

man who she could never have. For, although she might be an acceptable wife for a working man like David Archer, Anna knew clearly that her involvement in charity work and the *Gazette,* lack of family connections and the unfortunate incident in her past all placed her firmly outside the limits of suitability for the Earl of Treybourne.

Not that an offer of any kind had been tendered. Of all people, and after working so closely with the girls at the school, she knew that a few kisses, a caress or two and a few whispered exclamations did not an offer of marriage make.

Clarinda may have guessed at Anna's inclination toward Mr. Archer, but she would know better than to encourage a match with the earl. As would Aunt Euphemia. Even Julia at her young age understood the rules of polite society and the lines that were drawn regarding marriage. The only person not listening to the rules of the world in which she existed was her.

And the foolish heart that beat inside her, telling her even now to hope for a chance at something between them. Even as her mind knew of his deception. Even as she accepted their differences in opinion and values and rank and status. Even as the unworthy part of her past reminded her of the reason she could not marry someone like David, her heart beat out a steady rhythm of encouragement.

Foolish heart! If she kept going in this direction, she would lose the drive to use her knowledge of his true identity to gain an advantage in their war of words.

Anna looked up to see Aunt Euphemia's concerned expression and smiled. "An outing sounds wonderful."

If her acceptance lacked enthusiasm, her aunt plowed

ahead without noticing. Calling the maid over, they helped her into her undergarments, then the outfit they had chosen without her, and soon Anna found herself dressed, coiffed and ready to leave the house. With Julia leading the way, they climbed into Clarinda's carriage to find her there already. Soon, they were on their way out of the city and in the direction of Arthur's Seat, high above Edinburgh.

Doubtful that the day would stay as clear and pleasant as it began, Anna worried about the choice of location. Julia continued to chatter all the way along their journey. Arthur's Seat was a favorite place of Anna's, for one could see the entire city of Edinburgh and all the way to the Forth and almost into the Borders to the south. If the day were a clear one...

The carriage pulled to a halt and the coachman jumped down to assist them. No sooner had she stepped out and straightened her clothing and bonnet than Clarinda called out greetings to someone waiting.

"Ah, Mr. Archer! This is a splendid location, after all."

Anna grabbed for Clarinda's arm, missed and instead took hold of her skirts. Holding her from moving forward, she whispered in her ear.

"Clarinda! What do you think you are doing? Why is he here?" Anna dared not look at him. Trying to muster her anger, she tugged again until Clarinda turned to face her. "What is this about?"

"Mr. Archer leaves for London shortly and I thought you might need more time and exposure to make certain you wheedled enough information from him regarding Lord Treybourne." Clarinda whispered her words, but then shot a smile over Anna's head to the man no doubt approaching them.

"I have changed my mind over this matter, Clarinda," she whispered through her teeth now, for the earl was coming closer and would soon be able to hear her words.

"The hero!" Clarinda called out, smiling as he walked up to them and bowed over her hand, treating her as though she were superior in rank to him. And Clarinda had no idea. "I have heard a full report and so you cannot deny that you gallantly saved my friend's life in the storm yesterday."

He moved to greet her next, taking her hand and lifting it to his lips. If he lingered over it a few seconds more than he had spent on Clarinda's, no one mentioned it. For her part, Anna was finding it difficult to remain aloof, and when their gazes met, she held her breath.

"Miss Fairchild," he said softly, not quite releasing her hand. "I am pleased to see that you felt up to joining us today." He held her hand out to the side and examined her from head to toe, all in a polite guise that did not seem untoward at all. "I see no sign of lasting injury from our run-in with the storm and its fury. I am glad."

Her mind willed the rest of her to accept his words as the polite bantering that they were, but her body blossomed with heat at the very sight and sound of him. The skin on her hand where his lips had touched seemed sensitive, as did her own mouth and the place on her neck where he had caressed as he held her face and kissed her. Finally, the sound of intense coughing pushed through her reverie and gained her attention…and his.

"Miss Julia," he said, moving to her side and offering a warm greeting her sister. "And how do you fare on this beautiful day?"

Julia smiled and made her curtsy. "I am well, Mr. Archer. And you?" Anna noticed the pleasure in her sister's expression as she spoke with him and as he directed his full attention on her.

"Very well, now that the rains seems to have ended. I began to think I was going to sprout roots and grow leaves with all the water."

"Is what Lady MacLerie tells us true? Do you leave for London soon?"

How had she heard that when Clarinda had kept her voice down? Julia seemed quite capable of ferreting out information. Perhaps Anna should turn her loose to practice her skills on Lord Treybourne?

"I fear it is. I have left matters behind that must be handled without delay. I leave in the morning."

Now that she knew who he was, Anna picked up on all sorts of double entendres in his words. Even in his tone of voice.

"Oh, Mr. Archer!" Julia moaned out. "But we were just truly making your acquaintance."

Lord Treybourne laughed then, his face looking younger and full of life as he did. "Ah, Miss Julia. I think I will miss you most when I leave Edinburgh."

Aunt Euphemia muttered words under her breath at that comment and Anna strained to hear them. Lord Treybourne noticed them as well.

"I will miss all of you, and especially you, Miss Erskine."

The nerve of the man, flirting with her aging aunt as though he meant it. The strange thing was that she believed he was sincere in his liking, or in Aunt Euphemia's case, abiding, each of them.

Her aunt turned a becoming shade of pink and smiled at him. "Mr. Archer, it has been a pleasure to meet you during your stay here. Will you return to Edinburgh?"

"I believe I will, Miss Erskine," he said. Turning to look at her now, he continued, "There is so much beauty here, I do not think I could resist another visit."

Anna watched as Aunt Euphemia's bosom began to heave and she blinked rapidly at the man. Surely she did not believe such folderol? When he turned his gaze back to her and his intense blue eyes turned her stomach to mush, she understood her aunt's reaction. Just as he began to speak to her again, Julia grabbed his arm and tugged him in the direction of the last rise of the hill.

"Come, Mr. Archer. I want to show you where scholars believe the Votadini built a hill-fort centuries ago."

Anna watched as the two walked off together, Julia pointing out several piles of stone and Lord Treybourne nodding and looking as she did so, and considered that Lord Treybourne had been a willing participant in it. He did not seem false in his treatment or attitude toward Julia.

She let out a sigh as she realized that she knew not where the line between the truth and falsehoods lay. Did she judge him by his actions? His words? He had convincingly spoken of Lord Treybourne as a separate person from himself during their conversations. He had listened and discussed how he disagreed with the earl about the subject of the essays, even the basic tenets of society and the conditions of all His Majesty's subjects.

But, where did Lord Treybourne begin and Mr. Archer end? And the question that struck fear deep in her: Which man had she fallen in love with?

"You did not tell me he saved you during yesterday's storm," Aunt Euphemia huffed out as though insulted.

"Actually, I spoke to no one about what happened yesterday." She turned and looked at Clarinda, who was examining a rock near her foot with a newfound interest. "How did you hear about the incident?"

Clarinda directed her servants to begin setting up the meal and guided Anna and her aunt to a place more suited for a private conversation. From that spot, they could watch as Julia led Lord Treybourne along the highest parts of the hill.

"Mr. Archer sent word to me last evening about your near-brush with death, Anna. Although, and I must say he is admirable in his humility, he did not say anything about his role in your escape from that crumbling building that was struck by lightning." Aunt Euphemia gasped, pulled her handkerchief from the reticule dangling on her wrist and dabbed at her forehead.

"So, if he did not disclose the incident, who did?" *And what did they say about the rest of what had happened between them?*

"Mrs. Dobbs sent word that you had been in the midst of the storm and that you were distraught upon your return to the school. Anna, she worries about you and only brought it to my attention because she feared you suffered some harm."

Aunt Euphemia gasped again at this disclosure and Clarinda directed one of the servants to assist her to one of the chairs they had brought with them for just that purpose. Once the older woman was settled and being served something cool to drink, Anna turned to Clarinda and pursued the matter again.

"Obviously, Mrs. Dobbs imparted something to you that you wish to ask me to clarify."

"She said that your mouth, ahem, your lips were swollen. Now, how did she put it in her earthy way? Ah, yes. From the way your hair was loosened and your mouth appeared, she thought 'ye looked as though ye'd been weel-kissed.'"

She had been. Well-kissed. Though she could defend the way in which her hair came loose from the tightly wrapped style she favored most days.

"I was caught in the middle of a storm, Clarinda. I gave no thought to my appearance when the lightning bolts and rain were erupting around us."

"Us."

Anna wanted nothing so much as to reach over and wipe the smug expression from Clarinda's face, but her friend knew exactly what had happened. She just did not understand all the problems involved.

"So you *were* well-kissed?"

"That is not the point...."

"What is, then?"

"He lied to me. He continues to lie to me," Anna whispered even while she watched the man under discussion run across the hill with her little sister.

"And have you told him your truths?" Clarinda asked, meeting Anna's gaze evenly when she faced her.

That took the argument out of her. It was true. She was expecting him to divulge who he was and what his plans were without thought of exposing her own secrets. Clarinda, she was certain, referred to a particularly humiliating ordeal that Anna had faced in her first placement as a governess near Inverness. Not that it had left her unscarred, but it was one she knew Clarinda was familiar with, having witnessed the aftermath firsthand.

"Come now, Clarinda. Despite the rather lax approach to the rules of polite society that sometimes exists here in the north, not even you can tell me that explaining to a virtual stranger the loss of one's virtue to the master of the household while in his employ is a suitable topic of conversation."

Anna turned back to watch her sister's progress across the hilltop and came face-to-face with Lord Treybourne.

Had he heard her words? Her cheeks grew hot with a flaming blush at the very thought that she had revealed the most personal information. A glance at Clarinda found a slight shake telling her he had not heard her words.

"Has she tired you out then, Mr. Archer?" Anna complimented herself on her seamless use of the false name.

"And it is still early in the day, Miss Fairchild," he answered. "The dampness must be getting to me."

"Julia," Clarinda interrupted. "Please accompany me while we set up the table for our meal."

Julia knew that voice just as she did—it was the "I am Lady MacLerie and you are not" tone that commanded obedience from friend, foe or family alike. And, remarkably, she did not question or hesitate, marching off like a good little soldier and leaving Anna in awe of her friend's ability.

"If I was a man who gambled on such things," he began as they watched the two move off to where the MacLerie servants were unpacking a wagon of necessities, "I would place a bet that your sister lived in several other time periods before this one."

She smiled. "Julia is quite the student of history."

"More than that, she is an *aficionado* of it." He looked around at the edge of the hilltop and held out his arm. "Would you care for a more leisurely paced walk? I have not had a chance to savor such a view as this."

Anna's heart pounded and she wondered if he could feel it, being so close as they walked closer to the rim of Arthur's Seat. She tried to tell herself it was the height, for they stood hundreds of feet above the city now, but she knew it was more about the nearness of the man. Taking a deep breath, she calmed her thoughts and decided to focus on her original quest.

"So, you return to Lord Treybourne, then?" she asked. If he hesitated, she did not notice, choosing instead to think about the questions to ask.

"I return to London, Anna, and my duties there," he said, using her given name.

"Have you given up on finding Goodfellow?"

"I confess that seeking information on the man was foremost in my mind when gaining Lady MacLerie's cooperation today. But, once in your company and that of your sister and the others, I lost interest in him."

"Mr. Archer," she said, needing to direct his attention back to his duties, "I told you some things in confidence and now fear that Lord Treybourne will indeed discover them."

Now, she need only to wait and watch his reaction.

"Your causes are safe, Anna. I will not share what you told me."

Now she was in a quandary, for his words depended on her trust in him, and Anna could not say she did. She realized that he picked his words very carefully, not lying but not disclosing his real intentions.

"That requires that you be a man of honor," she tested.

"Have I done something that makes you doubt that?" he retorted. He released her arm and stepped away. "You speak of the liberties I took while we were alone yesterday."

She had not been referring to that, but if he wanted to think it, she would allow it.

"I will plead that I was overcome with relief at finding you and then removing you from danger, that I permitted my baser feelings through. Anna, I do not regret kissing you, but I do ask your pardon if it offended you."

"I was not asking you to apologize. Any sin against propriety was as much mine as yours."

"So now that we have decided that neither of us was offended by my kisses, may I say something else about yesterday?" Anna knew that this was more appropriate conversation for betrothed couples, and that did not describe them. However, his actions prior to their more personal moments had saved her from death or serious injury. "Of course you may. I owe you my life, so please speak freely."

"I…" he began and then stopped, as though searching for the words. Her own heart seemed to stutter as his words did. "There are so many things I would say if I could, Anna. But too many depend on my discretion, not the least of which is you. I must return to London, but there are many reasons I would stay if I could."

"Mr. Archer, a few kisses are hardly something to cause such consternation. I expected no promises, if that is your concern."

"You are misunderstanding me, Anna," he said, taking her hand in his. "I am only bothered because I sense there is a companionship and shared concerns and interests between us that I cannot allow to advance. In spite of any desire to do so on my own part. Too much and too many are at stake."

His words reflected her own when she'd first discovered his connection to Lord Treybourne. Now, he was saying that he felt something more between them, too? But, was it Mr. Archer or Lord Treybourne who felt it?

"I came here searching for Mr. Goodfellow and found you, instead. I regret that I cannot stay to see things progress between us."

"Anna!" Aunt Euphemia called out.

Apparently their discussion was at an end and she was no closer to discovering anything else about him, or even which man had engendered such feelings within her. She placed her hand on his arm and waited for his gaze to meet hers before speaking.

"For my part, I would wish that we had more time to further our acquaintance as well. I must ask, though. What will you tell Lord Treybourne about the *Gazette?* Or Goodfellow? What will your counsel be to him regarding the essays?"

He laughed then and it made her smile. So masculine yet with such a boyish quality. "It would seem that every time we share some intimacy—emotional or physical—the discussion comes back to those damned essays."

"We have not spoken of them. I thought that they were the reason you sought me out yesterday at the school." With the way her stomach was turning little flips inside, Anna feared she would reveal everything to him in a flash of weakness.

So, bringing up the magazine and its famous writer helped her regain the control she was quickly losing.

"Very well then," he began. "I thought that you were able to convey my concerns to Mr. Goodfellow more than adequately and he apparently was willing to forge ahead with the focus remaining on the issues."

"So, Lord Treybourne's answering article will be as balanced?" she asked, watching closely as he assembled his answer.

"I hope so."

The tone of his voice as he replied gave her pause, for he sounded very unsure of the certainty of it. Did he not write his own articles? She could not ask him that question without revealing that she knew who he was, so she asked another instead. "Does Lord Treybourne not control his own words? You mentioned those around him when we spoke of this before."

He guided her a few steps and then paused at the point where the city was directly before them. Old Town, New Town, Leith and the Firth, she could see it all from here. It was her favorite spot to use as an escape when the burdens she carried became too heavy. It was her thinking place and planning place. Now, even after he left, she would think of him when she came here.

"Political endeavors are rarely solitary exercises, Anna. The circle widens and widens until many are involved, some few holding power over the many. Lord Treybourne is not one of the many, as most think him to be."

She gasped, for he had just given her something to use against his own positions. "Is that somehow a bit disloyal to the man who employs you?"

"Lord Treybourne would be the first to admit it, if you spoke to him. He is a part of the whole, mayhap the recognizable one, the so-called torchbearer, but not the leader.

"His father, the Marquess of Dursby, leads the Tory causes. He is the one you and Nathaniel and Goodfellow must fear, or at the least, respect. He is the true puppet master for the party."

"Why are you telling me these things? You must know I will share them with Nathaniel and that Goodfellow will hear them, too."

"I knew the night of Lady MacLerie's party that he was there or had informants present. You," he said as he reached up and caressed her cheek with the back of his hand, "are one of those who help him in gathering information."

Torn between denying it and the risk of revealing even more to him, Anna chose another way. "A lady never tells, sir."

"Tell him what I have disclosed to you about the mechanics of the Tories. Tell him to use it if the need arises once I am gone back to my duties there."

"Anna!" Aunt Euphemia called to her. "Come, the meal is set!"

Still trying to understand his motives behind the revelations, Anna waved to her aunt and then turned back to Lord Treybourne. The only thing she knew to be true was his name.

"David, I am so confused," she said, finding the declaration not so painful after all.

"As am I, Anna. I wish…" he said as he had the night she discovered the truth about him. The night that everything in her life had turned upside down. "I wish…"

Clarinda's approach stopped anything more from being

said, but Anna understood what had just happened without any more words. David had said goodbye. There was no possibility of a future between them, not with all the reasons she knew about, and she was certain there were more from his point of view that she did not know. So, he had acknowledged that there were some of the softer feelings between them and said goodbye.

The most honorable thing he had done was to arm her with something to use if needed, if his father did not observe the bounds of battle that David had worked to establish.

"I know we did not give you time to eat this morning, so you must be famished." Clarinda walked between them and took Anna's arm. "Cook has prepared a lovely meal and Aunt Euphemia refuses to begin without you, informal meal or not, she says." After leading her a few steps away, she called back. "Mr. Archer, are you coming?"

So many emotions were coursing through her at this moment that Anna thought she would not be able to eat a morsel. But, once at table, and it was indeed a table brought there and set as though they were at home, the smells enticed her to try some of the dishes. Anna glanced back to see Lord Treybourne still standing at the edge, staring down at the city. Clarinda did not bother him with another call to eat, allowing him instead his privacy to consider whatever thoughts plagued him now.

Part of her wanted to join him there and tell him that she knew of his deception. Part of her wanted to go back to the time when she thought him Lord Treybourne's man. But, most disconcerting to her was the part that wanted to return to a time before any of this had happened and begin it all again differently. If only time travel, as he had suggested her sister did, truly existed. If only her heart were not breaking.

If only.

David stood at the rim looking over the entire city, and wondered what to do next. He hoped Anna understood his words, but feared she did not. Once back in London, he must do everything he could to protect all that she had accomplished here. Irony charged in again and he only knew that he was damned forever if his presence here caused her harm.

Accepting that he must return to the gathering that he had asked Lady MacLerie to arrange, David took a deep breath and walked back to the group. The lady had made an outstanding effort and could challenge any battlefield commanders on organization, arrangements, supplies and mustering the troops, and on such short notice. Lady MacLerie probably expected a different outcome than the one that was playing out before her, but nothing in her manner gave away any other reactions.

"Mr. Archer, there is a bench if you prefer to sit." She welcomed him and pointed to the seat open next to Anna. "Or, I can fix you a plate and you may pace around as men seem wont to do."

"I will join you at your lovely table, Lady MacLerie. I would hate to not partake of your wonderful arrangements after enlisting your help in setting this in motion."

"Mr. Archer, is there a place like this where you live in London?" Julia asked between forkfuls of a dish that smelled of roasted fowl.

He waited while Lady MacLerie filled his plate with a

wide variety and huge portions of everything prepared. He nodded his thanks and tasted one or two dishes. If nothing else, he could always fall back on proper manners, when all he wanted to do was scream out his rage against the way of things.

"Miss Julia, I can assure you that there is nothing to compare with this in London. We have greens and parklands, we even have some hills and valleys. But I suspect there is no other place in Great Britain that has this view."

The meal passed amiably with pleasant conversation and no one ever knew his torment at planning to leave behind the woman he loved.

Chapter Eighteen

"Have you ever seen such a crush at this time in the year?" Clarinda asked.

"No, of course not," Anna answered, completely disinterested in those who attended tonight's ball in the Assembly Rooms.

She had refused at first, as she always did. Then Clarinda had used tactics not shown before to force her compliance and attendance. Threats about leaving Aunt Euphemia behind for the whole of the winter when the MacLeries returned to their family estate were made. That respite, when her aunt visited the MacLeries, was the only time of the year when she answered to no one else and Anna knew her sanity would be in danger if she forfeited that visit.

Now, she stood just next to the front entrance watching as the latecomers jockeyed for a place inside. Not willing to exchange the only place where the air moved about and offered some relief from the heat, Anna remained there when Clarinda went off to dance or to speak to another of her friends or acquaintances.

"There is talk of Lord Treybourne's arrival in town."

Lord MacLerie pushed his way over to her and offered her a glass of lemonade. It was warm and watered down, but at the least it was wet and refreshing. As was his habit, he took a position with his back to the wall, using his height to gaze out over the rest of the crowds.

"Ah, but we two know that he has been here for some time," she replied, Planting a firm smile on her face, Anna met his startled stare. "The truth has a way of coming out, my lord."

"So it does," he said, nodding to her. "The gossip says that Dursby House was opened just two days ago and two of his lordship's friends are staying there already."

"Really? I wonder what Mr. Archer could tell us of the situation." There was a sarcastic edge to her voice that even she could hear, but she did not try to control or minimize it.

"I am sorry, Anna. Truly." He leaned down to keep his words from being overheard and whispered, "I thought I could protect you from his deception, and only added to your pain."

Tears gathered and she blinked them away. Crying had not helped. Anger had not helped. There was nothing that would help dull the pain of facing all of the aspects of this situation for her. Soon, she would return to her usual schedule, the one she carried out day after day, week after week, before he arrived. She would concentrate once again on the causes so important to her and Nathaniel. She would regain all of the control she'd lost because of him. Because of falling in love.

The next step was to gather her anger and direct it, with Goodfellow's help, at the person responsible for most of her misery. Lord Treybourne.

"Here comes Clarinda now. I will warn you that she is bringing two young men with her. Oh, too late to escape, for she is pointing at you."

Sometimes his height was an appreciated advantage for finding someone she was seeking. Now, though, it was simply annoying.

"Robert, I wanted to introduce you to two visitors from London. Lord Ellerton, Lord Hillgrove, this is my husband, Lord MacLerie And this is Miss Anna Fairchild."

She curtsied to them and accepted the introduction, but she did not fail to see the looks exchanged when her name was mentioned.

"They are Lord Treybourne's friends and staying at his family's home here." Clarinda whispered the information to her, but the stares and murmurs around them revealed their identities as they approached.

"There is much speculation, my lords, about whether or not the infamous Lord Treybourne will make an appearance in his adversary's stronghold. Can you offer any information about that?" she asked.

Did these two know about Lord Treybourne's plans to seek out Goodfellow here? Did they know of the false identity that he was employing?

"I fear I cannot offer any clarification at all, Miss Fairchild. We have spent a few weeks at the Dursby hunting box in the Cairngorms and are on our way back to London," Lord Ellerton replied.

"And you have not seen his lordship?" she asked again.

"The earl is quite busy, you know. With his position in Commons, family responsibilities and writing those articles,

the man barely sleeps." Lord Ellerton was looking quite uncomfortable at her direct questions. When he threw a glance
at his companion, the other one jumped into the conversation.

"Hasn't come hunting with us in years, has he, El-lerton?"
Lord Hillgrove asked his friend. Shaking their heads in
unison, she knew they'd seen him.

Robert must have felt some pity for them, for he asked them
about their estates and the talk turned to hunting, horses and
houses. Clarinda stepped over to fill the breach in conversation.

"They have seen him. They were boasting when I found
them at the refreshment tables," she said quietly.

Anna thought to confide in her friend, but hesitated to do
so now. Clarinda would not be pleased when she discovered
the truth about the man she seemed to be aiding in his pursuit
of her unmarried friend. Robert would bear some of the brunt
of it, but to inform her now would be unforgiveable.

Before she could respond, a footman made his way to
their little group and handed a note to Lord Ellerton. First his
lordship's face turned red and then he paled by the end of the
note. He handed it to his friend, who had the same reaction
before they explained that they must take their leave. Curious
to see the cause of it, Anna turned to follow them when
Clarinda stopped her.

"Leave it be, Anna."

"You do not understand, Clarinda. Lord Treybourne is
here, probably waiting for them outside."

A hand on her arm slowed her. "I could read the note. He
is there, and he told them to leave discreetly. He does not wish
to embarrass you by his presence."

"Clarinda," she repeated. One look at her friend's face and

she comprehended that she knew the truth, too. "How long have you known?"

"I am late to the game," she said. "I realized it yesterday after we returned from Arthur's Seat. Something your aunt said about men and their reputations. The thought occurred to me that Lord Treybourne would be a fool not to seek out Good-fellow on his own, without fanfare or attention. And from what little Robert has told me of the man, he is not a fool."

Anna nodded and lifted Clarinda's hand from her arm, freeing herself to follow the men outside. She had debated for days over the need to confront him with the knowledge she held. At first, she decided not to do it. Something in the way he spoke to her and the way he treated Julia told her that he was not trying to humiliate her by his deception. And unless his investigator had been more efficient than her efforts to block him, he did not know the full extent of her involvement in the publication.

Now though, this situation had fallen into her lap and her curiosity drove her on, out the doors, down the stone steps and onto the sidewalk. Lord Ellerton and Lord Hillgrove were making their way along the row of coaches there. A few minutes later, they climbed into the one carrying the Dursby crest and she could hear only voices from within—three voices. Tucking herself into the shadows at the edge of the building there, she tried to listen to their exchange.

Her name…she heard her name and Clarinda's. Then some muffled cursing…then nothing. She peeked out and watched as the third man climbed out on the street side of the coach and gave instructions to the driver. Too dark to catch a clear look at him, she knew him more by his height and build. He walked to the sidewalk and watched as the coach pulled off down the cobblestone street. He noticed her quickly and she saw it in his expression that changed from surprise to something resembling relief at her pres-ence there.

"Anna," he said as he walked to her side.

"Lord Treybourne," she replied. It was time, past time, for dissembling. "Did your friends do something wrong? You sounded irate with them."

"Anna, would you let me explain?" He reached for her and she stepped away. "Please?"

"I have been fearing this since I discovered who you really were and now that the moment has arrived, I find myself at a loss for words," she admitted. Anna wrapped her arms around herself. "I thought about an angry confrontation but I realized that would serve no purpose."

"How long have you known?" he asked.

"Since the night of the dinner. I heard you and Robert speaking outside."

"Why did you not ask me about it? Does Lord MacLerie know? Or Nathaniel?"

David moved closer then, but at a slow pace. She was distraught and skittish and he did not want to scare her away before he could explain. Her eyes grew glassy and she swayed a bit. When they were only an arm's length apart, he paused and waited. Her lack of reaction unnerved him more than any show of emotion could have and he felt it down into his soul.

"Yes, I spoke to Nathaniel about you and he promised not to let on." She glanced around the area, looking back down George Street toward the Assembly Rooms and then back toward him, all without ever meeting his gaze. "I do not even know if I can trust any answer you give me, my lord, but please just tell me why? Why did you do this?"

"David," he said. "My name is David."

"David Robert Henry George Lansdale, Earl of Treybourne, heir to the Marquess of Dursby." She looked at him then. "You see, I know all your names, my lord." A pause, haunted by a faint sob. "Just tell me why."

"Anna, you know most of this already. The pieces just do not fit together the right way. Your writer Goodfellow began making a mess of my father's political plans. His essays were firmly trouncing the heir to his titles, his wealth, his position, but most to his honor and reputation. When he began threatening to take action, I came here seeking the help of an old friend to cool the fires before they got out of control."

"Nathaniel?" she asked.

"Yes. My plan was to come here, discuss how best to handle the escalation my father was demanding and to discover, if I could, the identity of Mr. Goodfellow. Instead, upon my arrival, I was accosted by some mere woman who tried to pry my business out of me. Offended but intrigued, I tried to irritate her enough to stay away, however she was so different from the women that I, Lord Treybourne, meet and socialize with that she drew me to her."

"You are trying to level the blame for your deception on me?" Her voice was a bit stronger then.

"Not at all. My point is that, in spite of my efforts to the contrary, I was impressed by every detail I discovered about you—your work, your efforts at the school, your deep opinions about the issues of the day. Then it was too late. I feared that any sense of companionship or enjoyment between us would turn to hatred if you discovered who I was…who I am. Actually, I saw it happen every time my name was mentioned. Your attitude and even the expression in your eyes hardened." David shook his head and smiled at her. "I confess that I was enjoying our time together too much and did not want to lose it."

"And did you never think about the shock and humiliation I would suffer when I discovered that you were a hoax and I was in love with you?" Anger now laced her words. She clenched her hands into fists at her sides.

The words, even uttered in anger, took his breath away.

"You fell in love with Mr. Archer, not me," he said.

"Who is the man who shares my beliefs in the social ills of our country? Which man treated my sister with infinite patience and caring? Which man held me and kissed me with a passion I had not experienced before? Tell me, Lord Trey-bourne, which man did I so foolishly fall in love with?"

"You fell in love with the man who loves you in return. The man who, even knowing how you would react, could not stay away from you. The man who cannot offer you all that you deserve."

"I know my position, my lord, and I understand clearly that I am not suitable for an earl. It is no surprise to me at all. I just do not appreciate being played the fool."

"I was never doing that, Anna. Never. If anyone was the fool, it is I. Instead of telling you the truth, I lied. I do not blame you for not believing me now."

"So, tell me your truth now. David Archer raised hopes that I thought long dead—ones of a happy marriage, children, family and friends. Now those hopes are dashed to pieces by a man I thought I loved. Make me understand now why you did that."

Her plea tore his heart apart. Would knowing the truth help her now? Could it reduce the pain she would feel when he left? He would take the chance.

"My father has sworn to destroy anyone or anything that gets in the way of his political aims. Your publication is such a thing. I came here to try to calm the waters and take your publication out of his sight. Things became worse when I discovered that you funded your school with the profits from the magazine."

She gasped then and lost most of the color in her face. "You know?" Now she clenched her hands together before her.

"My investigators—"

"You had me investigated? You had no right—"

"I believe in knowing my enemies, Anna."

She turned away from him for a moment and then faced him. She gave every indication that she was bracing herself for some terrible disclosure.

"I found out that you own the magazine and the school. I discovered that you raised your sister from the time your mother died until you moved in with your aunt. I learned that you care about those less fortunate and would do anything to help them. I also realized that my very presence here would draw attention and my father would find out what I already knew and destroy everything you hold dear."

She looked near to fainting and he paused for a moment. Reaching out to her, he held her hand as he continued.

"It is not David Archer who is the façade—it is Lord Trey-bourne. We share the same opinions, you and I, about society and reform and so many other things. For many reasons, I support several similar charities in London, but I had to enter into a bargain with my father to gain access to my money. If I do not carry out the very public role he has carved out for me, the funding ceases and many people like the ones at your school will be abandoned."

She looked at him then and he knew she understood his dilemma now.

"If I continue to carrying out my father's bidding, I undermine the political battles to achieve the very causes I support. If I do not, those who depend on me for their living will have nothing."

"Damned if you do and damned if you do not."

"Exactly," he said. "And then, just when I was considering leaving it all behind, I met a young woman who put me to shame with her own efforts. Who learned to never give up. Who demonstrated a clear commitment to her causes that shamed me for only throwing money after mine."

"I am not so holy as that, my lord. There are flaws here, too," she whispered. "And now?"

Anna was reeling from his disclosures. It was much better and much worse in some ways. He had been dishonest and had even set men on her to discover her secrets. And although he had uncovered her business affairs, he had not found the personal ones. Or he had not said so.

A noise drew her attention and she noticed that Clarinda and Robert stood a short distance from them, engaged in some private conversation. She smiled at their concern, for their presence covered any insult to propriety, but they were far enough away not to hear the words spoken.

"My father clamors for the blood of a Scottish reformer

named Goodfellow and I must find a way to appease him." He slid his fingers around hers and squeezed. "I have thought of nothing else but offering you marriage, but it will bring his wrath down on you and everything you own. If he discovers that a woman owns the publication and that her writer has been insulting and defeating his heir, he will destroy it. He is powerful enough that a few words whispered in the right ears will dry up your funding for the school and wipe out your advertising and subscription income."

"So," she said, "if we were selfish enough to be together, everything we have worked for would be destroyed." That was the end result of this mess and Anna knew she could not be happy at the expense of others. "I could not do it. Not even to have you," she whispered.

"Nor I, no matter how much I want you at my side."

So much had been shared that she could say nothing else. As though they had sensed the end of the exchange, the MacLeries now walked up to her, and Clarinda opened her arms to Anna.

David did not offer an objection. He might have actually been relieved that she was taken care of, but Anna could not watch his face as they walked away to their coach, leaving him alone on the sidewalk.

Chapter Nineteen

"This is very strange, Robert."

Anna held out the note from the bank to him and waited as he read it.

"It would appear that the mortgage to the school has been paid off and the deed is being processed now," he replied.

"I can read the words, I do not understand how it is possible. Unless you did this?"

The MacLeries had extensive holdings of property and were one of the wealthiest families in Scotland. If anyone could afford to buy the mortgage, Robert was the one.

"Just tell her."

Anna turned at the sound of Clarinda's voice and watched as she entered her husband's office and sent his secretary out with a simple nod. When the door closed and the room filled with an air of unease, Anna faced Robert. "Tell me what?"

"I handled the transaction here on Treybourne's behalf."

Shocked at the disclosure, she sat down in the chair in front of the desk and looked from one to the other. There was more, she could see it in their expressions. "He holds the mortgage on the school?"

So, her worst fears would come true then? In spite of the apparent truce and the more amiable tone to the last two of their exchanges, his lordship was taking measures to strike at the magazine and her interests.

"You misunderstand this, Anna. Treybourne does not hold the mortgage. You own the property outright now."

"I do not understand. Why would he do such a thing?"

"Because it is what he does," Robert said softly.

The other two exchanged a few more glances over and around her and, despite not seeing them directly, she could feel their scrutiny. This was becoming commonplace whenever they shared company ever since…the day David left Edinburgh. Now, Clarinda's whispers drew her attention, but they ceased as soon as she looked over at her friend.

"Anna, did anything untoward happen between you and Mr. Archer the day he left for London?" Clarinda emphasized his name and narrowed her eyes at her husband in some meaningful gesture that only they understood.

"Untoward?"

"Anything of a personal nature, perhaps? Something that you might want to discuss with my wife in private?" Robert said, standing. She wanted to laugh at his discomfort and at the way that Clarinda caught off his escape by a sharp look and a shake of her head.

"David and I did not…" she began.

"Was there some insult to your honor, Anna?" she asked.

"Oh, please, Clarinda. You and Robert know the truth about my honor." Robert bristled as he always did when the past was raised in front of him, warning her that he would protect her now even if he had not protected her then. "There was no insult."

Anna stood and paced the room now.

"I still feel like such a fool. How could someone who prides herself on guiding young women in how to avoid such things have fallen for his lies so easily?"

Robert did stand then and he walked around the desk and put his hand on her shoulder. His strength and presence was reassuring to her even now when her gullibility was exposed.

"You were so busy falling in love that you did not notice his deception. And I suspect that Treybourne was so busy trying to keep up the deception, that he did not notice he was falling in love."

Anna took much comfort in his assessment and wanted to believe that when David, Lord Treybourne, said he felt the same way about her as she felt about him, he was not lying. Not that it would make things any different, but it would help her put this behind her if she did not feel used by him. Foolish, a dupe, stupid, certainly, but not used.

"But why did he need to pretend to be someone else? Was seeking a truce so demeaning to him that it was better to resort to subterfuge and lies?"

Her own words damned her as much as accused him. Had she not lied and covered her own identity as the owner of the magazine and as A. J. Goodfellow? If it was such a good thing, why had she not revealed all of it to him when he told her his reasons?

"Oh, please!" Clarinda exclaimed then. "Men and their pride, Anna. It always comes down to pride."

"There is more than that in Treybourne's case, my dear."

"There is?" They spoke at the same time.

"Nathaniel and I did not trust his lordship's motives and so I had someone gather more information about his practices and his past." Robert went back to the desk, tugged open one of the side drawers and lifted out a portfolio from within. "I received this recently from London."

Clarinda leaned over and reached for it, but Robert moved it under his hands. "There was no need, for it seems that Treybourne believed he owed you an explanation himself." He took another packet of papers from the drawer, this one already opened from the looks of it.

"You've read it?" she asked.

"Yes. In his communications with me, Treybourne suggested I do so in order to quiet any concerns I might have about his intentions or what effects this may have on you."

"Robert!" Clarinda moaned. "You read it before Anna?"

He took his wife by the hand and brought her to stand next to him. "When you extended your protection to her, she became my responsibility, Clarinda. I did so only because I would do so if she were my sister or yours."

Anna could not argue, especially not when she knew that his sentiments were genuine regarding her. The effect of his words on her friend were predictable. Clarinda brushed away a few tears and reached up to touch his face.

"Come. I think Anna will want privacy to consider his words."

"Anna?" Clarinda asked before allowing him to guide her out of the study.

She would expect a complete and thorough explanation and Anna would give it to her...later. For now, she wanted to read his letter alone. She nodded and Clarinda left without further argument. The door closed quietly and she walked to the other side of the desk and sat down. With a nervous tickle in her stomach, she peeled off the covering and began to read.

Miss Fairchild,
Anna,

As I write this I am struck by the recognition that this is actually the first time you will read my words. Not those of Lord Treybourne, but those of David Lansdale, the man who came to know you on his visit to Edinburgh. My perfidy and the deception I perpetrated on you has already been exposed and, although I tried to explain my reasons for it to you, I never did ask for your forgiveness for it. Of course, there are many good reasons why you should not grant it—Nathaniel and Lord MacLerie have no doubt informed you of several by this time.

You have probably discussed with Lord MacLerie or Nathaniel the reason why I hid my identity from you and others on my visit there. Although they have ventured their opinions, they were not privy to the true reasons which I would like to make known to you now. Lady MacLerie has probably tried to convince you that male pride is at the heart of it, and, to some extent, that is true.

It is difficult, as a peer of the realm, to be soundly trounced by one's opponent in public and then show up in their locale—it is like asking for one's person and reputation to be abused. So, arriving hat-in-hand on Mr. Goodfellow's doorstep—so to speak—was something better accomplished with some measure of discretion. Your presence and unexpected involvement there changed everything.

Anna sat back and smiled. This letter read as David himself spoke and was so completely different from his essays written each month. His mention of Nathaniel and Robert and Clarinda, and that he knew she would seek their advice, touched her somehow. Some of this was old ground gone over again, but she continued reading.

And now to the real reason for the charade of David Archer.

Just as you protected those endeavors and enterprises which you value with a heavy measure of secrecy and misdirection, so did I.

Due to irresponsible and heinous behavior on my part in my youth, a young woman was compromised and, as a result, died in childbirth. I realize now, after overhearing your words to Lady MacLerie and upon further discussion with her about your own personal situation and the women who you endeavor to help, that this is the most unforgivable act in your eyes. The only good thing that came from it was my own personal realization that I must make amends for my actions.

Her stomach clenched now at the thought that he had committed the same crime…act against some woman as had been done to her. How could he have? What had driven him to such a thing? How young had he been?

Now she understood his reaction upon first learning of the true nature of her school; and she knew he had overheard her disclosure about her own life. It was clear that his own guilt in some similar situation colored his actions.

And so, for a number of years I have supported through personal funding and oversight, two orphanages and a school for the unfortunates of society. These charities have grown and the cost of supporting them has soared due to the economic conditions in our nation, as you are well aware.

As a result, I entered into a bargain with my father, the Marquess of Dursby, whereby I would carry out certain public functions designed to promote his political agenda in return for a yearly allowance in an amount sufficient to continue those charities already mentioned. Making these arrangements more difficult is the fact that the marquess does not know of them. More to the point, much as you mentioned a fear that your interests would be destroyed, so too would these if my father were aware of them, for they are diametrically opposed to his own views of societal welfare and charity.

Recently, due to Mr. Goodfellow's very public success at undermining the Tory position, demands were made regarding the ongoing exchange of points of view—demands accompanied by the threat of a cessation of the agreed-upon allowance if success was not assured. In an attempt to know more about my enemy, and at the same time, recognizing that my opponent espoused my own personal views, I sought more information so that some agreement might be reached concerning the manner in which our discourse would continue.

Anna had held her breath for so long now, her chest hurt. Each line, each sentence, contained another shocking revelation about the man she thought she knew and his life and his causes. For exactly the opposite reasons, they stood on either side of the same issue and ended up pursuing the same ends. His motivation and hers, cause and effect, shameful and shamed, and yet the results of it were support for those who could not care for themselves.

The rest of this you already know. I appeared in Edinburgh, searching out Mr. Goodfellow, and discovered instead one Miss Anna Fairchild. In spite of my efforts to avoid, mislead and ignore this young woman, she became the reason I remained when I should have long before sought London. Like no one I had ever met before, and I confess that I expect to meet no one like her again, she supported those very things I hold dear and precious and did so in spite of all the strictures of society which should have stopped her.

Tears flowed now and Anna wiped them away to keep them from falling on the page as she finished his missive. To read of his thoughts about her tore at her bruised heart.

Because the danger facing your interests is due to my actions and those of my father's, I have taken steps to insure that your financial investments are secured against loss. Lord MacLerie has agreed to handle these arrangements and the deed for the property and building that houses your school will shortly be in your hand and control.

I will continue my bargain as I promised until I can secure funding in other ways or until my father tires of it. Please warn Mr. Goodfellow that I will not be such easy prey again.

There are many things I would like to say to you, but since Lord MacLerie will undoubtedly read this prior to you seeing it, I will only wish you well in your endeavors and in your life.

Anna glanced down to the bottom and his signature. She sobbed at the sight of it.

Yr. Servant— ~~Treybourne~~ —David

She moved all the papers aside, crossed her arms under her head and cried as she considered all he had said. Sometime later, she looked up to find Clarinda with the paper in hand. So much for privacy.

"Robert suggested I check on you."

"You read it?" Anna really needed no answer, for Clarinda's eyes were as swollen from crying as she imagined her own were.

"Every word of it. Twice." Clarinda dabbed at her eyes and wiped her nose. "More importantly, what are your thoughts on this? Does it tell you what you needed to know?"

Anna thought about how much more she'd learned about

David from this letter. It must be true or Robert would have said otherwise. She thought about that—she knew it was true without Robert's word on it for there were two things she understood about David before she read any of it. Despite his charade and his covering his identity, just as she had, under it all there was an honorable man.

The second thing she knew was that she still loved him.

"Yes," she answered.

"Is there anything you still need to know? Something that the letter does not speak to?"

She held out her hand and Clarinda reached across the desk to hold it. "He has secured the mortgage on the school. He has explained his actions and his reasons for them. His pretense, apparently undertaken for reasons similar to my own, can be understood in that light. The debate will continue and everyone and all the things I hold dear are taken care of." Anna took the letter from Clarinda and folded it back into the neat parcel it had been. "Everything is settled."

Anna could tell that her friend did not believe her words. She did not believe them, either, but she did think that the effort to accept it was the important thing. It would take time for everything to truly settle back into place.

She would go back to the schedule that had served her so well. She would continue the work she loved so much. And with every breath she took, she would miss the man she fell in love with and mourn for everything her life could have been.

"'Oh what a tangled web we weave….'" Anna whispered to herself as Clarinda left without another word.

Chapter Twenty

November, 1818 Lansdale Park England

His stomach rolled with nervousness as his coach-and-four drew up in front of their family estate. David gathered up the various packets and papers and placed them back in the leather case. It had taken nearly three months, but he was ready now. The coach stopped and several footmen ran to attend to the visitors. His coachmen had their instructions and would wait for him. He nodded to the other occupants of the coach and climbed out.

Walking up the immaculately groomed path to the ornate marble entryway, he paused ever so slightly as the huge front door to the manor house opened before him. The butler, one of the few servants he recognized, greeted him and directed him to the blue drawing room where his parents waited.

The sound of his riding boots echoed ahead and behind him as he walked the long hallway and stood outside the largest and most stately of all the rooms used to receive visitors. A footman immediately opened the door and announced his arrival.

"Treybourne," his mother said from her seat at the writing desk. He walked to her, bowed as was expected and then leaned over to kiss her cheek.

"Mother," he said, stepping back. "You look well. I think the country agrees with you." Of course, it was the expected and the polite thing to say, so he did. His only other choice would have been to remind her that she had died a bit more each day since Amelia's death four years ago and gave every appearance of it.

David presented himself before his father and bowed. "Sir."

"You look like some country rector, Treybourne. Why are you not dressed appropriately?"

If it had been another day, he might have responded differently, but David was so filled with anticipation that the insult washed over him. "I will be traveling the rest of the day, sir. I am dressed for that."

"Traveling? There are meetings scheduled. The ministers will be arriving this afternoon...."

"And I will be gone, sir."

"Treybourne?" His mother had risen from her seat and approached him. "Where are you going?"

"I am going to Scotland, Mother."

"Scotland?" his father asked. "I have not asked you to go to Scotland."

David lifted the case to the desk and opened it. "I have attempted to honor my agreement this last year, sir, but these last few months have proven to me that I was wrong to accept it in the first place." He held out a number of portfolios to his father and gave him a few moments to leaf through them.

"As you have frequently pointed out to me, Mr. Goodfellow bested my arguments in six issues straight and I have yet to recover my momentum in the discourse. Our approach to the situation has diverged and I am no longer willing to go after the man involved as an enemy."

"Treybourne, I will cut off your income if you do not—"

"I have spoken to the undersecretary who agrees that my effectiveness as a party spokesperson has diminished substantially and he was willing to consider an alternative. My suggestion of Lord Cunningham was accepted." David paused and handed him a list he'd drawn up of other potential Tory party members, but he knew that his father actually liked Cunningham.

"You spoke to the undersecretary?" His father was surprised—something not altogether known to him.

"I did. And in order to make the transition flow, I drafted two sample essays for Cunningham to use."

"You cannot do this."

"Actually, sir, I can. Once I reach my birthday, I will gain control of my inheritance from grandfather and not need your money. I have spent the last two months making arrangements for my financial commitments and I can manage all of them until that day without a penny from you."

"What? You cannot be serious about this!" His father shook his head. "Why? Why would you do something like this and not simply continue the arrangements we've made?"

"Because I am completely opposed to everything you support."

"That is nothing new between us. You have never agreed with any of my aims or purposes." His father brushed this objection aside as he had all the previous ones. "What has changed now?"

"I have discovered something I want more." It was a simple truth, but weren't all the important things in life only that? "Some*one* I want more."

"A woman? This is over that penniless Scottish bi—?"

His mother gasped. "Dursby!"

"Let me tell you what your son has been doing, Elizabeth. Treybourne went to Edinburgh to discover the identity of the writer who has been trouncing him in debate. When he couldn't find the person, he began sniffing around this…"

David grabbed his father by the lapels of his morning coat and shook him. "Do not speak of her in that way!" He shoved him back and tried to regain his control.

Instead of stopping his father, the shocking action goaded him on. "While you were…" He paused when David took a step toward him. "While you were off consulting old school friends, I found out who Goodfellow is."

"You did?" he asked.

"It is that woman, Fairchild is her name I believe. *She* is Goodfellow."

David stopped and realized what had been in front of him all along. He laughed, out loud, until his stomach ached and his father looked uneasy again. "Anna is A. J. Goodfellow!"

Now when he thought of the name, he realized that it was the first initials of her and Julia's names along with a play on words regarding portraying a man—a good fellow. He laughed again and, from the expressions of their faces, his parents thought he'd been driven around the bend.

"This is no matter of folly. You have been bested by a woman! A woman! A penniless commoner who purports her writings as a man's."

"On the contrary, sir, this is a matter of the most serious kind. And I will tell you that she is a better man than most men I know and she will make the perfect wife for me."

"I will not permit it!" His father's voice echoed now in the large chamber. "My solicitors—"

"Will inform you that there is nothing you can do to stop me. I am of age and do not need your permission."

"Treybourne," his mother whispered. "Married? David…" He walked over to her and knelt down next to her.

"I will bring her to meet you, Mother," he said, taking her hand and patting it. "But there is someone I would like you to meet right now. I know that you do not understand my motives, sir, but I want to share part of them with you."

"Motives? For turning your back on your family, your heritage? For refusing to honor your commitments? I do not care to know them. Your actions speak for themselves."

Most likely his father would not understand, but in the hopes that it might make some small difference, he walked over and gave instructions to one of the footman by the drawing room door. Some preparation was needed before the introduction.

"Actually, I believe my actions over these last few years uphold the family tradition. Acting honorably and carrying out one's duties is part of the Lansdale heritage."

He waited by the door for the footman's return with the other occupants of the coach. He spoke loud enough for his father to hear, but directed his words at his mother.

"Some years ago, after reprehensible behavior on my part, I

learned that owning up to one's responsibilities can bring about needed change. I think that discovering my daughter's existence and being able to save her and others from the life they were condemned to was as good a thing for me as it was for them."

"Daughter? You have a daughter?" she asked.

"Yes, Mother." He looked at the door as the footsteps in the hall grew louder. "Here, Mrs. Green, let me take her."

David leaned over and lifted Maddy's hand from her nurse's. She had fallen asleep in the coach just before they arrived and was only waking up now. "Come, sweet, there is someone I want you to meet," he whispered. She wrapped her other hand over his and allowed him to lead her across the room toward his mother.

He walked slowly over to his mother, crouching down so that he was closer. Maddy glanced at him, fear evident on her face as she whispered "Papa" and clutched at his arm.

"Mother, this is…" Before he could say her name, his mother shook her head as though seeing a ghost.

"Amelia?" Her shocked gaze revealed that his perception of the strong resemblance between his daughter and his deceased sister was correct. Her dark hair was a mass of curls that encircled a cherubic face and the blue eyes rimmed in even darker blue that proclaimed her a Lansdale. Exactly as his sister had looked at this same age.

"This is Maddy, my daughter," he said. "Maddy, this is my mother, Lady Dursby." Maddy leaned her head away from his shoulder and examined his mother before smiling. The smile was her mother's mark, the one he would always remember when he thought of Sarah.

He could see that his mother was fighting the urge to reach out to the child. She glanced from Maddy to his father and back again, clearly evaluating the risks involved with his displeasure against her own needs. She did not reach out after all, but she did offer a smile of her own to his daughter. David looked over at his father.

The marquess's face was a blank, nothing there—not his gaze or the set of his mouth or the countenance of his forehead gave away his thoughts. Or so it seemed, until his mother pleaded with him.

"John?"

His father's gaze was haunted by the same ghost as his mother's. They were both, they were all, remembering his younger sister now. A curt nod was all his father would give on it, but it was enough to free his mother to reach out to the child.

"Maddy is such a pretty name," she said, reaching out to touch her cheek, but then withdrawing her hand. "How old are you, child?"

"Almost eight, Lady Dursby."

David was so proud of her and knew that this had been the right thing to do. Even if his father would not relent, his mother's heart had softened already.

"Mrs. Green, would you take Maddy back to the coach? We will be leaving shortly."

"Certainly, my lord."

Before Mrs. Green could take her by the hand, Maddy stepped closer and kissed his mother on the cheek. Stunned, no one moved until the stillness became uncomfortable around them. What David feared the most was his mother's, and his father's, reaction to a gesture of such familiarity.

"Goodbye, Maddy," she finally whispered with a touch to Maddy's cheek.

The continued silence from his father was not a surprise, and yet it was. David watched as Mrs. Green took her hand and they walked from the room following the same footman who had escorted them here. When the door closed, he faced them.

"Her mother was a housemaid at the London house who I took a fancy to when I arrived home from the university. With no way to refuse my advances, she had no choice but to accept them."

This was certainly not the topic for mixed company, but his mother needed to know.

"She was turned out when her condition was obvious. I was on the continent and did not know."

"You are not the first nobleman to get a girl with child, Treybourne. It happens. It is the way of things. But, it is not something we talk about," his father answered.

He had hoped for too much. He thought that if he put a face on the tribulations of the poor and powerless, his father might at least consider that there were problems in how those in control handled them. He'd tried, now it was time to finish this.

"I tracked Sarah down when I returned to London, but by that time, it was too late. She died in childbirth and the babe nearly died with her. Maddy was a sickly baby and it was not certain that she would survive for the first three years."

"You have supported her since then?"

"Yes, and others like Sarah, as well."

"You are using money from my estates to fund poorhouses?"

"Yes, and more." David nodded to his mother. "And I will

continue. I have made arrangements to make certain that all of my interests can be supported until I come into my inheritance, sir."

"It is her fault," his father growled.

"Maddy's? Still blaming the innocent for our actions, sir?"

"That woman, the one in Edinburgh."

"Anna? No, sir, it is my fault. I had a conscience after seeing the travails I forced on one young woman, but didn't really know how to use it. Anna simply reminded me of how to live and live by it." David turned and walked to the door.

"You plan to marry her?"

"If she will have me." He smiled as he remembered telling her that marriage was not possible. "She may refuse me due to my deplorable behavior toward her. By the by, sir, my whereabouts in Edinburgh are no secret, my man-of-business in London can reach me if you need something."

"If you leave now, Treybourne, I will—"

"No, sir, you will not. You have nothing with which to threaten me now and if you threaten Anna or any of her interests or businesses or cause her any trouble at all, other than the essays, I will go to work for her and share all my knowledge of the Tory party's plans and projects."

That did the trick, for his father's mouth opened and shut several times before any sounds came out. He had no doubt that his father would try, but everything was now in place. Thomas had things strung out pretty tightly and he would not be able to expand any of the charities, but none would fail between now and the anniversary of his birth, when he came into his fortune.

A short farewell to his mother and he found himself nearly

running to get into the coach and be on his way. In some ways, this was the hardest of the meetings he had planned. But in so many other ways, the one awaiting him in Edinburgh would be much more important.

Chapter Twenty-One

Anna heard the commotion in the front office of the *Gazette* and hoped that Lesher would take care of it. Her patience was at its thinnest and Aunt Euphemia had complained of it several times over the last few weeks. Nathaniel took refuge in his club, a new one that had opened recently and was only for men, of course. "A place of refuge where we can discuss our political aspirations" is how he described it. "A place to drink, swear, gamble and hide from the women looking for them" were the words she'd used.

Part of the problem was that she missed Clarinda again. She and Robert had returned to the Highlands, but not before sharing their wonderful news—a child was expected in the spring. When Anna asked how long she'd known and not whispered it to her in confidence, Clarinda mentioned that with *the situation* as it was, she was not certain that they had the same views on procreation and did not want to upset Anna.

They'd gone from Nathaniel's phrase "their campaign" to

Clarinda's "the situation." Words were all that seemed to matter anymore and where once they filled her life and gave her purpose and joy, now they mocked her empty world. The exchange of essays had become mundane. It was as though neither had the passion to engage the other in the battles that had raged before.

The subscriptions were increasing and Anna was pleased with the content, and the advertisers seemed content with the layout and design. Even the changes she instituted to include book reviews and employment ads drew favorable notice. The *Scottish Monthly Gazette* was now the second leading periodical in Edinburgh and it was shipped to England, Wales and several other countries, according to the distributors' reports.

All in all it had been a successful year and all indications were that it would continue through the next year. The expansion of the school into a second building would be possible now due to all the...

The commotion now spread closer to the office door and Anna did not know whether to open it or bar it from intruders. Loud voices, some threatening words and some righteous anger, and a scuffling in the hall and Anna could stand it no longer. She walked around the desk to the door and pulled it open. The small group of men outside in the hallway stopped in an instant and some of them wore very guilty expressions.

"Mr. Lesher, is there some problem? It sounds like the time they took the cannon through the streets into Leith to defend the harbor. Are we under attack now?"

"Pardon, Miss Fairchild. I knew ye didna wish to be disturbed and we were just stoppin' him from doing just that."

"Him, Mr. Lesher? Who are you trying to stop?"

Anna rocked up onto her toes, trying to see over the three tall men directly in front of her to the one who stood at the back with his head tilted down. The others finally gave way and she caught a glimpse now. Her heart, that traitorous one beating in her breast, knew him before her eyes did. She rolled back down on her feet, hoping that she would be able to remain standing as he walked toward her.

"I came to discuss the quality of your publication and the possibility of finding employment here."

He seemed to take great satisfaction in shoving the last two men out of the way with more force than she thought necessary. But the closer he got, the more difficulty she had breathing. Soon, he was only inches from her and she drank in the sight of him. The silence in the hallway drew her from her stupor.

"Come in, please, and allow the men to get back to work."

She moved back and opened the door wider so he could enter. Lesher stood outside and watched as she began to close the door.

"I sent for Mr. Hobbs-Smith, miss. Just give a yell if ye need anything."

Did he not realize that the one thing, the one person, she needed the most was now in the room with her? And she knew it would gain her nothing but heartache. Anna nodded at Lesher and closed the door. If there were a hesitation in the time it took her to turn and face him, she did not think anyone would fault her for it. For she never thought to see him again, never thought that she would hear his voice or smell the scent of the soap with which he washed.

Now he was here and she could not find the words to begin. After you'd met someone, discovered that they were not the person you thought to be in some ways and were in other ways, fallen in love and made your peace with a solitary life after they left…well, what did one say? Anna fell back to the training of her early days. When in doubt, be polite.

"Good day, Lord Treybourne. I confess that you do not look anything as I imagined you would when I read your essays in *Whiteleaf's Review.* I had visualized someone older, stodgier even. Please sit." She pointed at the chair and took a seat behind the desk. Better than standing and letting him see how her legs threatened to give way.

"Good day to you as well—" he paused and lowered his voice "—Mr. Goodfellow." He knew! "I'd imagined you to have a long, narrow nose that you glared down as your gnarly fingers toiled over those essays of yours." He looked around as though being afraid of being overheard, and nodded. "Oily black hair and a grizzly beard, too."

She laughed in spite of herself at his fantastical description. "I see we each drew our own conclusions when we had no facts to go on." Anna remembered his words about employment and asked him, "What is this about seeking employment?"

"I understand your publication recently began to include employment inquiries and I came to see if Mr. Goodfellow could be replaced."

"Lord Treybourne, I cannot imagine that you need a job?"

He stopped and stared at her face, unable to believe it had been only a matter of several months since he had last seen her. He wanted to pull her close and hold her and whisper words he'd not been able to say to her now. But, was it too late?

"I cannot carry on the pretense of polite discussion, Anna. Not with you, not with so much at stake."

Her lip trembled a bit, but he could see no other sign that his presence was affecting her the way hers was tearing him apart piece by agonizing piece.

"Very well, Lord Treybourne, what should we be doing?" Her voice shook, too, so perhaps she did still have feelings for him?

"We need to speak on important matters. I need to ask if you read my letter?" He held his breath and waited. At her nod, he asked, "Have I lost every possible chance of being forgiven by you?"

"Forgiven, Lord Treybourne? From your greeting, I think that I might be the one asking for your pardon."

"But I lied and misrepresented myself to you as someone else," he argued.

"As did I," she replied.

"I used our acquaintance to gain information to use against you... I confess I did not know at the time that you were Mr. Goodfellow, but now I do and I..." He leaned forward and reached across the desk to take her hand. "I am sorry for not telling you the truth, Anna, from the beginning."

"As am I, for not only did I do the same, but I involved others to do it for me." He noticed the hint of tears in her brown eyes and hated knowing that she'd shed many tears because of him.

"Well, if you have your teaching slate close at hand, perhaps we should keep score of our sins?" He tried to jest, but all he wanted to do was fall on his knees before her and beg her to forgive him. "Misrepresentation, one point, lies, two," he offered. "I own a school and an orphanage," he began.

"I own a school and a magazine," she countered. "I think that gives me four points and you three. Shall we play to *vingt-et-un?*"

"Is being a fool a sin?" he asked.

"A fault, but not a sin," she answered.

"But if we are going to tally faults, you will need a larger slate." His biggest fault was in not seeing the whole woman before him. He'd parceled her into small pieces, ones that he needed at that particular moment. When he needed a diversion, he sought her out. When he needed information, he sought her out. When he now wanted her forgiveness, he sought her and prayed she could grant him that.

"You have the gravest expression on your face, Lord Trey bourne. I think you are losing the ambiance of the game."

"Anna, you were not a fool. It is not being foolish when someone sets out to deceive you."

She laughed then and it drifted off into something less about humor and more about a bitter taste left behind after something spoils. "What truly amazes me is how I missed all of the missteps and clues about who you really were. I have not been so foolish since…well, since my younger days."

"And as well-educated and informed and well-read as I am, I could not tell that the person writing the words as my opponent was challenging me to discover her secrets. How is that for being a fool?"

"We can agree that we were both fools. Is there anything we actually did well?"

"I know something we did exceedingly well, Anna." He lifted her hand now and placed it between his.

The warmth seeped into her and she remembered being

wrapped in his arms the day he saved her in the storm. He haunted her dreams and woke her in the middle of the night, with his name on her lips and his kisses branded onto her lips and skin by the memories of the passion of that day. If she held on to nothing else of him, those memories would be enough.

"We fell in love well."

"Very well, my lord."

"How could that have happened?"

"A friend of mine has an interesting theory about how it happened." Robert's words rang true as he spoke to her.

"Really? And what did Lady MacLerie have to say on the matter?"

She smiled at his understanding of her deepest, dearest friends. "Actually it was Lord MacLerie. He told me that I was so busy falling in love that I did not notice your deception."

"And my part in this?" he asked.

"That you were so busy trying to keep up the deception that you never noticed you were falling in love."

He stood then and walked to the window of the office. The weather outside was not pleasant—it never seemed to be when he was in Edinburgh and she supposed that nothing would ever convince him that brilliantly beautiful days filled with sunshine and warm breezes had ever occurred here.

"He is going to be insufferable when he learns that he was correct, is he not?"

"There is as much a chance of that being the case as there is—"

"Rain in Edinburgh?"

His smile was stunning and she could watch it over and over. His mouth curved and his eyes sparkled and her heart ached.

"I was going to say 'that he will make certain we admit it.' But rain in Edinburgh seems appropriate, too."

Lord Treybourne crossed the room in a few paces and crouched down next to her. Then, he said nothing, he only took her left hand, turned it over and placed his lips where he had that night so long ago. Her breath caught as she watched it and felt the shivers spread through her.

"I think that we knew all of this, the part about being in love when you left and when you wrote me your explanation. What has changed to bring you here?"

"I realized, after telling you that marriage was not possible, that I was worried about not being worthy or ready to marry you."

"Not ready? Not worthy? I think you are reversing our positions here. I know Clarinda spoke to you about my own history on the day we visited Arthur's Seat."

"I discovered that you lived by your conscience, but I was simply paying mine off, Anna. I was living comfortably, carrying on my life as it was meant to be, and allowing my father to provide the funds to the benefit of those he supported." He reached out and touched her cheek. "I want to follow your example and be part of the fight for what I believe in."

She shook her head. He was being so harsh a judge of himself, holding his behavior to a standard no one could meet. "How do you plan on doing this?" She remembered his first words upon seeing her in the hall and wondered at the connection.

"There will be a new opponent for Mr. Goodfellow in

Whiteleaf's beginning next month. I told my father that our bargain was over, that I was tired of living my life as a hypocrite and I was coming here to marry the woman who was a better man than most I know."

She tried to follow his confusing progression of thoughts, but she lost him after the part about telling his father. "Your father knows I am Goodfellow?" She began to tug her hand free of his. "This is not good."

"Actually he told me who Goodfellow was. I was still working under the assumption that it was MacLerie."

"Robert? You thought Robert wrote the essays? He would be so pleased to know that."

"Then let's keep it to ourselves, please. I could not tell if my father was more horrified by the fact that a woman bested his heir in their battle of words or that it might get out that a woman did it. His sense of honor and mine are not the same."

"Did you hear yourself? Why can you not accept that? Why can you not accept that your good works are what matters most?"

"I will try," he said, knowing that the worst was still to follow. "Nathaniel told me he offered you marriage."

"Nathaniel has offered me marriage several times a year for the last five. Ever since we began this endeavor."

"Will you accept his?" He would break every bone in the man's body if she preferred him.

"This is about my inability to marry you, David. I am completely unsuitable to marry an earl."

"I need you, Anna. I want you and I love you. I will wear down your resistance if it takes me years to do it. But, there is one matter that could be the thing that stops any chance of our happiness together."

She frowned at him and shook her head now. "I was not appropriate to marry you when you were simply the honorable Mr. Archer, or so I thought you to be, and I am less acceptable to be the wife of an earl who will inherit a marquessate at some time in his life."

"When I learned about you and all the things you do, your skills as a teacher, a writer, a financier, a manager, and even more important, that you work for the same things I do, I realized that the woman who I wanted the most as my wife would be the one woman who would hate me for what I did."

He leaned against the desk and watched her as he told her the rest of it, the part he dared not put in the letter and allow someone else to know before he could tell her.

"There was another result of what I did to the young maid in our household, the one I mentioned in my letter."

Her face lost all expression and he could not tell what she was thinking at all.

"I have a daughter, a lovely child named Maddy."

"A child," she whispered.

"I found her even as I discovered her mother's whereabouts, but it was too late for me to help Sarah. I took the baby and found an older couple who could not have children and they cared for her for me."

"You see her? You take care of her?"

"I took her from the terrible conditions in which I found her and she is now a happy, healthy girl." He would beg her if he had to. "Anna, I know that this is unfair, but I want her to be a part of my life. It could not happen in London, society does not want to see a lord's bastard about, but I discovered that here, it might be possible. Here, with the right woman to be at my side, I can make amends for what I did."

Anna had not spoken other than to ask him those questions. What was she thinking? Would she marry him even though he had committed against another woman the same sin that scarred her life?

"David, I think we are making a muddle out of this again. We are so busy living our mistakes and trying to make amends to everyone else, that we are not forgiving the one person who can let go of the past."

He smiled then. It was exactly what they were doing. "I can't forgive myself."

"Clarinda said once that I should let the past remain where it is and focus on the more difficult task of making a life to move away from it. I do love you, David, and if you are willing, I would like to try to live for the better part of ourselves instead of the worst."

"Anna, there is one more thing you need to know before you give your consent to this." He paused and looked at the door, for he heard the noises outside the office that foretold of the arrival of several people.

"Just as Treybourne and Goodfellow sought a truce, I want no more explanation, clarifications or rationalizations. We will have time for all of those later."

"No, Anna, this is more along the lines of an introduction."

The words were no sooner out than Nathaniel burst through the door, followed by Lesher and the same men who had tried to stop him the first time. The effect was ruined when Julia and Maddy skipped around them and into the room, making it a crowded and loud chamber. The introduction he had planned for so long and agonized over how to tell Anna about her was blown to bits when Julia called out his name and Maddy called him "Papa."

Nathaniel whined about losing Anna. Julia screamed about David joining her family. Maddy simply held on to Anna and did not say a word. In an instant, he had gone from single man, to husband of one, father of one and brother to another, and nothing could have pleased him more.

Chapter Twenty-Two

The wedding, although accomplished in some haste, took too long for him. It was a small, intimate gathering of friends and some of the bride's family and it took place in the morning room of their new house on the east side of the New Town. The sun shone, a miracle he did not yet believe could occur here in Edinburgh, and the beams of light danced around them as they made their promises before God and witnesses.

The girls had gone ahead with Lord and Lady MacLerie to their Highland estate, and that was their destination as soon as they had a brief private journey. He decided on the hunting box and now they sat in the large, comfortable and well-appointed coach of the Earl of Treybourne.

Leather covered the thick seat cushions and their padding made the journey over the roads north of the city in the Cairngorm Mountains a more pleasant one. It was his constant state of arousal that made each mile feel like twenty. He had planned to wait until they reached their destination for the night before touching her, but Anna had other ideas.

"Do you remember your hesitation to ride in a closed coach with me?"

"I was protecting your reputation, Anna."

"I have heard," she said, as she placed her hand on his thigh. His body hardened and surged against his pantaloons. "I have heard that great liberties can be taken in a closed carriage. Is it true, Lord Treybourne?"

"It is true, Lady Treybourne. And perhaps on the next part of our journey, I might demonstrate a few of them for you?"

Anna laughed at his suggestion, but her nod got him thinking of all sorts of liberties he would take with her, once she was his.

But he knew that something inside of him worried about the consummation of their vows. After all, she was not a virgin, he knew, but he knew nothing of how it had been accomplished and if she carried any hesitation about it. Or if using that part of him that was larger and more insistent would hurt her when he lost himself in the chaos of passion?

"You are thinking too much again, David."

"I am worried that it might be difficult for you when we…do…"

"Do you love me?" she asked him. "If you do, I have no fear of what is to happen."

"Did it hurt you?" He stammered out the words but could not complete the sentence.

"Clarinda says that—"

"I do not want to think about Clarinda when I am making you mine tonight, Anna. Please do not mention her name."

Anna laughed then and it was the most marvelous sound he'd ever heard. He drew her into his arms and opened the window coverings so that the daylight brightened the carriage and they could see the passing scenery.

To take his mind off the thought of Clarinda telling his wife of private matters of connubial felicity, he decided to tell her himself. One thing led to another and by the time they reached the hunting box, he discovered that he was just as affected by the plan and did not want to wait for the night. As though they knew, and they should have since it was their marriage trip, the servants disappeared as soon as they arrived and David was able to persuade, convince, cajole and seduce Anna into bed in the middle of the afternoon.

Shy about proceeding in the daylight, he closed the curtains around the bed, a throwback to an earlier time, and allowed her the shadows. It did not lessen his ardor or hers, and soon their clothes were gone, and they lay naked against each other.

"You are worrying."

"I—"

"David, join with me now," she urged.

She did worry, but his own concern eased hers. She knew he would have a care of her and that not even the mindless passion that seemed to envelop them when the touching and the kissing drove them mad frightened her now. There was an ache deep inside her, one that eased with the pleasure he gave her, but was not satisfied.

Part of her yearned for that completion, another part hoped it would never be fulfilled, that each time they shared the passion of their marriage, whether in bed or not, she would want it again and again. David seemed pleased by the way she let him control her body, and she wanted to give him back some measure of the happiness and joy he'd brought to her life.

She knew what to expect. The first time had not been so long ago that she could not remember it, but nothing was as it had been that time. Although she did not voice her true worry, she was concerned that she would not please him because of that other time. Now, as his body demanded its own satisfaction, she guided him between her thighs and to the place that still throbbed from the touch of his hands and his mouth just moments ago.

David brought her to fulfillment then and as she let her legs fall apart so that he could move closer, Anna felt him press his fullness against her and heard him whisper his love. He thrust his hardness deep within her, even against her womb, but there was no pain, just a fullness that felt wonderful. He moved then, lifting her hips with his hand beneath her bottom and sliding as far inside as he could. He moved in and back, pushing faster and harder and deeper with each thrust.

The sensation that built within her was different than the frantic one he caused with his fingers touching that spot between her legs. This time, with his arousal planted deep, removed and thrust in again and again, she grabbed for the bedcovers and moaned. It was deep, he was deep and it felt as though he rubbed against a place that itched with need. More and more, she felt the tension growing and she raised her hips to keep in rhythm with his movements.

Then, just when she had almost convinced herself that this was as pleasurable as it could be, her body tightened and exploded, tightened and exploded and arched as wave after wave of pleasure washed over her. Then with a final thrust against the very center of her, she felt his release and heard his cry of passion, too.

A short time passed and they lay with their bodies still joined. Anna could not keep a thought in her head, she could only feel the results of his loving. She ached and throbbed in places she did not know she had. Her legs and arms felt as if she had done two days of laundry herself. But her heart was lighter and happier than it had been in a long time.

"Are you well?" he whispered. She could hear the concern there.

"I am well," she said. "David, I feel healed by the love you shared."

He reached over and took her hand and placed it on his chest, over his own heart. "And you have helped me to heal as well, my sweet Anna."

And somewhere in the night, their old wounds and pains, their war of words became a thing of their past and they made plans on how to share the rest of their lives with each other.

Epilogue

Edinburgh, 1819

"It's here, Anna," he called out as he entered the *Gazette*'s office. "Is she in there, Lesher?"

"Aye, sir. I just left her sitting at the desk."

The door down the hall opened and he watched as his wife waddled down the corridor toward him. Her pregnancy was advanced now and it would not be long before they had a son to halt Robert's unstinting boasting about producing the best son in Edinburgh. Or perhaps it would be a girl, with soft brown eyes and a gentle smile? He only knew that whatever they were blessed with, he would give thanks to the Almighty for and spend his life taking care of.

"Here, love," he said. "I should have come to you." He guided her to a chair and handed her the magazine. "Do you remember how you ended the last one? Look how he copied you!"

In spite of her initial disbelief and even resistance, David had taken over the role of Mr. Goodfellow. He did not use the information he'd threatened to, but his essays were "written with the perspective of an insider" as his newest opponent complained. If anyone ever discovered the new identity of the reformist Scottish magazine's lead writer, word never spread.

They'd agreed to share the job since Anna truly enjoyed it, but soon, with the personal demands of a family and husband, the teaching duties at the school and her oversight of some of the charities they supported, she allowed him to write most of them. Certain subjects when raised were her special concerns and David would sit at night and watch the words come to her in a torrent.

She smiled so he knew she was pleased. She was not easily satisfied for she always wanted it to be more or better than the last, so David laughed. "You goaded the *puir mon,* as Mrs. Dobbs would say, into an unfair fight, Anna. This was only his third issue."

The first two had lasted six months and four and he had not told her that Cunningham only lasted that long because his first two essays were handed to him, completed before David had come north. This third man showed every sign of being the worthy opponent they needed to keep their issues in the public eye. The success of their magazine continued to grow as did the school and an orphanage. And his wife.

"What did Clarinda say about your symptoms?" he asked. He admired the woman's no-nonsense approach to childbearing and encouraged Anna to consult the same midwife who had attended her.

"I cannot believe you quote her as you do."

"Nor can I, but she does seem to know a great deal about

it. And if it helps you when your time, the time, comes, I am grateful."

"So," Anna said, using her husband's hand to aid her in standing next to him, "before you write this next rebuttal, I have to tell you something that may help you."

"*May* help me?"

"Or it may hinder you. I was not privy to how it worked the last time."

With her eclectic and wide-ranging areas of interest, he could not imagine what she wanted to tell him. "This is intriguing." He moved closer and she still pulled him down so that his ear was close to her mouth.

"How will you feel if you, the Earl of Treybourne, are beaten by another woman?" she whispered.

The information sank in and he was shocked by her suggestion. "A woman? It cannot be. How do you know? Or are you guessing?"

"I just thought I should warn you that your father is a quick study."

He looked at the essay again and then at his wife. Could she be correct? Who better to recognize the work of another of her gender? He laughed now as he realized it was possible.

"Perhaps there's hope for him yet?"

"There is hope for everyone. You taught me that."

David looked about him and knew that she had taught and given him more than he could ever repay. But he would continue to try every day of the rest of his life.

Author's Note

The early eighteenth century saw the beginning of great changes for Edinburgh, known as the "Athens of the North." Although the capital of the newly formed Union after 1707 was London, Edinburgh remained a center of power and influence in Scotland through the 18th and 19th centuries. When the population increased and the need for residential space soared in the early 1700s, a bold new plan of expansion was introduced. Eventually a new part of Edinburgh was built over the drained marshlands to the north of the existing royal burgh. The New Town, designed by James Craig in a balanced, grid-iron format, soon became the center of culture and wealth.

The architecture had an underlying uniformity to it and Robert Adams's palace-front design became a much-copied innovation. With a square to its east (St. Andrew's) and west (St. George's, later renamed Charlotte's), New Town boasted of evenly laid streets and both private residences and public buildings. Properties were "feued" much like medieval land where the owner paid an annual fee in gold, grain or service for the right to hold it. Many public buildings, such as the Assembly Rooms, were funded by taxes or by subscription fees.

Building the New Town took decades and it happened in several stages, beginning with St. Andrew's Square and finishing with St. George's. Most construction took place from 1767 and was completed in 1820—just in time for the visit of the former Prince Regent and now King George IV to Edinburgh in 1822. Outside influences, such as the American Revolution and the Napoleonic Wars, slowed building as well as the occasional lack of financial support.

While the Old Town remained the business, financial and industrial center of Scotland, the New Town became the center of wealth and culture. Now, almost two centuries later, many of its buildings have been restored and No.7 Charlotte Square is a wonderful example of the city in its prime.

For more information about Georgian Edinburgh, visit the National Trust for Scotland's Web site at www.nts.org.uk. For the purposes of my novel, I did speed up some of the construction in the New Town since I needed certain sections finished before they actually were.

The other thing that burgeoned were the publications for mostly political reasons, and two of the leading ones centered in Edinburgh were *Blackwood's Magazine* and *The Edinburgh Review*. This was also the beginnings of formal book reviews.

Unfortunately, the authors suffered for their political and social views as well as the quality (or lack of) in their writing. Reviewers tore apart novelists, poets and even other essayists based solely on with whom they spent their time and whether they were identified with the Whig or Tory party, with little time spent on the content of the work. Anyone believing that nasty reviews or contentious exchanges in publications are a modern invention should find a copy of *Blackwood's* at their nearest reference library or online and take a look. Writing and being reviewed, even in the 1800s, was not for the faint of heart!

* * * * *

Medieval
Lords & Ladies
COLLECTION

VOLUME FOUR
CHRISTMAS KNIGHTS
Share the magic of a
Medieval Christmas!

King's Pawn by Joanna Makepeace

The handsome Earl of Wroxeter, powerful and commanding, had no intention of marriage. But when the king ordered him to take a bride, he had no choice but to obey. Cressida, a beautiful innocent, caused fireworks at court. It was the Earl's task to rescue her…and make her every Christmas wish come true!

The Alchemist's Daughter by Elaine Knighton

A chance meeting in the Holy Land gave Isidora a means of escape. But she would have to watch her beloved Lucien continue the experiments that claimed her father's life. And how would such an exotic flower fare in the cold depths of an English winter?

Available 5th October 2007

www.millsandboon.co.uk

2 FREE

BOOKS AND A SURPRISE GIFT!

We would like to take this opportunity to thank you for reading this Mills & Boon® book by offering you the chance to take TWO more specially selected titles from the Historical series absolutely FREE! We're also making this offer to introduce you to the benefits of the Mills & Boon® Reader Service™—

- ★ FREE home delivery
- ★ FREE gifts and competitions
- ★ FREE monthly Newsletter
- ★ Exclusive Reader Service offers
- ★ Books available before they're in the shops

Accepting these FREE books and gift places you under no obligation to buy, you may cancel at any time, even after receiving your free shipment. Simply complete your details below and return the entire page to the address below. You don't even need a stamp!

YES! Please send me 2 free Historical books and a surprise gift. I understand that unless you hear from me, I will receive 4 superb new titles every month for just £3.69 each, postage and packing free. I am under no obligation to purchase any books and may cancel my subscription at any time. The free books and gift will be mine to keep in any case.

H7ZED

Ms/Mrs/Miss/Mr ....Initials ....

BLOCK CAPITALS PLEASE

Surname ....

Address ....

....

....Postcode.................................

Send this whole page to:
UK: FREEPOST CN81, Croydon, CR9 3WZ